M000191254

Deemed 'the father of the scientific detective story', **Richard Austin Freeman** had a long and distinguished career, not least as a writer of detective fiction. He was born in London, the son of a tailor who went on to train as a pharmacist. After graduating as a surgeon at the Middlesex Hospital Medical College, Freeman taught for a while and joined the colonial service, offering his skills as an assistant surgeon along the Gold Coast of Africa. He became embroiled in a diplomatic mission when a British expeditionary party was sent to investigate the activities of the French. Through his tact and formidable intelligence, a massacre was narrowly avoided. His future was assured in the colonial service. However, after becoming ill with blackwater fever, Freeman was sent back to England to recover and, finding his finances precarious, embarked on a career as acting physician in Holloway Prison. In desperation, he turned to writing and went on to dominate the world of British detective fiction, taking pride in testing different criminal techniques. So keen were his powers as a writer that part of one of his best novels was written in a bomb shelter.

As a Thief in the Night

R Austin Freeman

HOUSE OF
STRATUS

Copyright by W L Briant

All rights reserved. No part of this publication may be reproduced, stored in a
retrieval system, or transmitted, in any form, or by any means (electronic, mechanical,
photocopying, recording, or otherwise), without the prior permission of the
publisher. Any person who does any unauthorised act in relation to this publication
may be liable to criminal prosecution and civil claims for damages.

The right of R Austin Freeman to be identified as the author of this work
has been asserted.

This edition published in 2001 by House of Stratus, an imprint of
House of Stratus Ltd, Thirsk Industrial Park, York Road, Thirsk,
North Yorkshire, YO7 3BX, UK.
Also at: House of Stratus Inc., 2 Neptune Road, Poughkeepsie, NY 12601, USA.

www.houseofstratus.com

Typeset, printed and bound by House of Stratus.

A catalogue record for this book is available from the British Library
and the Library of Congress.

ISBN 0-7551-0347-5

This book is sold subject to the condition that it shall not be lent, resold, hired out,
or otherwise circulated without the publisher's express prior consent in any form of
binding, or cover, other than the original as herein published and without a similar
condition being imposed on any subsequent purchaser, or bona fide possessor.

This is a fictional work and all characters are drawn from the author's imagination.
Any resemblance or similarities to persons either living or dead are entirely coincidental.

CONTENTS

CHAPTER ONE

The Invalid

Looking back on events by the light of experience I perceive clearly that the thunder-cloud which burst on me and on those who were dear to me had not gathered unseen. It is true that it had rolled up swiftly; that the premonitory mutterings, now so distinct but then so faint and insignificant, gave but a brief warning. But that was of little consequence, since whatever warnings there were passed unheeded, as warnings commonly do, being susceptible of interpretation only by means of the subsequent events which they foreshadowed.

The opening scene of the tragedy – if I had but realized it – was the arrival of the Reverend Amos Monkhouse from his far-away Yorkshire parish at the house of his brother Harold. I happened to be there at the time; and though it was not my concern, since Harold had a secretary, I received the clergyman when he was announced. We knew one another well enough by name though we had never met, and it was with some interest and curiosity that I looked at the keen-faced, sturdy, energetic-looking parson and contrasted him with his physically frail and rather characterless brother. He looked at me, too, curiously and with a certain appearance of surprise, which did not diminish when I told him who I was.

"Ha!" said he, "yes. Mr Mayfield. I am glad to have the opportunity of making your acquaintance. I have heard a good deal about you from Harold and Barbara. Now I can fit you with a visible personality. By the way, the maid tells me that Barbara is not at home."

"No, she is away on her travels in Kent."

"In Kent!" he repeated, raising his eyebrows.

"Yes, on one of her political expeditions; organizing some sort of women's emancipation movement. I dare say you have heard about it."

He nodded a little impatiently. "Yes. Then I assume that Harold is not so ill as I had supposed?"

I was inclined to be evasive; for, to be quite candid, I had thought more than once that Barbara might properly have given a little less attention to her political hobbies and a little more to her sick husband. So I replied cautiously:

"I really don't quite know what his condition is. You see, when a man has chronically bad health, one rather loses count. Harold has his ups and downs, but he always looks pretty poorly. Just now, I should say he is rather below his average."

"Ha! Well, perhaps I had better go up and have a look at him. The maid has told him that I am here. I wonder if you would be so kind as to show me the way to his room. I have not been in this house before."

I conducted him up to the door of the bedroom and then returned to the library to wait for him and hear what he thought of the invalid. And now that the question had been raised, I was not without a certain uneasiness. What I had said was true enough. When a man is always ailing one gets to take his ill-health for granted and to assume that it will go on without any significant change. One repeats the old saying of "the creaking gate" and perhaps makes unduly light of habitual illness. Might it be that Harold was being a little neglected? He had certainly looked bad enough when I had called on him that morning. Was it possible that he was really seriously ill? Perhaps in actual danger?

I had just asked myself this question when the door was opened abruptly and the clergyman strode into the room. Something in his expression – a mingling, as it seemed, of anger and alarm – rather startled me; nevertheless I asked him calmly enough how he found his brother. He stared at me, almost menacingly, for a second or two; then slowly and with harsh emphasis he replied: "I am shocked at the change in him. I am horrified. Why, good God, Sir! the man is dying!"

"I think that can hardly be," I objected. "The doctor saw him this morning and did not hint at anything of the sort. He thought he was not very well but he made no suggestion as to there being any danger."

"How long has the doctor been attending him?"

"For something like twenty years, I believe; so by this time he ought to understand the patient's – "

"Tut-tut," the parson interrupted, impatiently, "what did you say yourself but a few minutes ago? One loses count of the chronic invalid. He exhausts our attention until, at last, we fail to observe the obvious. What is wanted is a fresh eye. Can you give me the doctor's address? Because, if you can, I will call on him and arrange a consultation. I told Harold that I wanted a second opinion and he made no objection; in fact he seemed rather relieved. If we get a really first-class physician, we may save him yet."

"I think you are taking an unduly gloomy view of Harold's condition," said I. "At any rate, I hope so. But I entirely agree with you as to the advisability of having further advice. I know where Dr Dimsdale lives so if you like I will walk round with you."

He accepted my offer gladly and we set forth at once, walking briskly along the streets, each of us wrapped in thought and neither speaking for some time. Presently I ventured to remark:

"Strictly, I suppose, we ought to have consulted Barbara before seeking another opinion."

"I don't see why," he replied. "Harold is a responsible person and has given his free consent. If Barbara is so little concerned about him as to go away from home – and for such a trumpery reason, too – I don't see that we need consider her. Still, as a matter of common civility, I might as well send her a line. What is her present address?"

"Do you know," I said, shamefacedly, "I am afraid I can't tell you exactly where she is at the moment. Her permanent address, when she is away on these expeditions, is the head-quarters of the Women's Friendship League at Maidstone."

He stopped for a moment and glowered at me with an expression of sheer amazement. "Do you mean to tell me," he exclaimed, "that she has gone away, leaving her husband in this condition, and that she is not even within reach of a telegram?"

"I have no doubt that a telegram or letter would be forwarded to her."

He emitted an angry snort and then demanded: "How long has she been away?"

"About a fortnight," I admitted, reluctantly.

"A fortnight!" he repeated in angry astonishment. "And all that time beyond reach of communication! Why the man might have been dead and buried and she none the wiser!"

"He was much better when she went away," I said, anxious to make the best of what I felt to be a rather bad case. "In fact, he seemed to be getting on quite nicely. It is only during the last few days that he has got this set-back. Of course, Barbara is kept informed as to his condition. Madeline sends her a letter every few days."

"But, my dear Mr Mayfield," he expostulated, "just consider the state of affairs in this amazing household. I came to see my brother, expecting – from the brief letter that I had from him – to find him seriously ill. And I do find him seriously ill; dangerously ill, I should say. And what sort of care is being taken of him? His wife is away from home, amusing herself with her platform fooleries, and has left no practicable address. His secretary, or whatever you call him, Wallingford, is not at home. Madeline is, of course, occupied in her work at the school. Actually, the only person in the house besides the servants is yourself – a friend of the family but not a member of the household at all. You must admit that it is a most astonishing and scandalous state of affairs."

I was saved from the necessity of answering this rather awkward question by our arrival at Dr Dimsdale's house; and, as it fortunately happened that the doctor was at home and disengaged, we were shown almost at once into his consulting room.

I knew Dr Dimsdale quite well and rather liked him though I was not deeply impressed by his abilities. However, his professional skill was really no concern of mine, and his social qualities were unexceptionable. In appearance and manner he had always seemed to me the very type of a high-class general practitioner, and so he impressed me once more as we were ushered into his sanctum. He shook hands with me genially, and as I introduced the Reverend Amos looked at him with a politely questioning expression. But the clergyman lost no time in making clear the purpose of his visit; in fact he came to the point with almost brutal abruptness.

"I have just seen my brother for the first time for several months and I am profoundly shocked at his appearance. I expected to find him ill, but I did not understand that he was so ill as I find him."

"No," Dr Dimsdale agreed, gravely, "I suppose not. You have caught him at a rather unfortunate time. He is certainly not so well today."

"Well!" exclaimed Amos. "To me he has the look of a dying man. May I ask what, exactly, is the matter with him?"

The doctor heaved a patient sigh and put his fingertips together.

"The word 'exactly,'" he replied, with a faint smile, "makes your question a little difficult to answer. There are so many things the matter with him. For the last twenty years, on and off, I have attended him, and during the whole of that time his health has been unsatisfactory − most unsatisfactory. His digestion has always been defective, his circulation feeble, he has had functional trouble with his heart, and throughout the winter months, more or less continuous respiratory troubles − nasal and pulmonary catarrh and sometimes rather severe bronchitis."

The Reverend Amos nodded impatiently. "Quite so, quite so. But, to come from the past to the present, what is the matter with him now?"

"That," the doctor replied suavely, "is what I was coming to. I mentioned the antecedents to account for the consequents. The complaints from which your brother has suffered in the past have been what are called functional complaints. But functional disease − if there really is such a thing − must, in the end, if it goes on long enough, develop into organic disease. Its effects are cumulative. Each slight illness leaves the bodily organs a little less fit."

"Yes?"

"Well, that is, I fear, what is happening in your brother's case. The functional illnesses of the past are tending to take on an organic character."

"Ha!" snorted the Reverend Amos. "But what is his actual condition now? To put it bluntly, supposing he were to die tonight, what would you write on the death certificate?"

"Dear me!" said the doctor. "That is putting it very bluntly. I hope the occasion will not arise."

"Still, I suppose you don't regard his death as an impossible contingency?"

"Oh, by no means. Chronic illness confers no immortality, as I have just been pointing out."

"Then, supposing his death to occur, what would you state to be the cause?"

Dr Dimsdale's habitual suavity showed a trace of diminution as he replied: "You are asking a very unusual and hardly admissible question, Mr Monkhouse. However, I may say that if your brother were to die tonight he would die from some definite cause, which would be duly set forth in the certificate. As he is suffering from chronic gastritis, chronic bronchial catarrh, functional disorder of the heart and several other morbid conditions, these would be added as contributory causes. But may I ask what is the object of these very pointed questions?"

"My object," replied Amos, "was to ascertain whether the circumstances justified a consultation. It seems to me that they do. I am extremely disturbed about my brother. Would you have any objection to meeting a consultant?"

"But not in the least. On the contrary, I should be very glad to talk over this rather indefinite case with an experienced physician who would come to it with a fresh eye. Of course, the patient's consent would be necessary."

"He has consented, and he agreed to the consultant whom I proposed – Sir Robert Detling – if you concurred."

"I do certainly. I could suggest no better man. Shall I arrange with him or will you?"

"Perhaps I had better," the parson replied, "as I know him fairly well. We were of the same year at Cambridge. I shall go straight on to him now and will let you know at once what arrangement he proposes."

"Excellent," said the doctor, rising with all his suavity restored. "I shall keep tomorrow as free as I can until I hear from you, and I hope he will be able to manage it so soon. I shall be glad to hear what he thinks of our patient, and I trust that the consultation may be helpful in the way of treatment."

He shook our hands heartily and conducted us to the street door, whence he launched us safely into the street.

"That is a very suave gentleman," Amos remarked as we turned away. "Quite reasonable, too; but you see for yourself that he has no real knowledge of the case. He couldn't give the illness an intelligible name."

"It seemed to me that he gave it a good many names, and it may well be that it is no more than he seems to think; a sort of collective illness, the resultant of the various complaints that he mentioned. However, we shall know more when Sir Robert has seen him; and meanwhile, I wouldn't worry too much about the apparent neglect. Your brother, unlike most chronic invalids, doesn't hanker for attention. He has all he wants and he likes to be left alone with his books. Shall you see him again today?"

"Assuredly. As soon as I have arranged matters with Detling I shall let Dr Dimsdale know what we have settled and I shall then go back and spend the evening with my brother. Perhaps I shall see you tomorrow?"

"No. I have to run down to Bury St Edmunds tomorrow morning and I shall probably be there three or four days. But I should very much like to hear what happens at the consultation. Could you send me a few lines? I shall be staying at the Angel."

"I will certainly," he replied, halting and raising his umbrella to signal an approaching omnibus. "Just a short note to let you know what Sir Robert has to tell us of poor Harold's condition."

He waved his hand, and stepping off the kerb, hopped on to the foot-board of the omnibus as it slowed own, and vanished into the interior. I stood for a few moments watching the receding vehicle, half inclined to go back and take another look at the sick man; but reflecting that his brother would be presently returning, I abandoned the idea and made my way instead to the Underground Railway station and there took a ticket for the Temple.

There is something markedly infectious in states of mind. Hitherto I had given comparatively little attention to Harold Monkhouse. He was a more or less chronic invalid, suffering now from one complaint and now from another, and evidently a source of no particular anxiety either to his friends or to his doctor. He was always pallid and sickly-looking, and if, on this particular morning, he had seemed to look more haggard and ghastly than usual, I had merely noted that he was "not so well today."

But the appearance on the scene of the Reverend Amos had put a rather different complexion on the affair. His visit to his brother had resulted in a severe shock, which he had passed on to me; and I had to admit that our interview with Dr Dimsdale had not been reassuring. For the fact which had emerged from it was that the doctor could not give the disease a name.

It was very disquieting. Supposing it should turn out that Harold was suffering from some grave, even some mortal disease, which ought to have been detected and dealt with months ago. How should we all feel? How, in particular, would Barbara feel about the easygoing way in which the illness had been allowed to drift on? It was an uncomfortable thought; and though Harold Monkhouse was really no concern of mine, excepting that he was Barbara's husband, it continued to haunt me as I sat in the rumbling train and as I walked up from the Temple station to my chambers in Fig Tree Court.

CHAPTER TWO

Barbara Monkhouse Comes Home

In the intervals of my business at Bury St Edmunds I gave more than a passing thought to the man who was lying sick in the house in the quiet square at Kensington. It was not that I had any very deep feeling for him as a friend, though I liked him well enough. But the idea had got into my mind that he had perhaps been treated with something less than ordinary solicitude; that his illness had been allowed to drift on when possibly some effective measures might have been taken for his relief. And as it had never occurred to me to make any suggestions on the matter or to interest myself particularly in his condition, I was now inclined to regard myself as a party to the neglect, if there had really been any culpable failure of attention. I therefore awaited with some anxiety the letter which Amos had promised to send.

It was not until the morning of my third day at Bury that it arrived; and when I had opened and read it I found myself even less reassured than I had expected.

"Dear Mayfield," it ran. "The consultation took place this afternoon and the result is, in my opinion, highly unsatisfactory. Sir Robert is, at present, unable to say definitely what is the matter with Harold. He states that he finds the case extremely obscure and reserves his opinion until the blood-films and other specimens which he took, have been examined and reported on by an expert pathologist. But on one point he is perfectly clear.

He regards Harold's condition as extremely grave – even critical – and he advised me to send a telegram to Barbara insisting on her immediate return home. Which I have done; and only hope it may reach her in the course of the day.

That is all I have to tell you and I think you will agree that it is not an encouraging report. Medical science must be in a very backward state if two qualified practitioners – one of them an eminent physician – cannot between them muster enough professional knowledge to say what is the matter with a desperately sick man. However, I hope that we shall have a diagnosis by the time you come back.

Yours sincerely,

AMOS MONKHOUSE."

I could not but agree, in the main, that my clerical friend's rather gloomy view was justified, though I thought that he was a trifle unfair to the doctors, especially to Sir Robert. Probably a less scientific practitioner, who would have given the condition some sort of name, would have been more satisfying to the parson. Meanwhile, I allowed myself to build on "the blood-films and other specimens" hopes of a definite discovery which might point the way to some effective treatment.

I despatched my business by the following evening and returned to London by the night train, arriving at my chambers shortly before midnight. With some eagerness I emptied the letter-cage in the hope of finding a note from Amos or Barbara; but there was none, although there were one or two letters from solicitors which required to be dealt with at once. I read these through and considered their contents while I was undressing, deciding to get up early and reply to them so that I might have the forenoon free; and this resolution I carried out so effectively that by ten o'clock in the morning I had breakfasted, answered and posted the letters, and was on my way westward in an Inner Circle train.

It was but a few minutes' walk from South Kensington Station to Hilborough Square and I covered the short distance more quickly than usual. Turning into the square, I walked along the pavement on the garden side, according to my habit, until I was nearly opposite the house. Then I turned to cross the road and as I did so, looked up at the house. And at the first glance I stopped short and stared in dismay: for the blinds were lowered in all the windows. For a couple of seconds I stood and gazed at this ominous spectacle; then I hurried across the road and, instinctively avoiding the knocker, gave a gentle pull at the bell.

The door was opened by the housemaid, who looked at me somewhat strangely but admitted me without a word and shut the door softly behind me. I glanced at her set face and asked in a low voice: "Why are all the blinds down, Mabel?"

"Didn't you know, Sir?" she replied, almost in a whisper. "It's the master – Mr Monkhouse. He passed away in the night. I found him dead when I went in this morning to draw up the blinds and give him his early tea."

I gazed at the girl in consternation, and after a pause she continued: "It gave me an awful turn, Sir, for I didn't see, at first, what had happened. He was lying just as he usually did, and looked as if he had gone to sleep, reading. He had a book in his hand, resting on the counterpane, and I could see that his candle-lamp had burned itself right out. I put his tea on the bedside table and spoke to him, and when he didn't answer I spoke again a little louder. And then I noticed that he was perfectly still and looked even paler and more yellow than usual and I began to feel nervous about him. So I touched his hand; and it was as cold as stone and as stiff as a wooden hand. Then I felt sure he must be dead and I ran away and told Miss Norris."

"Miss Norris!" I exclaimed.

"Yes, Sir. Mrs Monkhouse only got home about an hour ago. She was fearfully upset when she found she was too late. Miss Norris is with her now, but I expect she'll be awfully glad you've come. She was asking where you were. Shall I tell her you are here?"

"If you please, Mabel," I replied; and as the girl retired up the stairs with a stealthy, funereal tread, I backed into the open doorway of the dining room (avoiding the library, in case Wallingford should be there)

11

where I remained until Mabel returned with a message asking me to go up.

I think I have seldom felt more uncomfortable than I did as I walked slowly and softly up the stairs. The worst had happened – at least, so I thought – and we all stood condemned; but Barbara most of all. I tried to prepare some comforting, condolent phrases, but could think of nothing but the unexplainable, inexcusable fact that Barbara had of her own choice and for her own purposes, gone away leaving a sick husband and had come back to find him dead.

As I entered the pleasant little boudoir – now gloomy enough, with its lowered blinds – the two women rose from the settee on which they had been sitting together, and Barbara came forward to meet me, holding out both her hands.

"Rupert!" she exclaimed, "how good of you! But it is like you to be here just when we have need of you." She took both my hands and continued, looking rather wildly into my face: "Isn't it an awful thing? Poor, poor Harold! So patient and uncomplaining! And I so neglectful, so callous! I shall never, never forgive myself. I have been a selfish, egotistical brute."

"We are all to blame," I said, since I could not honestly dispute her self-accusations; "and Dr Dimsdale not the least. Harold has been the victim of his own patience. Does Amos know?"

"Yes," answered Madeline, "I sent him a telegram at half-past eight. I should have sent you one, too, but I didn't know that you had come back."

There followed a slightly awkward silence during which I reflected with some discomfort on the impending arrival of the dead man's brother, which might occur at any moment. It promised to be a somewhat unpleasant incident, for Amos alone had gauged the gravity of his brother's condition, and he was an outspoken man. I only hoped that he would not be too outspoken.

The almost embarrassing silence was broken by Barbara, who asked in a low voice: "Will you go and see him, Rupert?" and added: "You know the way and I expect you would rather go alone."

I said "yes" as I judged that she did not wish to come with me, and, walking out of the room, took my way along the corridor to the well-remembered door, at which I halted for a moment, with an unreasonable impulse to knock, and then entered. A solemn dimness pervaded the room, with its lowered blinds, and an unusual silence seemed to brood over it. But everything was clearly visible in the faint, diffused light – the furniture, the pictures on the walls, the bookshelves and the ghostly shape upon the bed, half-revealed through the sheet which had been laid over it.

Softly, I drew back the sheet, and the vague shape became a man; or rather, as it seemed, a waxen effigy, with something in its aspect at once strange and familiar. The features were those of Harold Monkhouse, but yet the face was not quite the face that I had known. So it has always seemed to me with the dead. They have their own distinctive character which belongs to no living man – the physiognomy of death; impassive, expressionless, immovable; fixed for ever, or at least, until the changes of the tomb shall obliterate even its semblance of humanity.

I stepped back a pace and looked thoughtfully at the dead man who had slipped so quietly out of the land of the living. There he lay, stretched out in an easy, restful posture, just as I had often seen him; the eyes half-closed and one long, thin arm lying on the counterpane, the waxen hand lightly grasping the open volume; looking – save for the stony immobility – as he might if he had fallen asleep over his book. It was not surprising that the housemaid had been deceived, for the surroundings all tended to support the illusion. The bedside table with its pathetic little provisions for a sick man's needs: the hooded candle-lamp, drawn to the table-edge and turned to light the book; the little decanter of brandy, the unused tumbler, the water-bottle, the watch, still ticking in its upright case, the candle-box, two or three spare volumes and the hand-bell for night use; all spoke of illness and repose with never a hint of death.

There was nothing by which I could judge when he had died. I touched his arm and found it rigid as an iron bar. So Mabel had found it some hours earlier, whence I inferred that death had occurred not much past midnight. But the doctors would be able to form a better opinion, if it should seem necessary to form any opinion at all. More to the point than the exact time of death was the exact cause. I recalled the blunt question that Amos had put to Dr Dimsdale and the almost indignant tone in which the latter had put it aside. That was less than a week ago; and now that question had to be answered in unequivocal terms. I found myself wondering what the politic and plausible Dimsdale would put on the death certificate and whether he would seek Sir Robert Detling's collaboration in the execution of that document.

I was about to replace the sheet when my ear caught the footsteps of some one approaching on tip-toe along the corridor. The next moment the door opened softly and Amos stole into the room. He passed me with a silent greeting and drew near the bed, beside which he halted with his hand laid on the dead hand and his eyes fixed gloomily on the yellowish-white, impassive face. He spoke no word, nor did I presume to disturb this solemn meeting and farewell, but silently slipped out into the corridor where I waited for him to come out.

Two or three minutes passed, during which I heard him, once or twice, moving softly about the room and judged that he was examining the surroundings amidst which his brother had passed the last few weeks of his life. Presently he came out, closing the door noiselessly behind him, and joined me opposite the window. I looked a little nervously into the stern, grief-stricken face, and as he did not speak, I said, lamely enough: "This is a grievous and terrible thing, Mr Monkhouse." He shook his head gravely. "Grievous indeed; and the more so if one suspects, as I do, that it need not have happened. However, he is gone and recriminations will not bring him back."

"No," I agreed, profoundly relieved and a little surprised at his tone; "whatever we may feel or think, reproaches and bitter words will bring no remedy. Have you seen Barbara?"

"No; and I think I won't – this morning. In a day or two, I hope I shall be able to meet and speak to her as a Christian man should.

Today I am not sure of myself. You will let me know what arrangements are made about the funeral?"

I promised that I would, and walked with him to the head of the stairs, and when I had watched him descend and heard the street door close, I went back to Barbara's little sitting-room.

I found her alone, and, when I entered she was standing before a miniature that hung on the wall. She looked round as I entered and I saw that she still looked rather dazed and strange. Her eyes were red, as if she had been weeping but they were now tearless, and she seemed calmer than when I had first seen her. I went to her side, and for a few moments we stood silently regarding the smiling, girlish face that looked out at us from the miniature. It was that of Barbara's step-sister, a very sweet, loveable girl, little more than a child, who had died some four years previously, and who, I had sometimes thought, was the only human creature for whom Barbara had felt a really deep affection. The miniature had been painted from a photograph after her death and a narrow plait of her gorgeous, red-gold hair had been carried round inside the frame.

"Poor little Stella!" Barbara murmured. "I have been asking myself if I neglected her, too. I often left her for days at a time."

"You mustn't be morbid, Barbara," I said. "The poor child was very well looked after and as happy as she could be made. And nobody could have done any more for her. Rapid consumption is beyond the resources of medical science at present."

"Yes, unfortunately." She was silent for a while. Then she said: "I wonder if anything could have been done for Harold. Do you think it possible that he might have been saved?"

"I know of no reason for thinking so, and now that he is gone I see no use in raising the question."

She drew closer to me and slipped her hand into mine.

"You will be with us as much as you can, Rupert, won't you? We always look to you in trouble or difficulty, and you have never failed us. Even now you don't condemn me, whatever you may think."

"No, I blame myself for not being more alert, though it was really Dimsdale who misled us all. Has Madeline gone to the school?"

"Yes. She had to give a lecture or demonstration, but I hope she will manage to get a day or two off duty. I don't want to be left alone with poor Tony. It sounds unkind to say so, for no one could be more devoted to me than he is. But he is so terribly high-strung. Just now, he is in an almost hysterical state. I suppose you haven't seen him this morning?"

"No. I came straight up to you." I had, in fact, kept out of his way, for, to speak the truth, I did not much care for Anthony Wallingford. He was of a type that I dislike rather intensely; nervous, high-strung, emotional and in an incessant state of purposeless bustle. I did not like his appearance, his manners or his dress. I resented the abject fawning way in which he followed Barbara about, and I disapproved of his position in this house; which was nominally that of secretary to Barbara's husband, but actually that of tame cat and generally useless hanger-on. I think I was on the point of making some disparaging comments on him, but at that moment there came a gentle tap at the door and the subject of my thoughts entered.

I was rather sorry that Barbara was still holding my hand. Of course, the circumstances were very exceptional, but I have an Englishman's dislike of emotional demonstrations in the presence of third parties. Nevertheless, Wallingford's behaviour filled me with amazed resentment. He stopped short with a face black as thunder, and, after a brief, insolent stare, muttered that he "was afraid he was intruding" and walked out of the room, closing the door sharply after him.

Barbara flushed (and I daresay I did, too), but made no outward sign of annoyance. "You see what I mean," she said. "The poor fellow is quite unstrung. He is an added anxiety instead of a help."

"I see that plainly enough," I replied, "but I don't see why he is unstrung, or why an unstrung man should behave like an ill-mannered child. At any rate, he will have to pull himself together. There is a good deal to be done and he will have to do some of it. I may assume, I suppose, that it will be his duty to carry out the instructions of the executors?"

"I suppose so. But you know more about such things than I do."

"Then I had better go down and explain the position to him and set him to work. Presently I must call on Mr Brodribb, the other executor, and let him know what has happened. But meanwhile there are certain things which have to be done at once. You understand?"

"Yes, indeed. You mean arrangements for the funeral. How horrible it sounds! I can't realize it yet. It is all so shocking and so sudden and unlooked-for. It seems like some dreadful dream."

"Well, Barbara," I said gently, "you shan't be troubled more than is unavoidable. I will see to all the domestic affairs and leave the legal business to Brodribb. But I shall want Wallingford's help, and I think I had better go down and see him now."

"Very well, Rupert," she replied with a sigh. "I shall lean on you now as I always have done in times of trouble and difficulty, and you must try to imagine how grateful I am since I can find no words to tell you."

She pressed my hand and released me, and I took my way down to the library with a strong distaste for my mission.

That distaste was not lessened when I opened the door and was met by a reek of cigarette smoke. Wallingford was sitting huddled up in an easy chair, but as I entered, he sprang to his feet and stood facing me with a sort of hostile apprehensiveness. The man was certainly unstrung; in fact he was on wires. His pale, haggard face twitched, his hands trembled visibly and his limbs were in constant, fidgety movement. But, to me, there seemed to be no mystery about his condition. The deep yellow stains on his fingers, the reek in the air and a pile of cigarette-ends in an ash-bowl were enough to account for a good deal of nervous derangement, even if there were nothing more – no drugs or drink.

I opened the business quietly, explaining what had to be done and what help I should require from him. At first he showed a tendency to dispute my authority and treat me as an outsider, but I soon made the position and powers of an executor clear to him. When I had brought him to heel I gave him a set of written instructions the following-out of which would keep him fairly busy for the rest of the day; and having set the dismal preparations going, I went forth from the house of mourning and took my way to New Square, Lincoln's Inn, where were the offices of Mr Brodribb, the family solicitor and my co-executor.

CHAPTER THREE

A Shock for the Mourners

It was on the day of the funeral that the faint, unheeded mutterings of the approaching storm began to swell into audible and threatening rumblings, though, even then, the ominous signs failed to deliver their full significance.

How well do I recall the scene in the darkened dining room where we sat in our sable raiment, "ready to wenden on our pilgrimage" to the place of everlasting rest and eternal farewell. There were but four of us, for Amos Monkhouse had not yet arrived, though it was within a few minutes of the appointed time to start; quite a small party; for the deceased had but few relatives, and no outsiders had been bidden.

We were all rather silent. Intimate as we were, there was no need to make conversation. Each, no doubt, was busy with his or her own thoughts, and as I recall my own they seem to have been rather trivial and not very suitable to the occasion. Now and again I stole a look at Barbara and thought what a fine, handsome woman she was, and dimly wondered why, in all the years that I had known her, I had never fallen in love with her. Yet so it was. I had always admired her; we had been intimate friends, with a certain amount of quiet affection, but nothing more − at any rate on my part. Of her I was not so sure. There had been a time, some years before, when I had had an uneasy feeling that she looked to me for something more than friendship. But she was always a reticent girl; very self-reliant and self-contained. I never knew a woman better able to keep her own counsel or control her emotions.

She was now quite herself again; quiet, dignified,, rather reserved and even a little inscrutable. Seated between Wallingford and Madeline, she seemed unconscious of either and quite undisturbed by the secretary's incessant nervous fidgeting and by his ill-concealed efforts to bring himself to her notice.

From Barbara my glance turned to the woman who sat by her side, noting with dull interest the contrast between the two; a contrast as marked in their bearing as in their appearance For whereas Barbara was a rather big woman, dark in colouring, quiet and resolute in manner, Madeline Norris was somewhat small and slight, almost delicately fair, rather shy and retiring, but yet with a suggestion of mental alertness under the diffident manner. If Barbara gave an impression of quiet strength, Madeline's pretty, refined face was rather expressive of subtle intelligence. But what chiefly impressed me at this moment was the curious inversion of their attitudes towards the existing circumstances; for whereas Barbara, the person mainly affected, maintained a quiet, untroubled demeanour, Madeline appeared to be overcome by the sudden catastrophe Looking at her set, white face and the dismay in her wide, grey eyes, and comparing her with the woman at her side, a stranger would at once have assumed the bereavement to be hers.

My observations were interrupted by Wallingford once more dragging out his watch.

"What on earth can have happened to Mr Amos?" he exclaimed. "We are due to start in three minutes. If he isn't here by then we shall have to start without him. It is perfectly scandalous! Positively indecent!. But there, it's just like a parson."

"My experience of parsons," said I, "is that they are, as a rule, scrupulously punctual. But certainly, Mr Amos is unpardonably late. It will be very awkward if he doesn't arrive in time. Ah, there he is," I added as the bell rang and a muffled knock at the street door was heard.

At the sound, Wallingford sprang up as if the bell had actuated a hidden spring in the chair, and darted over to the window, from which he peered out through the chink beside the blind.

"It isn't Amos," he reported. "It's a stranger, and a fool at that, I should say, if he can't see that all the blinds are down."

We all listened intently. We heard the housemaid's hurried footsteps, though she ran on tip-toe; the door opened softly, and then, after an interval, we heard some one ushered along the hall to the drawing room. A few moments later, Mabel entered with an obviously scandalized air.

"A gentleman wishes to speak to you, Ma'am," she announced.

"But, Mabel," said Barbara, "did you tell him what is happening in this house?"

"Yes, Ma'am, I explained exactly how things were and told him that he must call tomorrow. But he said that his business was urgent and that he must see you at once."

"Very well," said Barbara. "I will go and see what he wants. But it is very extraordinary."

She rose, and nearly colliding with Wallingford, who had rushed to open the door – which was, in fact, wide open – walked out quickly, closing the door after her. After a short interval – during which Wallingford paced the room excitedly, peered out of the window, sat down, got up again and looked at his watch – she came back, and, standing in the doorway, looked at me.

"Would you come here for a minute, Rupert," she said, quietly.

I rose at once and walked back with her to the drawing room, on entering which I became aware of a large man, standing monumentally on the hearth-rug and inspecting the interior of his hat. He looked to me like a plainclothes policeman, and my surmise was verified by a printed card which he presented and which bore the inscription "Sergeant J Burton."

"I am acting as coroner's officer," he explained in reply to my interrogatory glance, "and I have come to notify you that the funeral will have to be postponed as the coroner has decided to hold an inquest. I have seen the undertakers and explained matters to them."

"Do you know what reason there is for an inquest?" I asked. "The cause of death was certified in the regular way."

"I know nothing beyond my instructions, which were to notify Mrs Monkhouse that the funeral is put off and to serve the summonses for the witnesses. I may as well do that now."

With this he laid on the table six small blue papers, which I saw were addressed respectively to Barbara, Madeline, Wallingford, the housemaid, the cook and myself.

"Have you no idea at all why an inquest is to be held?" I asked as I gathered up the papers.

"I have no information," he replied, cautiously, "but I expect there is some doubt about the exact cause of death. The certificate may not be quite clear or it may be that some interested party has communicated with the coroner. That is what usually happens, you know, Sir. But at any rate," he added, cheerfully, "you will know all about it the day after tomorrow, which, you will observe, is the day fixed for the inquest."

"And what have we to do meanwhile?" Barbara asked. "The inquest will not be held in this house, I presume."

"Certainly not, Madam," the sergeant replied. "A hearse will be sent round tonight to remove the body to the mortuary, where the post mortem examination will be carried out, and the inquest will be held in the parish hall, as is stated on the summons. I am sorry that you should be put to this inconvenience," he concluded, moving tentatively towards the door, "but – er – it couldn't be helped, I suppose. Good morning, Madam."

I walked with him to the door and let him out, while Barbara waited for me in the hall, not unobserved by Wallingford, whose eye appeared in a chink beside the slightly open dining room door. I pointedly led her back into the drawing room and closed the door audibly behind us. She turned a pale and rather shocked face to me but she spoke quite composedly as she asked: "What do you make of it, Rupert? Is it Amos?"

I had already reluctantly decided that it must be. I say, reluctantly, because, if this were really his doing, the resigned tone of his last words to me would appear no less than sheer, gross hypocrisy.

"I don't know who else it could be," I answered. "The fact that he did not come this morning suggests that he at least knew what was happening. If he did, I think he might have warned us."

"Yes, indeed. It will be a horrid scandal; most unpleasant for us all, and especially for me. Not that I am entitled to any sympathy. Poor Harold! How he would have hated the thought of a public fuss over his dead body. I suppose we must go in now and tell the others. Do you mind telling them, Rupert?"

We crossed the hall to the dining room where we found the two waiting impatiently, Madeline very pale and agitated while Wallingford was pacing the room like a wild beast. Both looked at us with eager interrogation as we entered, and I made the announcement bluntly and in a dozen words.

The effect on both was electrical. Madeline, with a little cry of horror, sank, white-faced and trembling, into a chair. As for Wallingford, his behaviour was positively maniacal. After staring at me for a few moments with starting eyes and mouth agape, he flung up his arms and uttered a hoarse shout.

"This," he yelled, "is the doing of that accursed parson! Now we know why he kept out of the way – and it is well for him that he did!"

He clenched his fists and glared around him, showing his tobacco-stained teeth in a furious snarl while the sweat gathered in beads on his livid face. Then, suddenly, his mood changed and he dropped heavily on a chair, burying his face in his shaking hands. Barbara admonished him, quietly.

"Do try to be calm, Tony. There is nothing to get so excited about. It is all very unpleasant and humiliating, of course, but at any rate you are not affected. It is I who will be called to account."

"And do you suppose that doesn't affect me?" demanded Wallingford, now almost on the verge of tears.

"I am sure it does, Tony," she replied, gently, "but if you want to be helpful to me you will try to be calm and reasonable. Come, now," she added, persuasively, "let us put it away for the present. I must tell the servants. Then we had better have lunch and go our several ways to think the matter over quietly each of us alone. We shall only agitate one another if we remain together."

I agreed emphatically with this sensible suggestion. "Not," I added, "that there is much for us to think over. The explanations will have to come from Dimsdale. It was he who failed to grasp the seriousness of poor Harold's condition."

While Barbara was absent, breaking the news to the servants, I tried to bring Madeline to a more composed frame of mind. With Wallingford I had no patience. Men should leave hysterics to the other sex. But I was sorry for Madeline; and even if she seemed more overwhelmed by the sudden complications than the occasion justified, I told myself that the blow had fallen when she was already shaken by Harold's unexpected death.

The luncheon was a silent and comfortless function; indeed it was little more than an empty form. But it had the merit of brevity. When the last dish had been sent away almost intact, Wallingford drew out his cigarette case and we all rose.

"What are you going to do, Madeline?" Barbara asked.

"I must go to the school, I suppose, and let the secretary know that – that I may have to be absent for a day or two. It will be horrid. I shall have to tell him all about it – after having got leave for the funeral. But it will sound so strange, so extraordinary. Oh! It is horrible!"

"It is!" exclaimed Wallingford, fumbling with tremulous fingers at his cigarette case. "It is diabolical! A fiendish plot to disgrace and humiliate us. As to that infernal parson, I should like – "

"Never mind that, Tony," said Barbara; "and we had better not stay here, working up one another's emotions. What are you doing, Rupert?"

"I shall go to my chambers and clear off some correspondence."

"Then you might walk part of the way with Madeline and see if you can't make her mind a little more easy."

Madeline looked at me eagerly. "Will you, Rupert?" she asked.

Of course I assented, and a few minutes later we set forth together.

For a while she walked by my side in silence with an air of deep reflection, and I refrained from interrupting her thoughts, having no very clear idea as to what I should say to her. Moreover, my own mind was pretty busily occupied. Presently she spoke, in a tentative way, as if opening a discussion.

"I am afraid you must think me very weak and silly to be so much upset by this new trouble."

"Indeed, I don't," I replied. "It is a most disturbing and humiliating affair and it will be intensely unpleasant for us all, but especially for Barbara – to say nothing of Dimsdale."

"Dr Dimsdale is not our concern," said she, "but it will be perfectly horrible for Barbara. For she really has been rather casual, poor girl, and they are sure to make things unpleasant for her. It will be a most horrid scandal. Don't you think so?"

To be candid, I did. Indeed, I had just been picturing to myself the possibilities with an officious coroner – and he would not need to be so very officious, either – and one or two cross-grained jurymen. Barbara might be subjected to a very unpleasant examination. But I did not think it necessary to say this to Madeline. Sufficient for the day is the evil thereof. I contented myself with a vague agreement.

There was another interval of silence. Then, a little to my surprise, she drew closer to me, and, slipping her hand under my arm, said very earnestly: "Rupert, I want you to tell me what you really think. What is it all about?"

I looked down, rather disconcerted, into the face that was turned up to me so appealingly; and suddenly – and rather irrelevantly – it was borne in on me that it was a singularly sweet and charming face. I had never quite realized it before. But then she had never before looked at me quite in this way; with this trustful, coaxing, appealing expression.

"I don't quite understand you, Madeline," I said, evasively. "I know no more about it than you do."

"Oh, but you do, Rupert. You are a lawyer and you have had a lot of experience. You must have formed some opinion as to why they have decided to hold an inquest. Do tell me what you think."

The coaxing, almost wheedling tone, and the entreaty in her eyes, looking so earnestly into mine, nearly conquered my reserve. But not quite. Once more I temporized.

"Well, Madeline, we all realize that what Dimsdale has written on the certificate is little more than a guess, and quite possibly wrong; and even Detling couldn't get much farther."

"Yes, I realize that. But I didn't think that inquests were held just to find out whether the doctors' opinions were correct or not."

Of course she was perfectly right; and I now perceived that her thoughts had been travelling along the same lines as my own. An inquest would not be held merely to clear up an obscure diagnosis. There was certainly something more behind this affair than Dimsdale's failure to recognize the exact nature of the illness. There was only one simple explanation of the coroner's action, and I gave it – with a strong suspicion that it was not the right one.

"They are not, as a rule, excepting in hospitals. But this is a special case. Amos Monkhouse was obviously dissatisfied with Dimsdale, and with Barbara, too. He may have challenged the death certificate and asked for an inquest. The coroner would be hardly likely to refuse, especially if there were a hint of negligence or malpractice."

"Did Mr Amos say anything to you that makes you think he may have challenged the certificate?"

"He said very little to me at all," I replied, rather casuistically and suppressing the fact that Amos had explicitly accepted the actual circumstances and deprecated any kind of recrimination.

"I can hardly believe that he would have done it," said Madeline, "just to punish Barbara and Dr Dimsdale. It would be so vindictive, especially for a clergyman."

"Clergymen are very human sometimes," I rejoined; and, as, rather to my relief, we now came in sight of Madeline's destination, I adverted to the interview which she seemed to dread so much. "There is no occasion for you to go into details with the secretary," I said. "In fact you can't. The exact cause of death was not clear to the doctors and it has been considered advisable to hold an inquest. That is all you know, and it is enough. You are summoned as a witness and you are legally bound to attend, so you are asking no favour. Cut the interview dead short, and when you have done with it, try, like a sensible girl, to forget the inquest for the present. I shall come over tomorrow and then we can reconstitute the history of the case, so that we may go into the witness-box, or its equivalent, with a clear idea of what we have to tell. And now, good-bye, or rather au revoir!"

"Good-bye, Rupert." She took my proffered hand and held it as she thanked me for walking with her. "Do you know, Rupert," she added, "there is something strangely comforting and reassuring about you. We all feel it. You seem to carry an atmosphere of quiet strength and security. I don't wonder that Barbara is so fond of you. Not," she concluded, "that she holds a monopoly."

With this she let go my hand, and, with a slightly shy smile and the faintest suspicion of a blush, turned away and walked quickly and with an air quite cheerful and composed towards the gateway of the institution. Apparently, my society had had a beneficial effect on her nervous condition.

I watched her until she disappeared into the entry, and then resumed my journey eastward, rather relieved, I fear, at having disposed of my companion. For I wanted to think – of her among other matters; and it was she who first occupied my cogitations. The change from her usual matter-of-fact friendliness had rather taken me by surprise; and I had to admit that it was not a disagreeable surprise. But what was the explanation? Was this intimate, clinging manner merely a passing phase due to an emotional upset, or was it that the special circumstances had allowed feelings hitherto concealed to come to the surface? It was an interesting question, but one that time alone could answer; and as there were other questions, equally interesting and more urgent, I consigned this one to the future and turned to consider the others.

What could be the meaning of this inquest? The supposition that Amos had suddenly turned vindictive and resolved to expose the neglect, to which he probably attributed his brother's death, I could not entertain, especially after what he had said to me. It would have written him down the rankest of hypocrites. And yet he was in some way connected with the affair as was proved by his failure to appear at the funeral. As to the idea that the inquiry was merely to elucidate the nature of the illness, that was quite untenable. A private autopsy would have been the proper procedure for that purpose.

I was still turning the question over in my mind when, as I passed the Griffin at Temple Bar, I became aware of a tall figure some distance ahead walking in the same direction. The build of the man and his long, swinging stride seemed familiar. I looked at him more attentively; and just as he turned to enter Devereux Court I recognized him definitely as a fellow Templar named Thorndyke.

The chance encounter seemed a singularly fortunate one, and at once I quickened my pace to overtake him. For Dr Thorndyke was a medical barrister and admittedly the greatest living authority on medical jurisprudence. The whole subject of inquests and Coroners' Law was an open book to him. But he was not only a lawyer. He had, I understood, a professional and very thorough knowledge of pathology and of the science of medicine in general, so that he was the very man to enlighten me in my present difficulties.

I overtook him at the Little Gate of the Middle Temple and we walked through together into New Court. I wasted no time, but, after the preliminary greetings, asked him if he had a few minutes to spare. He replied, in his quiet, genial way: "But, of course, Mayfield. I always have a few minutes to spare for a friend and a colleague."

I thanked him for the gracious reply, and, as we slowly descended the steps and sauntered across Fountain Court, I opened the matter without preamble and gave him a condensed summary of the case; to which he listened with close attention and evidently with keen interest.

"I am afraid," he said, "that your family doctor will cut rather a poor figure. He seems to have mismanaged the case rather badly, to judge by the fact that the death of the patient took him quite by surprise. By the way, can you give me any idea of the symptoms – as observed by yourself, I mean?"

"I have told you what was on the certificate."

"Yes. But the certified cause of death appears to be contested. You saw the patient pretty often, I understand. Now what sort of appearance did he present to you?"

The question rather surprised me. Dimsdale's opinion might not be worth much, but the casual and inexpert observations of a layman would have seemed to me to be worth nothing at all. However, I tried to recall such details as I could remember of poor Monkhouse's appearance and his own comments on his condition and recounted them to Thorndyke with such amplifications as his questions elicited. "But," I concluded, "the real question is, who has set the coroner in motion and with what object?"

"That question," said Thorndyke, "will be answered the day after tomorrow, and there is not much utility in trying to guess at the answer in advance. The real question is whether any arrangements ought to be made in the interests of your friends. We are quite in the dark as to what may occur in the course of the inquest."

"Yes, I had thought of that. Some one ought to be present to represent Mrs Monkhouse. I suppose it would not be possible for you to attend to watch the case on her behalf?"

"I don't think it would be advisable," he replied. "You will be present and could claim to represent Mrs Monkhouse so far as might be necessary to prevent improper questions being put to her. But I do think that you should have a complete record of all that takes place. I would suggest that I send Holman, who does most of my shorthand reporting, with instructions to make a verbatim report of the entire proceedings. It may turn out to be quite unnecessary; but if any complications should arise, we shall have the complete depositions with the added advantage that you will have been present and will have heard all the evidence. How will that suit you?"

"If you think it is the best plan there is nothing more to say, excepting to thank you for your help."

"And give me a written note of the time and place to hand to Holman when I give him his instructions."

I complied with this request at once; and having by this time reached the end of the Terrace, I shook hands with him and walked

29

slowly back to my chambers in Fig Tree Court. I had not got much out of Thorndyke excepting a very useful suggestion and some valuable help; indeed, as I turned over his extremely cautious utterances and speculated on what he meant by "complications," I found myself rather more uncomfortably puzzled than I had been before I met him.

CHAPTER FOUR

"How, When and Where –"

It was on the second day after the interrupted funeral that the thunderbolt fell. I cannot say that it found me entirely unprepared, for my reflections during the intervening day had filled me with forebodings; and by Thorndyke that catastrophe was pretty plainly foreseen. But on the others the blow fell with devastating effect. However, I must not anticipate. Rather let me get back to a consecutive narration of the actual events.

On the day after the visit of the coroner's officer we had held, at my suggestion, a sort of family committee to consider what we knew of the circumstances and antecedents of Harold's death, so that we might be in a position to give our evidence clearly and readily and be in agreement as to the leading facts. Thus we went to the coroner's court prepared, at least, to tell an intelligible and consistent story.

As soon as I entered the large room in which the inquest was to be held, my forebodings deepened. The row of expectant reporters was such as one does not find where the proceedings are to be no more than a simple, routine inquiry. Something of public interest was anticipated, and these gentlemen of the Press had received a hint from some well-informed quarter. I ran my eye along the row and was somewhat relieved to observe Mr Holman, Thorndyke's private reporter, seated at the table with a large note-book and a half-dozen well-sharpened pencils before him. His presence – as, in a sense, Thorndyke's deputy – gave me the reassuring feeling that, if there were to be "complications," I should not have to meet them with my own limited knowledge and experience, but that there were reserves of special knowledge and weighty counsel on which I could fall back.

The coroner's manner seemed to me ominous. His introductory address to the jury was curt and ambiguous, setting forth no more than the name of the deceased and the fact that circumstances had seemed to render an inquiry advisable; and having said this, he proceeded forthwith (the jury having already viewed the body) to call the first witness, the Reverend Amos Monkhouse.

I need not repeat the clergyman's evidence in detail. When he had identified the body as that of his brother, Harold, he went on to relate the events which I have recorded: his visit to his sick brother, his alarm at the patient's appearance, his call upon Dr Dimsdale and his subsequent interview with Sir Robert Detling. It was all told in a very concise, matter-of-fact manner, and I noted that the coroner did not seek to amplify the condensed statement by any questions.

"At about nine o'clock in the morning of the 13th," the witness continued, "I received a telegram from Miss Norris informing me that my brother had died in the night. I went out at once and sent a telegram to Sir Robert Detling informing him of what had happened. I then went to number 16 Hilborough Square, where I saw the body of deceased lying in his bed quite cold and stiff. I saw nobody at the house excepting the housemaid and Mr Mayfield. After leaving the house I walked about the streets for several hours and did not return to my hotel until late in the afternoon. When I arrived there, I found awaiting me a telegram from Sir Robert Detling asking me to call on him without delay. I set forth at once and arrived at Sir Robert's house at half-past five, and was shown into his study immediately. Sir Robert then told me that he had come to the conclusion that the circumstances of my brother's death called for some investigation and that he proposed to communicate with the coroner. He urged me not to raise any objections and advised me to say nothing to anyone but to wait until the coroner's decision was made known. I asked him for his reasons for communicating with the coroner, but he said that he would rather not make any statement. I heard no more until the morning of the fifteenth, the day appointed for the funeral, when the coroner's officer called at my hotel to inform me that the funeral would not take place and to serve the summons for my attendance here as a witness."

When Amos had concluded his statement, the coroner glanced at the jury, and as no one offered to put any questions, he dismissed the witness and called the next – Mabel Withers – who, at once, came forward to the table. Having been sworn and having given her name, the witness deposed that she had been housemaid to deceased and that it was she who had discovered the fact of his death, relating the circumstances in much the same words as I have recorded. When she had finished her narrative, the coroner said: "You have told us that the candle in the deceased's lamp was completely burnt out. Do you happen to know how long one of those candles would burn?"

"Yes. About four hours."

"When did you last see deceased alive?"

"At half-past ten on Tuesday night, the twelfth. I looked in at his room on my way up to bed to see if he wanted anything, and I gave him a dose of medicine."

"What was his condition then?"

"He looked very ill, but he seemed fairly comfortable. He had a book in his hand but was not reading."

"Was the candle alight then?"

"No, the gas was alight. I asked him if I should turn it out but he said 'no.' He would wait until Miss Norris or Mr Wallingford came."

"Did you notice how much candle there was in the lamp then?"

"There was a whole candle. I put it in myself in the afternoon and it had not been lit. He used to read by the gas as long as it was alight. He only used the candle-lamp if he couldn't sleep and the gas was out."

"Could you form any opinion as to how long the candle had been burnt out?"

"It must have been out some time, for there was no smell in the room as there would have been if it had only been out a short time. The window was hardly open at all; only just a small crack."

"Do you know when deceased last took food?"

"Yes, he had his supper at eight o'clock; an omelette and a tiny piece of toast with a glass of milk."

"Who cooked the omelette?"

"Miss Norris."

"Why did Miss Norris cook it? Was the cook out?"

"No. But Miss Norris usually cooked his supper and sometimes made little dishes for his lunch. She is a very expert cook."

"Who took the omelette up to deceased?"

"Miss Norris. I asked if I should take his supper up, but she said she was going up and would take it herself."

"Was anyone else present when Miss Norris was cooking the omelette?"

"Yes, I was present and so was the cook."

"Did deceased usually have the same food as the rest of the household?"

"No, he usually had his own special diet."

"Who prepared his food, as a rule?"

"Sometimes the cook, but more often Miss Norris."

"Now, with regard to his medicine. Did deceased usually take it himself?"

"No, he didn't like to have the bottle on the bedside table, as it was rather crowded with his books and things. The bottle and the medicine-glass were kept on the mantelpiece and the medicine was given to him by whoever happened to be in the room when a dose was due. Sometimes I gave it to him; at other times Mrs Monkhouse or Miss Norris or Mr Wallingford."

"Do you remember when the last bottle of medicine came?"

"Yes. It came early in the afternoon of the day before he died. I took it in and carried it up at once."

When he had written down this answer, the coroner ran his eye through his previous notes and then glanced at the jury.

"Do any of you gentlemen wish to ask the witness any questions?" he enquired; and as no one answered, he dismissed the witness with the request that she would stay in the court in case any further testimony should be required of her. He then announced that he would take the evidence of Sir Robert Detling next in order to release him for his probably numerous engagements. Sir Robert's name was accordingly called and a grave-looking, elderly gentleman rose from near the doorway and walked up to the table. When the new witness had been sworn and the formal preliminaries disposed of, the coroner said: "I will ask you, Sir Robert, to give the jury an account of the circumstances which led to your making a certain communication to me."

Sir Robert bowed gravely and proceeded at once to make his statement in the clear, precise manner of a practised speaker.

"On Friday, the 8th instant, the Reverend Amos Monkhouse called on me to arrange a consultation with Dr Dimsdale who was in attendance on his brother, the deceased. I met Dr Dimsdale by appointment the following afternoon, the 9th, and with him made a careful examination of deceased. I was extremely puzzled by the patient's condition. He was obviously very seriously – I thought, dangerously – ill, but I was unable to discover any signs or symptoms that satisfactorily accounted for his grave general condition. I could not give his disease a name. Eventually, I took a number of blood-films and some specimens of the secretions to submit to a pathologist for examination and to have them tested for micro-organisms. I took them that night to Professor Garnett's laboratory, but the professor was unfortunately absent and not returning until the following night – Sunday. I therefore kept them until Sunday night when I took them to him and asked him to examine them with as little delay as possible. He reported on the following day that microscopical examination had not brought to light anything abnormal, but he was making cultures from the secretions and would report the result on Wednesday morning. On Wednesday morning at about half-past nine, I received a telegram from the Reverend Amos Monkhouse informing me that his brother had died during the night. A few minutes later, a messenger brought Professor Garnett's report; which was to the effect that no disease-bearing organisms had been found, nor anything abnormal excepting a rather singular scarcity of micro-organisms of any kind.

"This fact, together with the death of the patient, suddenly aroused my suspicions. For the absence of the ordinary micro-organisms suggested the presence of some foreign chemical substance. And now, as I recalled the patient's symptoms, I found them consistent with the presence in the body of some foreign substance. Instantly, I made my way to Professor Garnett's laboratory and communicated my suspicions to him. I found that he shared them and had carefully preserved the remainder of the material for further examination. We both suspected the presence of a foreign substance, and we both suspected it to be arsenic.

"The professor had at hand the means of making a chemical test, so we proceeded at once to use them. The test that we employed was the one known as Reinsch's test. The result showed a very appreciable amount of arsenic in the secretions tested. On this, I sealed up what was left of the specimens, and, after notifying Mr Monkhouse of my intention, reported the circumstances to the coroner."

When Sir Robert ceased speaking, the coroner bowed, and having written down the last words, reflected for a few moments. Then he turned to the jury and said: "I don't think we need detain Sir Robert any longer unless there are any questions that you would like to ask."

At this point the usual over-intelligent juryman interposed.

"We should like to know whether the vessels in which the specimens were contained were perfectly clean and free from chemicals."

"The bottles," Sir Robert replied, "were clean in the ordinary sense. I rinsed them out with clean water before introducing the material. But, of course, they could not be guaranteed to be chemically clean."

"Then doesn't that invalidate the analysis?" the juror asked.

"It was hardly an analysis," the witness replied. "It was just a preliminary test."

"The point which you are raising, Sir," said the coroner, "is quite a sound one but it is not relevant to this inquiry. Sir Robert's test was made to ascertain if an inquiry was necessary. He decided that it was, and we are now holding that inquiry. You will not form your verdict on the results of Sir Robert's test but on those of the post mortem examination and the special analysis that has been made."

This explanation appeared to satisfy the juror and Sir Robert was allowed to depart. The coroner once more seemed to consider awhile and then addressed the jury.

"I think it will be best to take next the evidence relating to the examination of the body. When you have heard that you will be better able to weigh the significance of what the other witnesses have to tell us. We will now take the evidence of Dr Randall."

As the new witness, a small, dry, eminently professional-looking man, stepped briskly up to the table, I stole a quick, rather furtive glance at my companions and saw my own alarm plainly reflected in their faces and bearing. Barbara, on my left hand, sat up stiffly, rigid as a statue, her face pale and set, but quite composed, her eyes fixed on the man who was about to be sworn. Madeline, on my right, was ghastly. But she, too, was still and quiet, sitting with her hands tightly clasped, as if to restrain or conceal their trembling, and her eyes bent on the floor. As to Wallingford, who sat on the other side of Barbara, I could not see his face, but by his foot, which I could see and hear, tapping quickly on the floor as if he were working a spinning-wheel, and his incessantly moving hands, I judged that his nerves were at full tension.

The new witness deposed that his name was Walter Randall, that he was a Bachelor of Medicine and police surgeon of the district and that he had made a careful examination of the body of deceased and that, with Dr Barnes, he had made an analysis of certain parts of that body.

"To anticipate a little," said the coroner, "did you arrive at an opinion as to the cause of death?"

"Yes. From the post mortem examination and the analysis taken together, I came to the conclusion that deceased died from the effects of arsenic poisoning."

"Have you any doubt that arsenic poisoning was really the cause of the deceased's death?"

"No, I have no doubt whatever."

The reply, uttered with quiet decision, elicited a low murmur from the jury and the few spectators, amidst which I heard Madeline gasp in a choking whisper, "Oh! God!" and even Barbara was moved to a low cry of horror. But I did not dare to look at either of them. As for me, the blow had fallen already. Sir Robert's evidence had told me all.

"You said," the coroner resumed, "that the post mortem and the analysis, taken together, led you to this conclusion. What did you mean by that?"

"I meant that the appearance of the internal organs, taken alone, would not have been conclusive. The conditions that I found were suggestive of arsenic poisoning but might possibly have been due to disease. It was only the ascertained presence of arsenic that converted the probability into certainty."

"You are quite sure that the conditions were not due to disease?"

"Not entirely. I would rather say that the effects of arsenical poisoning were added to and mingled with those of old-standing disease."

"Would you tell us briefly what abnormal conditions you found?"

"The most important were those in the stomach, which showed marked signs of inflammation."

"You are aware that the death certificate gives old-standing chronic gastritis as one of the causes of death?"

"Yes, and I think correctly. The arsenical gastritis was engrafted on an already existing chronic gastritis. That is what made the appearances rather difficult to interpret, especially as the post mortem appearances in arsenical poisoning are extraordinarily variable."

"What else did you find?"

"There were no other conditions that were directly associated with the poison. The heart was rather fatty and dilated, and its condition probably accounts for the sudden collapse which seems to have occurred."

"Does not collapse usually occur in poisoning by arsenic?"

"Eventually it does, but it is usually the last of a long train of symptoms. In some cases, however, collapse occurs quite early and may carry the victim off at once. That is what appears from the housemaid's evidence to have happened in this case. Death seems to have been sudden and almost peaceful."

"Were there any other signs of disease?"

"Yes, the lungs were affected. There were signs of considerable bronchial catarrh, but I do not regard this as having any connection with the effects of the poison. It appeared to be an old-standing condition."

"Yes," said the coroner. "The certificate mentions chronic bronchial catarrh of several years' standing. Did you find any arsenic in the stomach?"

"Not in the solid form and only a little more than a hundredth of a grain altogether. The stomach was practically empty. The other organs were practically free from disease, excepting, perhaps, the kidneys, which were congested but not organically diseased."

"And as to the amount of arsenic present?"

"The analysis was necessarily a rather hasty one and probably shows less than the actual quantity; but we found, as I have said, just over a hundredth of a grain in the stomach, one and a half grains in the liver, nearly a fifth of a grain in the kidneys and small quantities, amounting in all to two grains, in the blood and tissues. The total amount actually found was thus a little over three and a half grains – a lethal dose."

"What is the fatal dose of arsenic?"

"Two grains may prove fatal if taken in solution, as it appears to have been in this case. Two and a half grains, in a couple of ounces of fly-paper water, killed a strong, healthy girl of nineteen in thirty-six hours."

"And how long does a poisonous dose take to produce death?"

"The shortest period recorded is twenty minutes, the longest, over three weeks."

"Did you come to any general conclusion as to how long deceased had been suffering from the effects of arsenic and as to the manner in which it had been administered?"

"From the distribution of the poison in the organs and tissues and from the appearance of the body, I inferred that the administration of arsenic had been going on for a considerable time. There were signs of chronic poisoning which led me to believe that for quite a long time – perhaps months – deceased had been taking repeated small doses of the poison, and that the final dose took such rapid effect by reason of the enfeebled state of the deceased at the time when it was administered."

"And as to the mode of administration? Did you ascertain that?"

"In part, I ascertained it quite definitely. When the bearers went to the house to fetch the body, I accompanied them and took the opportunity to examine the bedroom. There I found on the mantelpiece a bottle of medicine with the name of deceased on the label and brought it away with me. It was an eight ounce bottle containing when full eight doses, of which only one had been taken. Dr Barnes and I, together, analyzed the remaining seven ounces of the medicine and obtained from it just over eleven grains of arsenic; that is a fraction over a grain and a half in each ounce dose. The arsenic was in solution and had been introduced into the medicine in the form of the solution known officially as Liquor Arsenicalis, or Fowler's Solution."

"That is perfectly definite," said the coroner. "But you said that you ascertained the mode of administration in part. Do you mean that you inferred the existence of some other vehicle?"

"Yes. A single dose of this medicine contained only a grain and a half of arsenic, which would hardly account for the effects produced or the amount of arsenic which was found in the body. Of course, the preceding dose from the other bottle may have contained the poison, too, or it may have been taken in some other way."

"What other way do you suggest?"

"I can merely suggest possibilities. A meal was taken about eight o'clock. If that meal had contained a small quantity of arsenic – even a single grain – that, added to what was in the medicine, would have been enough to cause death. But there is no evidence whatever that the food did contain arsenic."

"If the previous dose of medicine had contained the same quantity of the poison as the one that was last taken, would that account for the death of deceased?"

"Yes. He would then have taken over three grains in four hours – more than the minimum fatal dose."

"Did you see the other – the empty medicine bottle?"

"No. I looked for it and should have taken possession of it, but it was not there."

"Is there anything else that you have to tell us concerning your examination?"

"No, I think I have told you all I know about the case."

The coroner cast an interrogatory glance at the jury, and when none of them accepted the implied invitation, he released the witness and named Dr Barnes as his successor.

I need not record in detail the evidence of this witness. Having deposed that he was a Doctor of Science and lecturer in Chemistry at St Martha's Medical College, he proceeded to confirm Dr Randall's evidence as to the analysis, giving somewhat fuller and more precise details. He had been present at the autopsy, but he was not a pathologist and was not competent to describe the condition of the body. He had analyzed the contents of the medicine bottle with Dr Randall's assistance and he confirmed the last witness's statement as to the quantity of arsenic found and the form in which it had been introduced – Fowler's Solution.

"What is the strength of Fowler's Solution?"

"It contains four grains of arsenic – or, more strictly, of arsenious acid – to the fluid ounce. So that, as the full bottle of medicine must have contained just over twelve and a half grains of arsenious acid, the quantity of Fowler's Solution introduced must have been a little over three fluid ounces; three point fourteen, to be exact."

"You are confident that it was Fowler's Solution that was used?"

"Yes; the chemical analysis showed that; but in addition, there was the colour and the smell. Fowler's Solution is coloured red with Red Sandalwood and scented with Tincture of Lavender as a precaution against accidents. Otherwise it would be colourless, odourless and tasteless, like water."

On the conclusion of Dr Barnes' evidence, the coroner remarked to the jury: "I think we ought to be clear on the facts with regard to this medicine. Let Mabel Withers be recalled."

Once more the housemaid took her place by the table and the coroner resumed the examination.

"You say that the last bottle of medicine came early in the afternoon. Can you tell us the exact time?"

"It was about a quarter to three. I remember that because when I took up the new bottle, I asked Mr Monkhouse if he had had his medicine and he said that his brother, Mr Amos Monkhouse, had given him a dose at two o'clock just before he left."

"Did you open the fresh bottle?"

"I took off the paper wrapping and the cap but I didn't take the cork out."

"Was the old bottle empty then?"

"No; there was one dose left in it. That would be due at six o'clock."

"Do you know what became of the old bottle?"

"Yes. When I had given him his last dose – that was out of the new bottle – I took the old bottle away and washed it at once."

"Why did you wash the bottle?"

"The used medicine bottles were always washed and sent back to Dr Dimsdale."

"Did you send back the corks, too?"

"No, the corks were usually burned in the rubbish destructor."

"Do you know what happened to this particular cork?"

"I took it down with me in the morning and dropped it in the bin which was kept for the rubbish to be taken out to the destructor. The cork must have been burned with the other rubbish the same day."

"When you gave deceased that last dose of medicine from the new bottle, did you notice anything unusual about it? Any smell, for instance?"

"I noticed a very faint smell of lavender. But that was not unusual. His medicine often smelt of lavender."

"Do you know if the previous bottle of medicine smelt of lavender?"

"Yes, it did. I noticed it when I was washing out the bottle."

"That, gentlemen," said the coroner, as he wrote down the answer, "is a very important fact. You will notice that it bears out Dr Randall's opinion that more than one dose of the poison had been given; that, in fact, a number of repeated small doses had been administered. And, so far as we can see at present, the medicine was, at least, the principal medium of its administration. The next problem that we have to solve is how the poison got into the medicine. If none of you wish to put any questions to the very intelligent witness whom we have just been examining, I think we had better call Dr Dimsdale and hear what he has to tell us."

The jury had no questions to put to Mabel but were manifestly all agog to hear Dr Dimsdale's evidence. The housemaid was accordingly sent back to her seat, and the doctor stepped briskly – almost too briskly, I thought – up to the table.

CHAPTER FIVE

Madeline's Ordeal

I was rather sorry for Dimsdale. His position was a very disagreeable one and he fully realized it. His patient had been poisoned before his very eyes and he had never suspected even grave illness. In a sense, the death of Harold Monkhouse lay at his door and it was pretty certain that every one present would hold him accountable for the disaster. Indeed, it was likely that he would receive less than justice. Those who judged him would hardly stop to reflect on the extraordinary difficulties that beset a busy medical man whose patient is being secretly poisoned; would fail to consider the immense number of cases of illness presented to him in the course of years of practice and the infinitely remote probability that any one of them is a case of poison. The immense majority of doctors pass through the whole of their professional lives without meeting with such a case; and it is not surprising that when the infinitely rare contingency arises, it nearly always takes the practitioner unawares. My own amazement at this incredible horror tended to make me sympathetic towards Dimsdale and it was with some relief that I noted the courteous and considerate manner that the coroner adopted in dealing with the new witness.

"I think," the former observed, "that we had better, in the first place, pursue our inquiries concerning the medicine. You have heard the evidence of Dr Randall and Dr Barnes. This bottle of medicine, before any was taken from it, contained twelve and a half grains of arsenious acid, in the form of just over three fluid ounces of Fowler's Solution. Can you suggest any explanation of that fact?"

"No," replied Dimsdale, "I cannot."

"What should the bottle have contained? What was the composition of the medicine?"

"The medicine was just a simple, very mild tonic and alternative. The bottle contained twenty-four minims of Tincture of Nux Vomica, sixteen minims of Liquor Arsenicalis, half a fluid ounce of Syrup of Bitter Orange to cover the taste of the Nux Vomica and half an ounce of Compound Tincture of Cardamoms. So that each dose contained three minims of Tincture of Nux Vomica and two minims of Liquor Arsenicalis."

"Liquor Arsenicalis is another name for Fowler's Solution I understand?"

"Yes, it is the official name; the other is the popular name."

"Who supplied this medicine?"

"It was supplied by me."

"Do you usually supply your patients with medicine?"

"No. Only a few of my old patients who prefer to have their medicine from me. Usually, I write prescriptions which my patients have made up by chemists."

"This bottle, then, was made up in your own dispensary?"'

"Yes."

"Now, I put it to you, Dr Dimsdale: this medicine did actually contain Fowler's Solution, according to the prescription. Is it not possible that some mistake may have occurred in the amount put into the bottle?"

"No, it is quite impossible."

"Why is it impossible?"

"Because I made up this particular bottle myself. As my dispenser is not a qualified pharmacist, I always dispense, with my own hands, any medicines containing poisons. All dangerous drugs are kept in a poison cupboard under lock and key, and I carry the key on my private bunch. This is the key, and as you see, the lock is a Yale lock."

45

He held up the bunch with the little flat key separated, for the coroner's and the jurymen's inspection.

"But," said the coroner, "you have not made it clear that a mistake in the quantity was impossible."

"I was coming to that," replied Dimsdale. "The poisons in the cupboard are, of course, powerful drugs which are given only in small doses, and a special measure-glass is kept in the cupboard to measure them. This glass holds only two drachms – a hundred and twenty minims, that is, a quarter of an ounce. Now, the analysts found in this bottle three fluid ounces of Fowler's Solution. But to measure out that quantity, I should have had to fill the measure-glass twelve times! That is impossible. No one could do such a thing as that inadvertently, especially when he was dispensing poisons.

"But that is not all. The poison bottles are all quite small. The one in which the Liquor Arsenicalis is kept is a four ounce bottle. It happened that I had refilled it a few days previously and it was full when I dispensed this medicine. Now, obviously, if I had put three ounces of the Liquor into the medicine bottle, there would have remained in the dispensing bottle only one ounce. But the dispensing bottle is still practically full. I had occasion to use it this morning and I found it full save for the few minims that had been taken to make up the deceased's medicine.

"And there is another point. This medicine was coloured a deepish pink by the Tincture of Cardamoms. But if it had contained three ounces of Fowler's Solution in addition, it would have been a deep red of quite a different character. But I clearly remember the appearance of the bottle as it lay on the white paper when I was wrapping it up. It had the delicate pink colour that is imparted by the cochineal in the Tincture of Cardamoms."

The coroner nodded as he wrote down the reply, and enquired: "Would any of you, gentlemen, like to ask any questions concerning the bottle of medicine?"

"We should like to know, Sir," said the foreman, "whether this bottle of medicine ever left the doctor's hands before it was sent to deceased?"

"No, it did not," replied Dimsdale. "As the dispenser was absent, I put up the bottle entirely myself. I put in the cork, wrote the label, tied on the paper cap, wrapped the bottle up, sealed the wrapping, addressed it and gave it to the boy to deliver."

The foreman expressed himself as fully satisfied with this answer and the coroner then resumed: "Well, we seem to have disposed of the medicine so far as you are concerned, Doctor. We will now go on to consider the condition of deceased during the last few days. Did no suspicion of anything abnormal ever occur to you?"

"No, I neither perceived nor suspected anything abnormal."

"Is that not rather remarkable? I realize that poisoning would be the last thing that you would be looking for or expecting. But when it occurred, is it not a little strange that you did not recognize the symptoms?"

"Not at all," replied Dimsdale. "There was nothing to recognize. The classical symptoms of arsenic poisoning were entirely absent. You will remember that Sir Robert Detling had no more suspicion than I had."

"What are the classical symptoms, as you call them, of arsenic poisoning?"

"The recognized symptoms – which are present in the immense majority of cases – are acute abdominal pain and tenderness, intense thirst, nausea, vomiting and purging; the symptoms, in fact, of extreme irritation of the stomach and intestines. But in the case of deceased, these symptoms were entirely absent. There was, in my opinion, nothing whatever in his appearance or symptoms to suggest arsenic poisoning. His condition appeared in no way different from what I had known it to be on several previous occasions; just a variation for the worse of his ordinary ill-health."

"You do not doubt that arsenic poisoning was really the cause of his death?"

"The analysis seems to put the matter beyond question; otherwise – I mean apart from the analysis – I would not have entertained the idea of arsenic poisoning for a moment."

"But you do not dispute the cause of death?"

"No. Arsenic is extraordinarily variable in its effects, as Dr Randall mentioned, both on the dead body and on the living. Very anomalous cases of arsenic poisoning have been mistaken, during life, for opium poisoning."

The coroner wrote down the answer and having glanced over his notes, asked: "What was the condition of deceased when his wife went away from home?"

"He was much better. In fact his health seemed to be improving so much that I hoped he would soon be about again."

"And how soon after his wife's departure did his last attack begin?"

"I should hardly call it an attack. It was a gradual change for the worse. Mrs Monkhouse went away on the 29th of August. On the 2nd of September deceased was not so well and was extremely depressed and disappointed at the relapse. From that time his condition fluctuated, sometimes a little better and sometimes not so well. On the 8th he appeared rather seriously ill and was no better on the 9th, the day of the consultation with Sir Robert Detling After that he seemed to improve a little, and the slight improvement was maintained up to the 12th. His death came, at least to me, as quite a surprise."

"You spoke just now of several previous occasions on which attacks – or, if you prefer it, relapses – of a similar kind occurred. Looking back on those relapses by the light of what we now know, do you say that they were quite similar, in respect of the symptoms, to the one which ended in the death of deceased?"

"I should say they were identically similar. At any rate, I can recall no difference."

"Did any of them seem to be as severe as the fatal one?"

"Yes; in fact the last of them – which occurred in June – seemed to be more severe, only that it was followed by improvement and recovery. I have here the section of my card-index which relates to deceased. In the entry dated June 19 you will see that I have noted the patient's unsatisfactory condition."

He handed a small pack of index-cards to the coroner, who examined the upper card intently and then, with a sudden raising of the eyebrows, addressed the jury.

"I had better read out the entry. The card is headed 'Harold Monkhouse' and this entry reads: 'June 19. Patient very low and feeble. No appetite. Considerable gastric discomfort and troublesome cough. Pulse 90, small, thready. Heart sounds weak. Sending report to Mrs Monkhouse.'"

He laid the cards down on the table, and, looking fixedly at Dimsdale, repeated: "'Sending report to Mrs Monkhouse.' Where was Mrs Monkhouse?"

"Somewhere in Kent, I believe. I sent the report to the headquarters of the Women's Freedom League in Knightrider Street, Maidstone, from whence I supposed it would be forwarded to her."

For some seconds after receiving this answer the coroner continued to gaze steadily at the witness. At length he observed: "This is a remarkable coincidence. Can you recall the condition of deceased when Mrs Monkhouse went away on that occasion?"

"Yes. I remember that he was in comparatively good health. In fact, his improved condition furnished the opportunity for Mrs Monkhouse to make her visit to Maidstone."

"Can you tell us how soon after her departure on that occasion the relapse occurred?"

"I cannot say definitely, but my impression is that the change for the worse began a few days after she went away. Perhaps I might be able to judge by looking at my notes."

The coroner handed him back the index-cards, which he looked through rapidly. "Yes," he said, at length, "here is an entry on June 11 of a bottle of tonic medicine for Mrs Monkhouse. So she must have been at home on that date; and as it was a double-sized bottle, it was probably for her to take away with her."

"Then," said the coroner, "it is clear that, on the last two occasions, the deceased was comparatively well when his wife left home, but had a serious relapse soon after she went away. Now, what of the previous relapses?"

"I am afraid I cannot remember. I have an impression that Mrs Monkhouse was away from home when some of them occurred, but at this distance of time, I cannot recollect clearly. Possibly Mrs Monkhouse, herself, may be able to remember."

"Possibly," the coroner agreed, rather drily, "but as the point is of considerable importance, I should be glad if you would presently look through your case-cards and see if you can glean any definite information on the subject. Meanwhile we may pass on to one or two other matters. First as to the medicine which you prescribed for deceased; it contained, as you have told us, a certain amount of Fowler's Solution, and you considered deceased to be suffering from chronic gastritis. Is Fowler's Solution usually given in cases of gastritis?"

"No. It is usually considered rather unsuitable. But deceased was very tolerant of small doses of arsenic. I had often given it to him before as a tonic and it had always seemed to agree with him. The dose was extremely small – only two minims."

"How long have you known deceased?"

"I have known, and attended him professionally about twenty years."

"From your knowledge of him, should you say that he was a man who was likely to make enemies?"

"Not at all. He was a kindly, just and generous man, amiable and even-tempered; rather reserved and aloof; not very human, perhaps, and somewhat self-contained and solitary. But I could not imagine him making an enemy and, so far as I know, he never did."

The coroner reflected awhile after writing down this answer and then turned to the jury.

"Are there any questions that you wish to put to the witness, gentlemen?"

The jury consulted together for a few moments, and the foreman then replied: "We should like to know, Sir, if possible, whether Mrs Monkhouse was or was not away from home when the previous relapses occurred."

"I am afraid," said Dimsdale, "that I cannot be more explicit as the events occurred so long ago. The other witnesses – the members of the household – would be much more likely to remember. And I would urge you not to detain me from my professional duties longer than is absolutely necessary."

Hereupon a brief consultation took place between the coroner and the jury, with the result that Dimsdale was allowed to go about his business and Barbara was summoned to take his place. I had awaited this stage of the proceedings with some uneasiness and was now rather surprised and greatly relieved at the coroner's manner towards her; which was courteous and even sympathetic. Having expressed his and the jury's regret at having to trouble her in the very distressing circumstances, he proceeded at once to clear off the preliminaries, eliciting the facts that she was 32 years of age and had been married a little over three years, and then said: "Dr Dimsdale has told us that on the occasion of the attack or relapse in June last you were away from home, but he is not certain about the previous ones. Can you give us any information on the subject?"

"Yes," she replied, in a quiet, steady voice, "I recall quite clearly at least three previous occasions on which I went away from home leaving my husband apparently well – as well as he ever was – and came back to find him quite ill. But I think there were more than three occasions on which this happened, for I remember having once accused him, facetiously, of saving up his illnesses until I was out of the house."

"Can you remember if a serious relapse ever occurred when you were at home?"

"Not a really serious one. My husband's health was always very unstable and he often had to rest in bed for a day or two. But the really bad attacks of illness seem always to have occurred when I was away from home."

"Did it never strike you that this was a very remarkable fact?"

"I am afraid I did not give the matter as much consideration as I ought to have done. Deceased was always ailing, more or less, and those about him came to accept his ill-health as his normal condition."

"But you see the significance of it now?"

Barbara hesitated and then replied in a low voice and with evident agitation: "I see that it may have some significance, but I don't in the least understand it. I am quite overwhelmed and bewildered by the dreadful thing that has happened."

"Naturally, you are," the coroner said in a sympathetic tone, "and I am most reluctant to trouble you with questions under circumstances that must be so terrible to you. But we must find out the truth if we can."

"Yes, I realize that," she replied, "and thank you for your consideration."

The coroner bowed, and after a brief pause, asked: "Did it never occur to you to engage a nurse to attend to deceased?"

"Yes. I suggested it more than once to deceased, but he wouldn't hear of it. And I think he was right. There was nothing that a nurse could have done for him. He was not helpless and he was not continuously bed-ridden. He had a bell-push by his bedside and his secretary or the servants were always ready to do anything that he wanted done. The housemaid was most attentive to him. But he did not want much attention. He kept the books that he was reading on his bedside table and he liked to be left alone to read in peace. He felt that the presence of a nurse would have been disturbing."

"And at night?"

"At night his bell-push was connected with a bell in the secretary's bedroom. But he hardly ever used it. If his candle-lamp burned out he could put in a fresh candle from the box on his table; and he never seemed to want anything else."

"Besides deceased and yourself, who were the inmates of the house?"

"There was my husband's secretary, Mr Wallingford, Miss Norris, the cook, Anne Baker, the housemaid, Mabel Withers, and the kitchenmaid, Doris Brown."

"Why did deceased need a secretary? Did he transact much business?"

"No. The secretary wrote his few business letters, kept the accounts and executed any commissions, besides doing the various things that the master of the house would ordinarily have done. He is the son of an old friend of my husband's and he came to us when his father died."

"And Miss Norris? What was her position in the household?"

"She lived with us as a guest at my husband's invitation. She was the daughter of his first wife's sister, and he, more or less informally, adopted her as he had no children of his own."

"Deceased was a widower, then, when you married him?"

"Yes. His wife had been dead about two years."

'What was his age when he died?"

"He had just turned fifty-seven."

"On what sort of terms was deceased with the members of his household?"

"On the best of terms with them all. He was an undemonstrative man and rather cool and reserved with strangers and distinctly solitary and self-contained. But he was a kind and generous man and all the household, including the servants, were devoted to him."

"Was deceased engaged in any business or profession?"

"No, he had independent means, inherited from his father."

"Would you describe him as a wealthy man?"

"I believe he was quite well off, but he never spoke of his financial affairs to me, or to anybody but his lawyers."

"Do you know how his property is disposed of?"

"I know that he made a will, but I never enquired about the terms of it and he never told me."

"But surely you were an interested party."

"It was understood that some provision would be made for me if I survived him. That was all that concerned me. Deceased was not a man with whom it was necessary to make conditions; and I have some small property of my own. Mr Mayfield, who is present, of course, knows what the provisions of the will are as he is one of the executors."

Once more the coroner paused to look over his notes. Then he glanced inquiringly at the jury, and, when the foreman shook his head, he thanked Barbara and dismissed her; and as she walked back to her chair, pale and grave but perfectly composed, I found myself admiring her calm dignity and only hoping that the other witnesses would make as good a figure. But this hope was no sooner conceived than it was shattered. The next name that was called was Madeline Norris and for a few moments there was no response. At length Madeline rose slowly, ashen and ghastly of face, and walked unsteadily to the table. Her appearance – her deathly pallor and her trembling hands – struck me with dismay; and what increased my concern for the unfortunate girl was the subtle change in manner that I detected in the jury and the coroner. The poor girl's manifest agitation might surely have bespoken their sympathy; but not a sign of sympathy was discernible in their faces – nothing but a stony curiosity.

Having been sworn – on a testament which shook visibly in her grasp – she deposed that her name was Madeline Norris and her age twenty-seven.

"Any occupation?" the coroner enquired drily without looking up.

"I am a teacher at the Westminster College of Domestic Science."

"Teacher of what?"

"Principally of cookery and kitchen management, especially invalid cookery."

"Are you, yourself, a skilled cook?"

"Yes. It is my duty to demonstrate to the class."

"Have you ever cooked or prepared food for the deceased?"

"Yes. I usually cooked his meals when I was in the house at meal times."

"It has been stated that you prepared the last meal that deceased took. Is that correct?"

"Yes. I cooked an omelette for his supper."

"Will you describe to us the way in which you prepared that omelette?"

Madeline considered for a few moments and then replied in a low, shaky voice: "It was just a simple omelette. I first rubbed the pan with a cut clove of garlic and put in the butter to heat. Then I broke an egg into a cup, separated the yolk from the white, and, having beaten them up separately, mixed them and added a very small portion of pounded anchovy, a pinch or two of finely chopped parsley and a little salt. I cooked it in the usual way and turned it out on a hot plate which I covered at once."

"Who took it up to deceased?"

"I did. I ran straight up with it and sat and talked to deceased while he ate it."

"Did you meet anyone on your way up or in the bedroom?"

"No. There was nobody on the stairs, and the deceased was alone."

"Did deceased take anything to drink with his supper?"

"Yes. He had a glass of chablis. I fetched the bottle and the glass from the dining room and poured out the wine for him."

"Did you meet anybody in the dining room or coming or going?"

"No, I met nobody."

"Can you think of any way in which any poison could have got into the omelette or into the wine?"

"No. Nothing could possibly have got into the omelette. As to the wine, I poured it from the bottle into a clean glass. But the bottle was already open and had been in the cellaret since lunch."

"Now, with regard to the medicine. Did you give deceased any on the day before his death?"

"Yes. I gave him a dose soon after I came in – about six o'clock. That was the last dose in the bottle."

"Did you notice anything unusual about the medicine?"

"No. It was similar to what he had been taking for some days past."

"What was the medicine like?"

"It was nearly colourless with the faintest tinge of red and smelled slightly of lavender and bitter orange."

"Was there anything that caused you to notice particularly, on this occasion, the appearance and smell of the medicine?"

"No. I noticed the colour and the smell when I opened the, bottle on the previous morning to give deceased a dose."

"Did you examine the new bottle which had just been sent?"

"Yes. I looked at it and took out the cork and smelled it and tasted it."

"What made you do that?"

"I noticed that it seemed to contain Tincture of Cardamoms and I smelled and tasted it to find out if the other ingredients had been changed."

"And what conclusion did you arrive at?"

"That they had not been changed. I could taste the Nux Vomica and smell the orange and the Liquor Arsenicalis – at least the lavender"

"Did you realize what the lavender smell was due to?"

"Yes. I recognized it as the smell of Liquor Arsenicalis. I knew that deceased was taking Liquor Arsenicalis because I had asked Dr Dimsdale about it when I first noticed the smell."

The coroner wrote down this answer and then, raising his head, looked steadily at Madeline for some seconds without speaking; and the jury looked harder still. At length the former spoke, slowly, deliberately, emphatically.

"You have told us that you examined this medicine to find out what it contained, and that you were able to recognize Tincture of Cardamoms by its colour and Liquor Arsenicalis by its smell. It would seem, then, that you know a good deal about drugs. Is that so?"

"I know something about drugs. My father was a doctor and he taught me simple dispensing so that I could help him."

The coroner nodded. "Was there any reason why you should have taken so much interest in the composition of deceased's medicine?"

Madeline did not answer immediately. And as she stood trembling and hesitating in evident confusion, the coroner gazed at her stonily, and the jury craned forward to catch her reply.

"I used to examine his medicine," she replied at length, in a low voice and a reluctant and confused manner, "because I knew that it often contained Liquor Arsenicalis and I used to wonder whether that was good for him. I understood from my father that it was a rather irritating drug, and it did not seem very suitable for a patient who suffered from gastritis."

There was a pause after she had spoken and something in the appearance of the inquisitors almost as if they had been a little disappointed by this eminently reasonable answer. At length the coroner broke the silence by asking, with a slight softening of manner: "You have said that the change in colour of the last medicine led you to taste and smell it to ascertain if the other ingredients had been changed. You have said that you decided that they had not been changed. Are you sure of that? Can you swear that the smell of lavender was not stronger in this bottle than in the previous ones?"

"It did not seem to me to be stronger."

"Supposing the bottle had then contained as much Liquor Arsenicalis as was found in it by the analysts, would you have been able to detect it by the smell or otherwise?"

"Yes, I feel sure that I should. The analysts found three ounces of Liquor Arsenicalis; that would be nearly half the bottle. I am sure I should have detected that amount, not only by the strong smell but by the colour, too."

"You are sure that the colour of this medicine was due to Cardamoms only?"

"Yes, that is to cochineal. I recognized it at once. It is perfectly unmistakable and quite different from the colour of Red Sandalwood, with which Liquor Arsenicalis is coloured. Besides, this medicine was only a deepish pink in colour. But if three ounces of Liquor Arsenicalis had been in the bottle, the medicine would have been quite a dark red."

"You have had some experience in dispensing. Do you consider it possible that the Liquor Arsenicalis could have been put into the medicine by mistake when it was being made up?"

"It would be quite impossible if a minim measure-glass was used, as the glass would have had to be filled twelve times. But this is never done. One does not measure large quantities in small measures. Three ounces would be measured out in a four or five ounce measure, as a rule, or, possibly in a two ounce measure, by half refilling it."

"Might not the wrong measure-glass have been taken up by mistake?"

"That is, of course, just possible. But it is most unlikely; for the great disproportion between the large measure-glass and the little stock-bottle would be so striking that it could hardly fail to be noticed."

"Then, from your own observation and from Dr Dimsdale's evidence, you reject the idea that a mistake may have been made in dispensing this bottle of medicine?"

"Yes, entirely. I have heard Dr Dimsdale's evidence and I examined the medicine. I am convinced that he could not have made a mistake under the circumstances that he described and I am certain that the medicine that I saw did not contain more than a small quantity – less than a drachm – of Liquor Arsenicalis."

"You are not forgetting that the analysts actually found the equivalent of three ounces of Liquor Arsenicalis in the bottle?"

"No. But I am sure it was not there when I examined the bottle."

The coroner wrote down this answer with a deliberate air, and, when he had finished, turned to the jury.

"I think we have nothing more to ask this witness, unless there is any point that you want made more clear."

There was a brief silence. Then the super-intelligent juryman interposed.

"I should like to know if this witness ever had any Liquor Arsenicalis in her possession."

The coroner held up a warning hand to Madeline, and replied: "That question, Sir, is not admissible. It is a principle of English law that a witness cannot be compelled to make a statement incriminating him – or herself. But an affirmative answer to this question would be an incriminating statement."

"But I am perfectly willing to answer the question," Madeline said eagerly. "I have never had in my possession any Liquor Arsenicalis or any other preparation of arsenic."

"That answers your question, Sir," said the coroner, as he wrote down the answer, "and if you have nothing more to ask, we can release the witness."

He handed his pen to Madeline, and when she had signed her depositions – a terribly shaky signature it must have been – she came back to her chair, still very pale and agitated, but obviously relieved at having got through the ordeal. I had taken her arm as she sat down and was complimenting her on the really admirable way in which she had given her evidence, when I heard the name of Anthony Wallingford called and realized that another unpleasant episode had arrived.

CHAPTER SIX

The Verdict

I had not been taking much notice of Wallingford, my attention being occupied with the two women when it strayed from the proceedings. Beyond an irritated consciousness of his usual restless movements, I had no information as to how the soul-shaking incidents of this appalling day were affecting him. But when he rose drunkenly and, grasping the back of his chair, rolled his eyes wildly round the Court, I realized that there were breakers ahead.

When I say that he rose drunkenly, I use the word advisedly. Familiar as I was with his peculiarities – his jerkings, twitchings and grimacings – I saw, at once, that there was something unusual both in his face and in his bearing; a dull wildness of expression and an uncertainty of movement that I had never observed before. He had not come to the Court with the rest of us, preferring, for some reason, to come alone. And I now suspected that he had taken the opportunity to fortify himself on the way.

I was not the only observer of his condition. As he walked, with deliberate care, from his seat to the table, I noticed the coroner eyeing him critically and the jury exchanging dubious glances and whispered comments. He made a bad start by dropping the book on the floor and sniggering nervously as he stooped to pick it up; and I could see plainly, by the stiffness of the coroner's manner that he had made an unfavourable impression before he began his evidence.

"You were secretary to the deceased?" said the coroner, when the witness had stated his name, age (33) and occupation. "What was the nature of your duties?"

"The ordinary duties of a secretary," was the dogged reply.

"Will you kindly give us particulars of what you did for deceased?"

"I opened his business letters and answered them and some of his private ones. And I kept his accounts and paid his bills."

"What accounts would those be? Deceased was not in business, I understand?"

"No, they were his domestic accounts; his income from investments and rents and his expenditure."

"Did you attend upon deceased personally; I mean in the way of looking after his bodily comfort and supplying his needs?"

"I used to look in on him from time to time to see if he wanted anything done. But it wasn't my business to wait on him. I was his secretary, not his valet."

"Who did wait on him, and attend to his wants?"

"The housemaid, chiefly, and Miss Norris, and of course, Mrs Monkhouse. But he didn't usually want much but his food, his medicine, a few books from the library and a supply of candles for his lamp. His bell-push was connected with a bell in my room at night, but he never rang it."

"Then, practically, the housemaid did everything for him?"

"Not everything. Miss Norris cooked most of his meals, we all used to give him his medicine, I used to put out his books and keep his fountain pen filled, and Mrs Monkhouse kept his candle-box supplied. That was what he was most particular about as he slept badly and used to read at night."

"You give us the impression, Mr Wallingford," the coroner said, drily, "that you must have had a good deal of leisure."

"Then I have given you the wrong impression. I was kept constantly on the go, doing jobs, paying tradesmen, shopping and running errands."

"For whom?"

"Everybody. Deceased, Mrs Monkhouse, Miss Norris and even Dr Dimsdale. I was everybody's servant."

"What did you do for Mrs Monkhouse?"

"I don't see what that has got to do with this inquest?"

"That is not for you to decide," the coroner said, sternly. "You will be good enough to answer my question."

Wallingford winced as if he had had his ears cuffed. In a moment, his insolence evaporated and I could see his hands shaking as he, evidently, cudgelled his brains for a reply. Suddenly he seemed to have struck an idea.

"Shopping of various kinds," said he; "for instance, there were the candles for deceased. His lamp was of German make and English lamp-candles wouldn't fit it. So I used to have to go to a German shop at Sparrow Corner by the Tower, to get packets of Schneider's stearine candles. That took about half a day."

The coroner, stolidly and without comment, wrote down the answer, but my experience as a counsel told me that it had been a dummy question, asked to distract the witness's attention and cover a more significant one that was to follow. For that question I waited expectantly, and when it came my surmise was confirmed.

"And Dr Dimsdale? What did you have to do for him?"

"I used to help him with his books sometimes when he hadn't got a dispenser. I am a pretty good accountant and he isn't."

"Where does Dr Dimsdale do his bookkeeping?"

"At the desk in the surgery."

"And is that where you used to work?"

"Yes."

"Used Dr Dimsdale to work with you or did you do the books by yourself?"

"I usually worked by myself."

"At what time in the day used you to work there?"

"In the afternoon, as a rule."

"At what hours does Dr Dimsdale visit his patients?"

"Most of the day He goes out about ten and finishes about six or seven."

"So that you would usually be alone in the surgery?"

"Yes, usually."

As the coroner wrote down the answer I noticed the super-intelligent juryman fidgeting in his seat. At length he burst out: "Is the poison cupboard in the surgery?"

The coroner looked interrogatively at Wallingford, who stared at him blankly in sudden confusion.

"You heard the question? Is the poison cupboard there?"

"I don't know. It may be. It wasn't any business of mine."

"Is there any cupboard in the surgery? You must know that."

"Yes, there is a cupboard there, but I don't know what is in it."

"Did you never see it open?"

"No. Never."

"And you never had the curiosity to look into it?"

"Of course I didn't. Besides I couldn't. It was locked."

"Was it always locked when you were there?"

"Yes, always."

"Are you certain of that?"

"Yes, perfectly certain."

Here the super-intelligent juror looked as if he were about to spring across the table as he demanded eagerly: "How does the witness know that that cupboard was locked?"

The coroner looked slightly annoyed. He had been playing his fish carefully and was in no wise helped by this rude jerk of the line. Nevertheless, he laid down his pen and looked expectantly at the witness. As for Wallingford, he was struck speechless. Apparently his rather muddled brain had suddenly taken in the import of the question, for he stood with dropped jaw and damp, pallid face, staring at the juryman in utter consternation.

"Well," said the coroner, after an interval, "how did you know that it was locked?"

Wallingford pulled himself together by an effort and replied: "Why, I knew — I knew, of course, that it must be locked."

"Yes; but the question is, how did you know?"

"Why it stands to reason that it must have been locked."

"Why does it stand to reason? Cupboards are not always locked."

"Poison cupboards are. Besides, you heard Dimsdale say that he always kept this cupboard locked. He showed you the key."

Once more the coroner, having noted the answer, laid down his pen and looked steadily at the witness.

"Now, Mr Wallingford," said he, "I must caution you to be careful as to what you say. This is a serious matter, and you are giving evidence on oath. You said just now that you did not know whether the poison cupboard was or was not in the surgery. You said that you did not know what was in that cupboard. Now you say that you knew the cupboard must have been locked because it was the poison cupboard. Then it seems that you *did* know that it was the poison cupboard. Isn't that so?"

"No. I didn't know then. I do now because I heard Dimsdale say that it was."

"Then, you said that you were perfectly certain that the cupboard was always locked whenever you were working there. That meant that you knew positively, as a fact, that it *was* locked. Now you say that you knew that it must be locked. But that is an assumption, an opinion, a belief. Now, a man of your education must know the difference between a mere belief and actual knowledge. Will you, please, answer definitely: Did you, or did you not, know as a fact whether that cupboard was or was not locked?"

"Well, I didn't actually know, but I took it for granted that it was locked."

"You did not try the door?"

"Certainly not. Why should I?"

"Very well. Does any gentleman of the jury wish to ask any further questions about this cupboard?"

There was a brief silence. Then the foreman said: "We should like the witness to say what he means and not keep contradicting himself."

"You hear that, Sir," said the coroner. "Please be more careful in your answers in future. Now, I want to ask you about that last bottle of medicine. Did you notice anything unusual in its appearance?"

"No. I didn't notice it at all. I didn't know that it had come"

"Did you go into deceased's room on that day – the Wednesday?"

"Yes, I went to see deceased in the morning about ten o'clock and gave him a dose of his medicine; and I looked in on him in the evening about nine o'clock to see if he wanted anything, but he didn't."

"Did you give him any medicine then?"

"No. It was not due for another hour."

"What was his condition then?"

"He looked about the same as usual. He seemed inclined to doze, so I did not stay long."

"Is that the last time you saw him alive?"

"No. I looked in again just before eleven. He was then in much the same state – rather drowsy – and, at his request, I turned out the gas and left him."

"Did you light the candle?"

"No, he always did that himself, if he wanted it."

"Did you give him any medicine?"

"No. He had just had a dose."

"Did he tell you that he had?"

"No. I could see that there was a dose gone."

"From which bottle was that?"

"There was only one bottle there. It must have been the new bottle, as only one dose had been taken."

"What colour was the medicine?"

Wallingford hesitated a moment or two as if suspecting a trap. Then he replied, doggedly: "I don't know. I told you I didn't notice it."

"You said that you didn't notice it at all and didn't know that it had come. Now you say that you observed that only one dose had been taken from it and that you inferred that it was the new bottle. Which of those statements is the true one?"

"They are both true," Wallingford protested in a whining tone. "I meant that I didn't notice the medicine particularly and that I didn't know when it came."

"That is not what you said," the coroner rejoined. "However, we will let that pass. Is there anything more that you wish to ask this witness, gentlemen? If not, we will release him and take the evidence of Mr Mayfield."

I think the jury would have liked to bait Wallingford but apparently could not think of any suitable questions. But they watched him malevolently as he added his – probably quite illegible – signature to his depositions and followed him with their eyes as he tottered shakily back to his seat. Immediately afterwards my name was called and I took my place at the table, not without a slight degree of nervousness; for, though I was well enough used to examinations, it was in the capacity of examiner, not of witness, and I was fully alive to the possibility of certain pitfalls which the coroner might, if he were wide enough awake, dig for me. However, when I had been sworn and had given my particulars (Rupert Mayfield, 35, Barrister-at-Law, of No. 64 Fig Tree Court, Inner Temple) the coroner's conciliatory manner led me to hope that it would be all plain sailing.

"How long have you known deceased?" was the first question.

"About two and a half years," I replied.

"You are one of the executors of his will, Mrs Monkhouse has told us."

"Yes."

"Do you know why you were appointed executor after so short an acquaintance?"

"I am an old friend of Mrs Monkhouse. I have known her since she was a little girl. I was a friend of her father – or rather, her step-father."

"Was it by her wish that you were made executor?"

"I believe that the suggestion came from the deceased's family solicitor, Mr Brodribb, who is my co-executor. But probably he was influenced by my long acquaintance with Mrs Monkhouse."

"Has probate been applied for?"

"Yes."

"Then there can be no objections to your disclosing the provisions of the will. We don't want to hear them in detail, but I will ask you to give us a general idea of the disposal of deceased's property."

"The gross value of the estate is about fifty-five thousand pounds, of which twelve thousand represents real property and forty-three thousand personal. The principal beneficiaries are: Mrs Monkhouse, who receives a house valued at four thousand pounds and twenty thousand pounds in money and securities; the Reverend Amos Monkhouse, land of the value of five thousand and ten thousand invested money; Madeline Norris, a house and land valued at three thousand and five thousand in securities; Anthony Wallingford, four thousand pounds. Then there are legacies of a thousand pounds each to the two executors, and of three hundred, two hundred and one hundred respectively to the housemaid, the cook and the kitchen-maid. That accounts for the bulk of the estate. Mrs Monkhouse is the residuary legatee."

The coroner wrote down the answer as I gave it and then read it out slowly for me to confirm, working out, at the same time, a little sum on a spare piece of paper – as did also the intellectual juryman.

"I think that gives us all the information we want," the former remarked, glancing at the jury; and as none of them made any comment, he proceeded: "Did you see much of deceased during the last few months?"

"I saw him usually once or twice a week. Sometimes oftener. But I did not spend much time with him. He was a solitary, bookish man who preferred to be alone most of his time."

"Did you take particular notice of his state of health?"

"No, but I did observe that his health seemed to grow rather worse lately."

"Did it appear to you that he received such care and attention as a man in his condition ought to have received?"

"It did not appear to me that he was neglected."

"Did you realize how seriously ill he was?"

"No, I am afraid not. I regarded him merely as a chronic invalid."

"It never occurred to you that he ought to have had a regular nurse?"

"No, and I do not think he would have consented. He greatly disliked having anyone about his room."

"Is there anything within your knowledge that would throw any light on the circumstances of his death?"

"No. Nothing."

"Have you ever known arsenic in any form to be used in that household for any purpose; any fly-papers, weed-killer or insecticides, for instance?"

"No, I do not remember ever having seen anything used in that household which, to my knowledge or belief, contained arsenic."

"Do you know of any fact or circumstance which, in your opinion, ought to be communicated to this Court or which might help the jury in arriving at their verdict?"

"No, I do not."

This brought my examination to an end. I was succeeded by the cook and the kitchenmaid, but, as they had little to tell, and that little entirely negative, their examination was quite brief. When the last witness was dismissed, the coroner addressed the jury.

"We have now, gentlemen," said he, "heard all the evidence that is at present available, and we have the choice of two courses; which are, either to adjourn the inquiry until further evidence is available, or to find a verdict on the evidence which we have heard. I incline strongly to the latter plan. We are now in a position to answer the questions, how, when and where the deceased came by his death, and when we have done that, we shall have discharged our proper function. What is your feeling on the matter, gentlemen?"

The jury's feeling was very obviously that they wished to get the inquiry over and go about their business, and when they had made this clear, the coroner proceeded to sum up.

"I shall not detain you, gentlemen, with a long address. All that is necessary is for me to recapitulate the evidence very briefly and point out the bearing of it.

"First as to the cause of death. It has been given in evidence by two fully qualified and expert witnesses that deceased died from the effects of poisoning by arsenic. That is a matter of fact which is not disputed and which you must accept, unless you have any reasons for rejecting their testimony, which I feel sure you have not. Accepting the fact of death by poison, the question then arises as to how the poison came to be taken by deceased. There are three possibilities: he may have taken it himself, voluntarily and knowingly; he may have taken it by accident or mischance; or it may have been administered to him knowingly and maliciously by some other person or persons. Let us consider those three possibilities.

"The suggestion that deceased might have taken the poison voluntarily is highly improbable in three respects. First, since deceased was mostly bed-ridden, it would have been almost impossible for him to have obtained the poison. Second, there is the nature of the poison. Arsenic has often been used for homicidal poisoning but seldom for suicide; for an excellent reason. The properties of arsenic which commend it to poisoners – its complete freedom from taste and the indefinite symptoms that it produces – do not commend it to the suicide. He has no need to conceal either the administration or its results. His principal need is rapidity of effect. But arsenic is a relatively slow poison and one which usually causes great suffering. It is not at all suited to the suicide. Then there is the third objection that the mode of administration was quite unlike that of a suicide. For the latter usually takes his poison in one large dose, to get the business over; but here it was evidently given in repeated small doses over a period that may have been anything from a week to a year. And, finally, there is not a particle of evidence in favour of the supposition that deceased took the poison himself.

"To take the second case, that of accident: the only possibility known to us is that of a mistake in dispensing the medicine. But the evidence of Dr Dimsdale and Miss Norris must have convinced you that the improbability of a mistake is so great as to be practically negligible. Of course, the poison might have found its way accidentally into the medicine or the food or both in some manner unknown to us. But while we admit this, we have, in fact, to form our decision on what is known to us, not what is conceivable but unknown.

"When we come to the third possibility, that the poison was administered to deceased by some other person or persons with intent to compass his death, we find it supported by positive evidence. There is the bottle of medicine for instance It contained a large quantity of arsenic in a soluble form But two witnesses have sworn that it could not have contained, and, in fact, did not contain that quantity of arsenic when it left Dr Dimsdale's surgery or when it was delivered at deceased's house. Moreover, Miss Norris has sworn that she examined this bottle of medicine at six o'clock in the evening and that it did not then contain more than a small quantity – less than a drachm – of Liquor Arsenicalis. She was perfectly positive. She spoke with expert knowledge. She gave her reasons, and they were sound reasons. So that the evidence in our possession is to the effect that at six o'clock in the afternoon, that bottle of medicine did not contain more than a drachm – about a teaspoonful – of Liquor Arsenicalis; whereas at half-past ten, when a dose from the bottle was given to deceased by the housemaid, it contained some three ounces – about six tablespoonfuls. This is proved by the discovery of the poison in the stomach of deceased and by the exact analysis of the contents of the bottle. It follows that, between six o'clock and half-past ten, a large quantity of arsenical solution must have been put into the bottle. It is impossible to suppose that it could have got in by accident. Somebody must have put it in; and the only conceivable object that the person could have had in putting that poison into the bottle would be to cause the death of deceased.

"But further; the evidence of the medical witnesses proves that arsenic had been taken by deceased on several previous occasions. That, in fact, he had been taking arsenic in relatively small doses for some time past – how long we do not know – and had been suffering from chronic arsenical poisoning. The evidence, therefore, points very strongly and definitely to the conclusion that some person or persons had been, for some unascertained time past, administering arsenic to him.

"Finally, as to the identity of the person or persons who administered the poison, I need not point out that we have no evidence. You will have noticed that a number of persons benefit in a pecuniary sense by deceased's death. But that fact establishes no suspicion against any of them in the absence of positive evidence; and there is no positive evidence connecting any one of them with the administration of the poison. With these remarks, gentlemen, I leave you to consider the evidence and agree upon your decision."

The jury did not take long in arriving at their verdict. After a few minutes' eager discussion, the foreman announced that they had come to an unanimous decision.

"And what is the decision upon which you have agreed?" the coroner asked.

"We find," was the reply, "that deceased died from the effects of arsenic, administered to him by some person or persons unknown, with the deliberate intention of causing his death."

"Yes," said the coroner; "that is, in effect, a verdict of wilful murder against some person or persons unknown. I agree with you entirely. No other verdict was possible on the evidence before us. It is unfortunate that no clue has happened as to the perpetrator of this abominable crime, but we may hope that the investigations of the police will result in the identification and conviction of the murderer."

The conclusion of the coroner's address brought the proceedings to an end, and as he finished speaking, the spectators rose and began to pass out of the Court. I remained for a minute to speak a few words to Mr Holman and ask him to transcribe his report in duplicate. Then, I, too, went out to find my three companions squeezing into a taxicab which had drawn up opposite the entrance, watched with ghoulish curiosity by a quite considerable crowd. The presence of that crowd informed me that the horrible notoriety which I had foreseen had even now begun to envelop us. The special editions of the evening papers were already out, with, at least, the opening scenes of the inquest in print. Indeed, during the short drive to Hilborough Square, I saw more than one news-vendor dealing out papers to little knots of eager purchasers, and once, through the open window, a stentorian voice was borne in with hideous distinctness, announcing: "Sensational Inquest! Funeral stopped!"

71

I glanced from Wallingford, cowering in his corner, to Barbara, sitting stiffly upright with a slight frown on her pale face. As she caught my eye, she remarked bitterly: "It seems that we are having greatness thrust upon us."

CHAPTER SEVEN

The Search Warrant

The consciousness of the horrid notoriety that had already attached itself to us was brought home to me once more when the taxi drew up at the house in Hilborough Square. I stepped out first to pay the driver, and Barbara following, with the latch-key ready in her hand, walked swiftly to the door, looking neither to the right nor left, opened it and disappeared into the hall; while the other two, lurking in the cab until the door was open, then darted across the pavement, entered and disappeared also. Nor was their hasty retreat unjustified. Lingering doggedly and looking about me with a sort of resentful defiance, I found myself a focus of observation. In the adjoining houses, not a window appeared to be unoccupied. The usually vacant foot-way was populous with loiterers whose interest in me and in the ill-omened house was undissembled; while raucous voices, strange to those quiet precincts, told me that the astute news-vendors had scented and exploited a likely market.

With ill-assumed indifference I entered the house and shut the door – perhaps rather noisily; and was about to enter the dining room when I heard hurried steps descending the stairs and paused to look up. It was the woman – the cook's sister, I think – who had been left to take care of the house while the servants were absent; and something of eagerness and excitement in her manner caused me to walk to the foot of the stairs to meet her.

"Is anything amiss?" I asked in a low voice as she neared the bottom of the flight.

She held up a warning finger, and coming close to me, whispered hoarsely: "There's two gentlemen upstairs, Sir, leastways they look like gentlemen, but they are really policemen."

"What are they doing upstairs?" I asked.

"Just walking through the rooms and looking about. They came about a quarter of an hour ago, and when I let them in they said they were police officers and that they had come to search the premises."

"Did they say anything about a warrant?"

"Oh, yes, Sir. I forgot about that. One of them showed me a paper and said it was a search warrant. So of course I couldn't do anything. And then they started going through the house with their note-books like auctioneers getting ready for a sale."

"I will go up and see them," said I; "and meanwhile you had better let Mrs Monkhouse know. Where did you leave them?"

"In the large back bedroom on the first floor," she replied. "I think it was Mr Monkhouse's."

On this I began quickly to ascend the stairs, struggling to control a feeling of resentment which, though natural enough, I knew to be quite unreasonable. Making my way direct to the dead man's room, I entered and found two tall men standing before an open cupboard. They turned on hearing me enter and the elder of them drew a large wallet from his pocket.

"Mr Mayfield, I think, Sir," said he. "I am Detective Superintendent Miller and this is Detective-Sergeant Cope. Here is my card and this is the search warrant, if you wish to see it."

I glanced at the document and returning it to him asked: "Wouldn't it have been more in order if you had waited to show the warrant to Mrs Monkhouse before beginning your search?"

"That is what we have done," he replied, suavely. "We have disturbed nothing yet. We have just been making a preliminary inspection. Of course," he continued, "I understand how unpleasant this search is for Mrs Monkhouse and the rest of your friends, but you, Sir, as a lawyer will realize the position. That poor gentleman was poisoned with arsenic in this house. Somebody in this house had arsenic in his or her possession and we have got to see if any traces of it are left. After all, you know, Sir, we are acting in the interests of everybody but the murderer."

This was so obviously true that it left me nothing to say. Nor was there any opportunity, for, as the superintendent concluded, Barbara entered the room. I looked at her a little anxiously as I briefly explained the situation. But there was no occasion. Pale and sombre of face, she was nevertheless perfectly calm and self-possessed and greeted the two officers without a trace of resentment; indeed, when the superintendent was disposed to be apologetic, she cut him short by exclaiming energetically: "But, surely, who should be more anxious to assist you than I? It is true that I find it incredible that this horrible crime could have been perpetrated by any member of my household. But it was perpetrated by somebody. And if, either here or elsewhere, I can help you in any way to drag that wretch out into the light of day, I am at your service, no matter who the criminal may be. Do you wish anyone to attend you in your search?"

"I think, Madam, it would be well if you were present, and perhaps Mr Mayfield. If we want any of the others, we can send for them. Where are they now?"

"Miss Norris and Mr Wallingford are in the dining room. The servants have just come in and I think have gone to the kitchen or their sitting room"

"Then," said Miller, "we had better begin with the dining room"

We went down the stairs, preceded by Barbara, who opened the dining room door and introduced the visitors to the two inmates in tones as quiet and matter-of-fact as if she were announcing the arrival of the gas-fitter or the upholsterer. I was sorry that the other two had not been warned, for the announcement took them both by surprise and they were in no condition for surprises of this rather alarming kind. At the word "search," Madeline started up with a smothered exclamation and then sat down again, trembling and pale as death; while as for Wallingford, if the two officers had come to pinion him and lead him forth to the gallows, he could not have looked more appalled.

Our visitors were scrupulously polite, but they were also keenly observant and I could see that each had made a mental note of the effect of their arrival. But, of course, they made no outward sign of interest in any of us but proceeded stolidly with their business; and I noticed that, before proceeding to a detailed inspection, they opened their note-books and glanced through what was probably a rough inventory, to see that nothing had been moved in the interval since their preliminary inspection.

The examination of the dining room was, however, rather perfunctory. It contained nothing that appeared to interest them, and after going through the contents of the sideboard cupboards methodically, the superintendent turned a leaf of his note-book and said: "I think that will do, Madam. Perhaps we had better take the library next. Who keeps the keys of the bureau and the cupboard?"

"Mr Wallingford has charge of the library," replied Barbara. "Will you give the superintendent your keys, Tony?"

"There's no need for that," said Miller. "If Mr Wallingford will come with us, he can unlock the drawers and cupboard and tell us anything that we want to know about the contents."

Wallingford rose with a certain alacrity and followed us into the library, which adjoined the dining room. Here the two officers again consulted their note-books, and having satisfied themselves that the room was as they had left it, began a detailed survey, watched closely and with evident anxiety by Wallingford. They began with a cupboard, or small armoire, which formed the upper member of a large, old-fashioned bureau. Complying with Miller's polite request that it might be unlocked, Wallingford produced a bunch of keys, and, selecting from it, after much nervous fumbling, a small key, endeavoured to insert it into the keyhole; but his hand was in such a palsied condition that he was unable to introduce it.

"Shall I have a try, Sir?" the superintendent suggested, patiently, adding with a smile, "I don't smoke quite so many cigarettes as you seem to."

His efforts, however, also failed, for the evident reason that it was the wrong key. Thereupon he looked quickly through the bunch, picked out another key and had the cupboard open in a twinkling, revealing a set of shelves crammed with a disorderly litter of cardboard boxes, empty ink-bottles, bundles of letters and papers and the miscellaneous rubbish that accumulates in the receptacles of a thoroughly untidy man. The superintendent went through the collection methodically, emptying the shelves, one at a time, on to the flap of the bureau, where he and the sergeant sorted the various articles and examining each, returned it to the shelf. It was a tedious proceeding and, so far as I could judge, unproductive, for, when all the shelves had been looked through and every article separately inspected, nothing was brought to light save an empty foolscap envelope which had apparently once contained a small box and was addressed to Wallingford, and two pieces of what looked like chemist's wrapping-paper, the creases in which showed that they had been small packets. These were not returned to the shelves, but, without comment, enclosed in a large envelope on which the superintendent scribbled a few words with a pencil and which was then consigned to a large handbag that the sergeant had brought in with him from the hall.

The large drawers of the bureau were next examined. Like the shelves, they were filled with a horrible accumulation of odds and ends which had evidently been stuffed into them to get them out of the way. From this collection nothing was obtained which interested the officers, who next turned their attention to the small drawers and pigeonholes at the back of the flap. These, however, contained nothing but stationery and a number of letters, bills and other papers, which the two officers glanced through and replaced. When all the small drawers and pigeonholes bad been examined, the superintendent stood up, fixing a thoughtful glance at the middle of the range of drawers; and I waited expectantly for the next development. Like many old bureaus, this one had as a central feature a nest of four very small drawers enclosed by a door. I knew the arrangement very well, and so, apparently, did the superintendent; for, once more opening the top drawer, he pulled it right out and laid it on the writing flap. Then, producing from his pocket a folding foot-rule, he thrust it into one of the pigeonholes, showing a depth of eight and a half inches, and then into the case of the little drawer, which proved to be only a fraction over five inches deep.

"There is something more here than meets the eye," he remarked pleasantly. "Do you know what is at the back of those drawers, Mr Wallingford?"

The unfortunate secretary, who had been watching the officer's proceedings with a look of consternation, did not reply for a few moments, but remained staring wildly at the aperture from which the drawer had been taken out.

"At the back?" he stammered, at length. "No, I can't say that I do. It isn't my bureau, you know. I only had the use of it."

"I see," said Miller. "Well, I expect we can soon find out."

He drew out a second drawer and, grasping the partition between the two, gave a gentle pull, when the whole nest slid easily forward and came right out of its case. Miller laid it on the writing flap, and, turning it round, displayed a sliding lid at the back, which he drew up; when there came into view a set of four little drawers similar to those in front but furnished with leather tabs instead of handles. Miller drew out the top drawer and a sudden change in the expression on his face told me that he had lighted on something that seemed to him significant.

"Now I wonder what this is?" said he, taking from the drawer a small white-paper packet. "Feels like some sort of powder. You say you don't know anything about it, Mr Wallingford?"

Wallingford shook his head but made no further reply, whereupon the superintendent laid the packet on the flap and very carefully unfolded the ends – it had already been opened – when it was seen that the contents consisted of some two or three teaspoonfuls of a fine, white powder.

"Well," said Miller, "we shall have to find out what it is. Will you pass me that bit of sealing-wax, Sergeant?"

He reclosed the packet with the greatest care and having sealed both the ends with his signet-ring, enclosed it in an envelope and put it into his inside breast pocket. Then he returned to the little nest of drawers. The second drawer was empty, but on pulling out the third, he uttered an exclamation.

"Well, now! Look at that! Somebody seems to have been fond of physic. And there's no doubt as to what this is. Morphine hydrochlor, a quarter of a grain."

As he spoke, he took out of the drawer a little bottle filled with tiny white discs or tablets and bearing on the label the inscription which the superintendent had read out. Wallingford gazed at it with a foolish expression of surprise as Miller held it up for our – and particularly Wallingford's – inspection; and Barbara, I noticed, cast at the latter a side-long, inscrutable glance which I sought in vain to interpret.

"Morphine doesn't seem much to the point," Miller remarked as he wrapped the little bottle in paper and bestowed it in his inner pocket, "but, of course, we have only got the evidence of the label. It may turn out to be something else, when the chemical gentlemen come to test it."

With this he grasped the tab of the bottom drawer and drew the latter out; and in a moment his face hardened. Very deliberately, he picked out a small, oblong envelope, which appeared once to have contained a box or hard packet, but was now empty. It had evidently come through the post and was addressed in a legible business hand to "A Wallingford Esq., 16 Hilborough Square." Silently the superintendent held it out for us all to see, as he fixed a stern look on Wallingford. "You observe, Sir," he said, at length, "that the post-mark is dated the 20th of August; only about a month ago. What have you to say about it?"

"Nothing," was the sullen reply. "What comes to me by post is my affair. I am not accountable to you or anybody else."

For a moment, the superintendent's face took on a very ugly expression. But he seemed to be a wise man and not unkindly, for he quickly controlled his irritation and rejoined without a trace of anger, though gravely enough: "Be advised by me, Mr Wallingford, and don't make trouble for yourself. Let me remind you what the position is. In this house a man has died from arsenic poisoning. The police will have to find out how that happened and if anyone is open to the suspicion of having poisoned him. I have come here today for that purpose with full authority to search this house. In the course of my search I have asked you for certain information, and you have made a number of false statements. Believe me, Sir, that is a very dangerous thing to do. It inevitably raises the question why those false statements should have been made. Now, I am going to ask you one or two questions. You are not bound to answer them, but you will be well advised to hold nothing back, and, above all, to say nothing that is not true. To begin with that packet of powder. What do you say that packet contains?"

Wallingford, who characteristically, was now completely cowed by the superintendent's thinly-veiled threats, hung his head for a moment and then replied, almost inaudibly, "Cocaine."

"What were you going to do with cocaine?" Miller asked.

"I was going to take a little of it for my health."

The superintendent smiled faintly as he demanded: "And the morphine tablets?"

"I had thought of taking one of them occasionally to – er – to steady my nerves."

Miller nodded, and casting a swift glance at the sergeant, asked: "And the packet that was in this envelope: what did that contain?"

Wallingford hesitated and was so obviously searching for a plausible lie that Miller interposed, persuasively: "Better tell the truth and not make trouble"; whereupon Wallingford replied in a barely audible mumble that the packet had contained a very small quantity of cocaine.

"What has become of that cocaine?" the superintendent asked.

"I took part of it; the rest got spilt and lost."

Miller nodded rather dubiously at this reply and then asked: "Where did you get this cocaine and the morphine?"

Wallingford hesitated for some time and at length, plucking up a little courage again, replied: "I would rather not answer that question.

It really has nothing to do with your search. You are looking for arsenic."

Miller reflected for a few moments and then rejoined, quietly: "That isn't quite correct, Mr Wallingford. I am looking for anything that may throw light on the death of Mr Monkhouse. But I don't want to press you unduly, only I would point out that you could not have come by these drugs lawfully. You are not a doctor or a chemist. Whoever supplied you with them was acting illegally and you have been a party to an illegal transaction in obtaining them. However, if you refuse to disclose the names of the persons who supplied them, we will let the matter pass, at least for the present; but I remind you that you have had these drugs in your possession and that you may be, and probably will be compelled to give an account of the way in which you obtained them."

With that he pocketed the envelope, closed the drawers and turned to make a survey of the room. There was very little in it, however, for the bureau and its surmounting cupboard were the only receptacles in which anything could be concealed, the whole of the walls being occupied by open book-shelves about seven feet high. But even these the superintendent was not prepared to take at their face value. First, he stood on a chair and ran his eye slowly along the tops of all the shelves; then he made a leisurely tour of the room, closely inspecting each row of books, now and again taking one out or pushing one in against the back of the shelves. A set of box-files was examined in detail, each one being opened to ascertain that it contained nothing but papers, and even one or two obvious portfolios were taken out and inspected. Nothing noteworthy, however, was brought to light by this rigorous search until the tour of inspection was nearly completed. The superintendent was, in fact, approaching the door when his attention was attracted by a row of books which seemed to be unduly near the front edge of the shelf. Opposite this he halted and began pushing the books back, one at a time. Suddenly I noticed that one of the books, on being pushed, slid back about half an inch and stopped as if there were something behind it. And there was. When the superintendent grasped the book and drew it out, there came into view, standing against the back of the shelf, a smallish bottle, apparently empty, and bearing a white label.

"Queer place to keep a bottle," Miller remarked, adding, with a smile, "unless it were a whiskey bottle, which it isn't." He drew it out, and after looking at it suspiciously and holding it up to the light, took out the cork and sniffed at it. "Well," he continued, "it is an empty bottle and it is labelled 'Benzine.' Do you know anything about it, Mr Wallingford?"

"No, I don't," was the reply. "I don't use benzine, and if I did I should not keep it on a book-shelf. But I don't see that it matters much. There isn't any harm in benzine, is there?"

"Probably not," said Miller; "but, you see, the label doesn't agree with the smell. What do you say, Mrs Monkhouse?"

He once more drew out the cork and held the bottle towards her. She took it from him and having smelled at it, replied promptly: "It smells to me like lavender. Possibly the bottle has had lavender water in it, though I shouldn't, myself, have chosen a benzine bottle to keep a perfume in."

"I don't think it was lavender water," said the superintendent. "That, I think, is nearly colourless. But the liquid that was in this bottle was red. As I hold it up to the light, you can see a little ring of red round the edge of the bottom. I daresay the chemists will be able to tell us what was in the bottle, but the question now is, who put it there? You are sure you can't tell us anything about it, Mr Wallingford?"

"I have never seen it before, I assure you," the latter protested almost tearfully. "I know nothing about it, whatsoever. That is the truth, Superintendent; I swear to God it is."

"Very well, Sir," said Miller, writing a brief note on the label and making an entry in his note-book. "Perhaps it is of no importance after all. But we shall see. I think we have finished this room. Perhaps, Sergeant, you might take a look at the drawing room while I go through Mr Monkhouse's room. It will save time. And I needn't trouble you anymore just at present, Mr Wallingford."

The secretary retired, somewhat reluctantly, to the dining room while Barbara led the way to the first floor. As we entered the room in which that unwitnessed tragedy had been enacted in the dead of the night, I looked about me with a sort of shuddering interest. The bed had been stripped, but otherwise nothing seemed to be changed since I had seen the room but a few days ago when it was still occupied by its dread tenant. The bedside table still bore its pathetic furnishings; the water-bottle, the little decanter, the books, the candle-box, the burnt-out lamp, the watch – though that ticked no longer, but seemed, with its motionless hands, to echo the awesome stillness that pervaded that ill-omened room.

As the superintendent carried out his methodical search, joined presently by the sergeant, Barbara came and stood by me with her eyes fixed gloomily on the table.

"Were you thinking of him, Rupert?" she whispered. "Were you thinking of that awful night when he lay here, dying, all alone, and I – Oh! the thought of it will haunt me every day of my life until my time comes, too, however far off that may be."

I was about to make some reply, as consolatory as might be, when the superintendent announced that he had finished and asked that Wallingford might be sent for to be present at the examination of his room. I went down to deliver the message, and, as it would have appeared intrusive for me to accompany him, I stayed in the dining room with Madeline, who, though she had recovered from the shock of the detectives' arrival, was still pale and agitated.

"Poor Tony seemed dreadfully upset when he came back just now," she said. "What was it that happened in the library?"

"Nothing very much," I answered. "The superintendent unearthed his little stock of dope; which, of course, was unpleasant for him, but it would not have mattered if he had not been fool enough to lie about it. That was a fatal thing to do, under the circumstances."

As Wallingford seemed not to have said anything about the bottle, I made no reference to it, but endeavoured to distract her attention from what was going on in the house by talking of other matters. Nor was it at all difficult; for the truth is that we all, with one accord, avoided any reference to the horrible fact which was staring us in the face, and of which we must all have been fully conscious. So we continued a somewhat banal conversation, punctuated by pauses in which our thoughts stole secretly back to the hideous realities, until, at length, Wallingford returned, pale and scowling, and flung himself into an arm-chair. Madeline looked at him inquiringly, but as he offered no remark but sat in gloomy silence, smoking furiously, she asked him no questions, nor did I.

A minute or two later, Barbara came into the room, quietly and with an air of calm self-possession that was quite soothing in the midst of the general emotional tension.

"Do you mind coming up, Madeline?" she said. "They are examining your room and they want you to unlock the cupboard. You have your keys about you, I suppose?"

"Yes," Madeline replied, rising and taking from her pocket a little key-wallet. "That is the key. Will you take it up to them?"

"I think you had better come up yourself," Barbara replied. "It is very unpleasant but, of course, they have to go through the formalities, and we must not appear unwilling to help them."

"No, of course," said Madeline. "Then I will come with you, but I should like Rupert to come, too, if he doesn't mind. Will you?" she asked, looking at me appealingly. "Those policemen make me feel so nervous."

Of course, I assented at once; and as Wallingford, muttering "Damned impertinence! Infernal indignity!" rose to open the door for us, we passed out and took our way upstairs.

"I am sorry to trouble you, Miss Norris," said Miller, in a suave tone, as we entered, "but we must see everything if only to be able to say that we have. Would you be so kind as to unlock this cupboard?"

He indicated a narrow cupboard which occupied one of the recesses by the chimney-breast, and Madeline at once inserted the key and threw open the door. The interior was then seen to be occupied by shelves, of which the lower ones were filled, tidily enough, with an assortment of miscellaneous articles – shoes, shoe-trees, brushes, leather bags, cardboard boxes, note-books and other "oddments" –

while the top shelf seemed to have been used as a repository for jars, pots and bottles, of which several appeared to be empty. It was this shelf which seemed to attract the superintendent's attention and he began operations by handing out its various contents to the sergeant, who set them down on a table in orderly rows. When they were all set out and the superintendent had inspected narrowly and swept his hand over the empty shelf, the examination of the jars and bottles began.

The procedure was very methodical and thorough. First, the sergeant picked up a bottle or jar, looked it over carefully, read the label if there was one, uncovered or uncorked it, smelled it and passed it to the superintendent, who, when he had made a similar inspection, put it down at the opposite end of the table.

"Can you tell us what this is?" Miller asked, holding out a bottle filled with a thickish, nearly black liquid.

"That is caramel," Madeline replied. "I use it in my cookery classes and for cooking at home, too."

The superintendent regarded the bottle a little dubiously but set it down at the end of the table without comment. Presently he received from the sergeant a glass jar filled with a brownish powder.

"There is no label on this," he remarked, exhibiting it to Madeline.

"No," she replied. "It is turmeric. That also is used in my classes; and that other is powdered saffron."

"I wonder you don't label them," said Miller. "It would be easy for a mistake to occur with all these unlabelled bottles."

"Yes," she admitted, "they ought to be labelled. But I know what each of them is, and they are all pretty harmless. Most of them are materials that are used in cookery demonstrations, but that one that you have now is French chalk, and the one the sergeant has is pumice-powder."

"H'm," grunted Miller, dipping his finger into the former and rubbing it on his thumb; "what would happen if you thickened a soup with French chalk or pumice-powder? Not very good for the digestion, I should think."

"No, I suppose not," Madeline agreed, with the ghost of a smile on her pale face. "I must label them in future."

During this colloquy I had been rapidly casting my eye over the collection that still awaited examination, and my attention had been almost at once arrested by an empty bottle near the end of the row. It looked to me like the exact counterpart of the bottle which had been found in the library; a cylindrical bottle of about the capacity of half a pint, or rather less, and like the other, labelled in printed characters 'Benzine.'

But mine was not the only eye that had observed it. Presently, I saw the sergeant pick it up – out of its turn – scrutinize it suspiciously, hold it up to the light, take out the cork and smell both it and the bottle, and then, directing the latter, telescope-fashion, towards the window, inspect the bottom by peering in through the mouth. Finally, he clapped in the cork with some emphasis, and with a glance full of meaning handed the bottle to the superintendent.

The latter repeated the procedure in even more detail. When he had finished, he turned to Madeline with a distinctly inquisitorial air.

"This bottle, Miss Norris," said he, "is labelled 'Benzine.' But it was not benzine that it contained. Will you kindly smell it and tell me what you think it did contain. Or perhaps you can say off-hand."

"I am afraid I can't," she replied. "I have no recollection of having had any benzine and I don't remember this bottle at all. As it is in my cupboard I suppose I must have put it there, but I don't remember having ever seen it before. I can't tell you anything about it."

"Well, will you kindly smell it and tell me what you think it contained?" the superintendent persisted, handing her the open bottle. She took it from him apprehensively, and, holding it to her nose, took a deep sniff; and instantly her already pale face became dead white to the very lips.

"It smells of lavender," she said in a faint voice.

"So I thought," said Miller. "And now, Miss Norris, if you will look in at the mouth of the bottle against the light you will see a faint red ring round the bottom. Apparently, the liquid that the bottle contained was a red liquid. Moreover, if you hold the bottle against the light and look through the label, you can see the remains of another label under it. There is only a tiny scrap of it left, but it is enough for us to see that it was a red label. So it would seem that the liquid was a poisonous liquid – poisonous enough to require a red poison label. And then you notice that this red poison label seems to have been scraped off and the benzine label stuck on over the place where it had been, although, as the lavender smell and the red stain clearly show, the bottle never had any benzine in it at all. Now, Miss Norris, bearing those facts in mind, I ask you if you can tell me what was in that bottle."

"I have told you," Madeline replied with unexpected firmness, "that I know nothing about this bottle. I have no recollection of ever having seen it before. I do not believe that it ever belonged to me. It may have been in the cupboard when I first began to use it. At any rate, I am not able to tell you anything about it"

The superintendent continued to look at her keenly, still holding the bottle. After a few moments' silence he persisted: "A red, poisonous liquid which smells of lavender. Can you not form any idea as to what it was?"

I was about to enter a protest – for the question was really not admissible – when Madeline, now thoroughly angry and quite self-possessed, replied, stiffly: "I don't know what you mean. I have told you that I know nothing about this bottle. Are you suggesting that I should try to guess what it contained?"

"No," he rejoined hastily; "certainly not. A guess wouldn't help us at all. If you really do not know anything about the bottle, we must leave it at that. You always keep this cupboard locked, I suppose?"

"Usually. But I am not very particular about it. There is nothing of value in the cupboard, as you see, and the servants are quite trustworthy. I sometimes leave the key in the door, but I don't imagine that anybody ever meddles with it."

The superintendent took the key out of the lock and regarded it attentively. Then he examined the lock itself, and I also took the opportunity of inspecting it. Both the lock and the key were of the simplest kind, just ordinary builder's fittings, which, so far as any real security was concerned, could not be taken seriously. In the absence of the key, a stiff wire or a bent hair-pin would probably have shot the little bolt quite easily, as I took occasion to remark to the superintendent, who frankly agreed with me.

The bottle having been carefully wrapped up and deposited in the sergeant's hand-bag, the examination was resumed; but nothing further of an interesting or suspicious character was discovered among the bottles or jars. Nor did the sorting-out of the miscellaneous contents of the lower shelves yield anything remarkable with a single exception. When the objects on the lowest shelf had been all taken out, a small piece of white paper was seen at the back, and on this Miller pounced with some eagerness. As he brought it out I could see that it was a chemist's powder paper, about six inches square (when Miller had carefully straightened it out), and the creases which marked the places where it had been folded showed that it had contained a mass of about the bulk of a dessert-spoonful. But what attracted my attention – and the superintendent's – was the corner of a red label which adhered to a torn edge in company with a larger fragment of a white label on which the name or description of the contents had presumably been written or printed. Miller held it out towards Madeline, who looked at it with a puzzled frown.

"Do you remember what was in this paper, Miss Norris?" the former asked.

"I am afraid I don't," she replied.

"H'm," grunted Miller; "I should have thought you would. It seems to have been a good-sized powder and it had a poison label in addition to the descriptive label. I should have thought that would have recalled it to your memory."

"So should I," said Madeline. "But I don't remember having bought any powder that would be labelled 'poison.' It is very odd; and it is odd that the paper should be there. I don't usually put waste paper into my cupboard."

"Well, there it is," said Miller; but if you can't remember anything about it, we must see if the analysts can find out what was in it." With which he folded it and having put it into an envelope, bestowed it in his pocket in company with his other treasures.

This was the last of the discoveries. When they had finished their inspection of Madeline's room the officers went on to Barbara's, which they examined with the same minute care as they had bestowed on the others, but without bringing anything of interest to light. Then they inspected the servants' bedrooms and finally the kitchen and the other premises appertaining to it, but still without result. It was a tedious affair and we were all relieved when, at last, it came to an end. Barbara and I escorted the two detectives to the street door, at which the superintendent paused to make a few polite acknowledgments.

"I must thank you, Madam," said he, "for the help you have given us and for the kind and reasonable spirit in which you have accepted a disagreeable necessity. I assure you that we do not usually meet with so much consideration. A search of this kind is always an unpleasant duty to carry out and it is not made any more pleasant by a hostile attitude on the part of the persons concerned."

"I can understand that," replied Barbara; "but really the thanks are due from me for the very courteous and considerate way in which you have discharged what I am sure must be a most disagreeable duty. And of course, it had to be; and I am glad that it has been done so thoroughly. I never supposed that you would find what you are seeking in this house. But it was necessary that the search should be made here if only to prove that you must look for it somewhere else."

"Quite so, Madam," the superintendent returned, a little drily; "and now I will wish you good afternoon and hope that we shall have no further occasion to trouble you."

As I closed the street door and turned back along the hall, the dining room door – apparently already ajar – opened and Madeline and Wallingford stepped out; and I could not help reflecting, as I noted their pale, anxious faces and shaken bearing, how little their appearance supported the confident, optimistic tone of Barbara's last remarks But, at any rate, they were intensely relieved that the ordeal was over, and Wallingford even showed signs of returning truculence.

Whatever he was going to say, however, was cut short by Barbara, who, passing the door and moving towards the staircase, addressed me over her shoulder.

"Do you mind coming up to my den, Rupert? I want to ask your advice about one or two things."

The request seemed a little inopportune; but it was uttered as a command and I had no choice but to obey. Accordingly, I followed Barbara up the stairs, leaving the other two in the hall, evidently rather disconcerted by this sudden retreat. At the turn of the stairs I looked down on the two pale faces. In Madeline's I seemed to read a new apprehensiveness, tinged with suspicion; on Wallingford's a scowl of furious anger which I had no patience to seek to interpret.

CHAPTER EIGHT

Thorndyke Speaks Bluntly

When I had entered the little sitting room and shut the door, I turned to Barbara, awaiting with some curiosity what she had to say to me. But for a while she said nothing, standing before me silently, and looking at me with a most disquieting expression. All her calm self-possession had gone. I could read nothing in her face but alarm and dismay.

"It is dreadful, Rupert!" she exclaimed, at length, in a half-whisper. "It is like some awful dream! What can it all mean? I don't dare to ask myself the question."

I shook my head, for I was in precisely the same condition. I did not dare to weigh the meaning of the things that I had seen and heard.

Suddenly, the stony fixity of her face relaxed and with a little, smothered cry she flung her arm around my neck and buried her face on my shoulder.

"Forgive me, Rupert, dearest, kindest friend," she sobbed. "Suffer a poor lonely woman for a few moments. I have only you, dear, faithful one; only your strength and steadfastness to lean upon. Before the others I must needs be calm and brave, must cloak my own fears to support their flagging courage But it is hard, Rupert; for they see what we see and dare not put it into words. And the mystery, Rupert, the horrible shadow that is over us all! In God's name, what can it all mean?"

"That is what I ask myself, Barbara, and dare not answer my own question."

She uttered a low moan and clung closer to me, sobbing quietly. I was deeply moved, for I realized the splendid courage that enabled her to go about this house of horror, calm and unafraid; to bear the burden of her companions' weakness as well as her own grief and humiliation. But I could find nothing to say to her. I could only offer her a silent sympathy, holding her head on my shoulder and softly stroking her hair while I wondered dimly what the end of it all would be.

Presently she stood up, and, taking out her handkerchief, wiped her eyes resolutely and finally.

"Thank you, dear Rupert," she said, "for being so patient with me. I felt that I had come to the end of my endurance and had to rest my burden on you. It was a great relief. But I didn't bring you up here for that. I wanted to consult you about what has to be done. I can't look to poor Tony in his present state."

"What is it that has to be done?" I asked.

"There is the funeral. That has still to take place."

"Of course it has," I exclaimed, suddenly taken aback; for amidst all the turmoils and alarms, I had completely lost sight of this detail. "I suppose I had better call on the undertaker and make the necessary arrangements."

"If you would be so kind, Rupert, and if you can spare the time. You have given up the whole day to us already."

"I can manage," said I. "And as to the time of the funeral, I don't know whether it could be arranged for the evening. It gets dark pretty early."

"No, Rupert," she exclaimed, firmly. "Not in the evening. Certainly not. I will not have poor Harold's body smuggled away in the dark like the dishonoured corpse of some wretched suicide. The funeral shall take place at the proper time, if I go with it alone."

"Very well, Barbara. I will arrange for us to start at the time originally fixed. I only suggested the evening because – well, you know what to expect."

"Yes, only too well! But I refuse to let a crowd of gaping sight-seers intimidate me into treating my dead husband with craven disrespect."

"Perhaps you are right," said I with secret approval of her decision, little as I relished the prospect that it opened. "Then I had better go and make the arrangements at once. It is getting late. But I am loath to leave you alone with Madeline and Wallingford."

"I think, perhaps, we shall be better alone for the present, and you have your own affairs to attend to. But you must have some food before you go. You have had nothing since the morning, and I expect a meal is ready by now."

"I don't think I will wait, Barbara," I replied. "This affair ought to be settled at once. I can get some food when I have dispatched the business."

She was reluctant to let me go. But I was suddenly conscious of a longing to escape from this house into the world of normal things and people; to be alone for a while with my own thoughts, and, above all, to take counsel with Thorndyke. On my way out I called in at the dining room to make my adieux to Madeline and Wallingford. The former looked at me, as she shook my hand, very wistfully and I thought a little reproachfully.

"I am sorry you have to go, Rupert," she said. "But you will try to come and see us tomorrow, won't you? And spend as much time here as you can."

I promised to come at some time on the morrow; and having exchanged a few words with Wallingford, took my departure, escorted to the street door by the two women.

The closing of the door, sounding softly in my ears, conveyed a sense of relief of which I felt ashamed. I drew a deep breath and stepped forward briskly with a feeling of emancipation that I condemned as selfish and disloyal even as I was sensible of its intensity. It was almost with a sense of exhilaration that I strode along, a normal, unnoticed wayfarer among ordinary men and women, enveloped by no cloud of mystery, overhung by no shadow of crime. There was the undertaker, indeed, who would drag me back into the gruesome environment, but I would soon have finished with him, and then, for a time, at least, I should be free.

I finished with him, in fact, sooner than I had expected, for he had already arranged the procedure of the postponed funeral and required only my assent; and when I had given this, I went my way breathing more freely but increasingly conscious of the need for food.

Yet, after all, my escape was only from physical contact. Try as I would to forget for a while the terrible events of this day of wrath, the fresh memories of them came creeping back in the midst of those other thoughts which I had generated by a deliberate effort. They haunted me as I walked swiftly through the streets, they made themselves heard above the rumble of the train, and even as I sat in a tavern in Devereux Court, devouring with ravenous appreciation a well-grilled chop, accompanied by a pint of claret, black care stood behind the old-fashioned, high-backed settle, an unseen companion of the friendly waiter.

The lighted windows of Thorndyke's chambers were to my eyes as the harbour lights to the eyes of a storm-beaten mariner. As I emerged from Fig Tree Court and came in sight of them, I had already the feeling that the burden of mystery and vague suspicion was lightened; and I strode across King's Bench Walk with the hopeful anticipation of one who looks to shift his fardel on to more capable shoulders.

The door was opened by Thorndyke, himself; and the sheaf of papers in his hand suggested that he was expecting me.

"Are those the depositions?" I asked as we shook hands.

"Yes," he replied. "I have just been reading through them and making an abstract. Holman has left the duplicate at your chambers."

"I suppose the medical evidence represents the 'complications' that you hinted at? You expected something of the kind?"

"Yes. An inquest in the face of a regular death certificate suggested some pretty definite information; and then your own account of the illness told one what to expect."

"And yet," said I, "neither of the doctors suspected anything while the man was alive."

"No; but that is not very remarkable. I had the advantage over them of knowing that a death certificate had been challenged. It is always easier to be wise after than before the event."

"And now that you have read the depositions, what do you think of the case? Do you think, for instance, that the verdict was justified?"

"Undoubtedly," he replied. "What other verdict was possible on the evidence that was before the court? The medical witness swore that deceased died from the effects of arsenic poisoning. That is an inference, it is true. The facts are that the man died and that a poisonous quantity of arsenic was found in the body. But it is the only reasonable inference and we cannot doubt that it is the true one. Then again as to the question of murder as against accident or suicide, it is one of probabilities. But the probabilities are so overwhelmingly in favour of murder that no others are worth considering. No, Mayfield, on the evidence before us, we have to accept the verdict as expressing the obvious truth."

"You think it impossible that there can be any error or fallacy in the case?"

"I don't say that," he replied. "I am referring exclusively to the evidence which is set forth in these depositions. That is all the evidence that we possess. Apart from the depositions we have no knowledge of the case at all; at least I have none, and I don't suppose you have any."

"I have not. But I understand that you think it at least conceivable that there may be, after all, some fallacy in the evidence of wilful murder?"

"A fallacy," he replied, "is always conceivable. As you know, Mayfield, complete certainty, in the most rigorous sense, is hardly ever attainable in legal practice. But we must be reasonable. The law has to be administered; and if certainty, in the most extreme, academic sense, is unattainable, we must be guided in our action by the highest degree of probability that is within our reach."

"Yes, I realize that. But still you admit that a fallacy is conceivable. Can you, just for the sake of illustration, suggest any such possibility in the evidence that you have read?"

"Well," he replied, "as a matter of purely academic interest, there is the point that I mentioned just now. The body of this man contained a lethal quantity of arsenic. With that quantity of poison in his body, the man died. The obvious inference is that those two facts were connected as cause and effect. But it is not absolutely certain that they were. It is conceivable that the man may have died from some natural cause overlooked by the pathologist – who was already aware of the presence of arsenic, from Detling's information; or again it is conceivable that the man may have been murdered in some other way – even by the administration of some other, more rapidly acting poison, which was never found because it was never looked for. These are undeniable possibilities. But I doubt if any reasonable person would entertain them, seeing that they are mere conjectures unsupported by any sort of evidence. And you notice that the second possibility leaves the verdict of wilful murder unaffected."

"Yes, but it might transfer the effects of that verdict to the wrong person."

"True," he rejoined with a smile. "It might transfer them from a poisoner who had committed a murder to another poisoner who had only attempted to commit one; and the irony of the position would be that the latter would actually believe himself to be the murderer. But as I said, this is mere academic talk. The coroner's verdict is the reality with which we have to deal."

"I am not so sure of that, Thorndyke," said I, inspired with a sudden hope by his "illustration." "You admit that fallacies are possible and you are able to suggest two off-hand. You insist, very properly, that our opinions at present must be based exclusively on the evidence given at the inquest. But, as I listened to that evidence, I had the feeling – and I have it still – that it did not give a credible explanation of the facts that were proved. I had – and have – the feeling that careful and competent investigation might bring to light some entirely new evidence."

"It is quite possible," he admitted, rather drily.

"Well, then," I pursued, "I should wish some such investigation to be made. I can recall a number of cases in which the available evidence, as in the present case, appeared to point to a certain definite conclusion, but in which investigations undertaken by you brought out a body of new evidence pointing in a totally different direction. There was the Hornby case, the case of Blackmore, deceased, the Bellingham case and a number of others in which the result of your investigations was to upset completely a well-established case against some suspected individual."

He nodded, but made no comment, and I concluded with the question: "Well, why should not a similar result follow in the present case?"

He reflected for a few moments and then asked: "What is it that is in your mind, Mayfield? What, exactly do you propose?"

"I am proposing that you should allow me to retain you on my own behalf and that of other interested parties to go thoroughly into this case."

"With what object?"

"With the object of bringing to light the real facts connected with the death of Harold Monkhouse."

"Are you authorized by any of the interested parties to make this proposal?"

"No; and perhaps I had better leave them out and make the proposal on my own account only."

He did not reply immediately but sat looking at me steadily with a rather inscrutable expression which I found a little disturbing. At length he spoke, with unusual deliberation and emphasis.

"Are you sure, Mayfield, that you want the real facts brought to light?"

I stared at him, startled and a good deal taken aback by his question, and especially by the tone in which it was put.

"But, surely," I stammered, in reply. "Why not?"

"Don't be hasty, Mayfield," said he. "Reflect calmly and impartially before you commit yourself to any course of action of which you cannot foresee the consequences. Perhaps I can help you. Shall we, without prejudice and without personal bias, take a survey of the *status quo* and try to see exactly where we stand?"

"By all means," I replied, a little uncomfortably.

"Well," he said, "the position is this. A man has died in a certain house, to which he has been confined as an invalid for some considerable time. The cause of his death is stated to be poisoning by arsenic. That statement is made by a competent medical witness who has had the fullest opportunity to ascertain the facts. He makes the statement with complete confidence that it is a true statement, and his opinion is supported by those of two other competent professional witnesses. It is an established fact, which cannot be contested, that the body of deceased contained sufficient arsenic to cause his death. So far as we can see, there is not the slightest reason to doubt that the man died from arsenical poisoning.

"When we come to the question, 'How did the arsenic find its way into the man's body?' there appears to be only one possible answer. Suicide and accident are clearly excluded. The evidence makes it practically certain that the poison was administered to him by some person or persons with the intent to compass his death; and the circumstances in which the poisoning occurred make it virtually certain that the arsenic was administered to this man by some person or persons customarily and intimately in contact with him.

"The evidence shows that there were eight persons who would answer this description; and we have no knowledge of the existence of any others. Those persons are: Barbara Monkhouse, Madeline Norris, Anthony Wallingford, the housemaid, Mabel Withers, the cook, the kitchenmaid, Dr Dimsdale and Rupert Mayfield. Of these eight persons the police will assume that one, or more, administered the poison; and, so far as we can see, the police are probably right."

I was rather staggered by his bluntness. But I had asked for his opinion and I had got it. After a brief pause, I said: "We are still, of course, dealing with the depositions. On those, as you say, a presumption of guilt lies against these eight persons collectively. That doesn't carry us very far in a legal sense. You can't indict eight persons as having among them the guilty party. Do you take it that the presumption of guilt lies more heavily on some of these persons than on others?"

"Undoubtedly," he replied. "I enumerated them merely as the body of persons who fulfilled the necessary conditions as to opportunity and among whom the police will – reasonably – look for the guilty person. In a sense, they are all suspect until the guilt is fixed on a particular person. They all had, technically, a motive, since they all benefited by the death of deceased. Actually, none of them has been shown to have any motive at all in an ordinary and reasonable sense. But for practical purposes, several of them can almost be put outside the area of suspicion; the kitchenmaid, for instance, and Dr Dimsdale and yourself."

"And Mrs Monkhouse," I interposed, "seeing that she appears to have been absent and far away on each occasion when the poison seems to have been administered."

"Precisely," he agreed. "In fact, her absence would seem to exclude her from the group of possible suspects. But apart from its bearing on herself, her absence from home on these occasions has a rather important bearing on some of the others."

"Indeed!" said I, trying rapidly to judge what that bearing might be.

"Yes, it is this: the fact that the poisoning occurred – as it appears – only when Mrs Monkhouse was away from home, suggests not only that the poisoner was fully cognizant of her movements, which all the household would be, but that her presence at home would have hindered that poisoner from administering the poison. Now, the different persons in the house would be differently affected by her presence. We need not pursue the matter any further just now, but you must see that the hindrance to the poisoning caused by Mrs Monkhouse's presence would be determined by the nature of the relations between Mrs Monkhouse and the poisoner."

"Yes, I see that."

"And you see that this circumstance tends to confirm the belief that the crime was committed by a member of the household?"

"I suppose it does," I admitted, grudgingly.

"It does, certainly," said Thorndyke; "and that being so, I ask you again: do you think it expedient that you should meddle with this case? If you do, you will be taking a heavy responsibility; for I must remind you that you are not proposing to employ me as a counsel, but as an investigator who may become a witness. Now, when I plead in court, I act like any other counsel; I plead my client's case frankly as an advocate, knowing that the judge is there to watch over the interests of justice. But as an investigator or witness I am concerned only with the truth. I never give *ex parte* evidence. If I investigate a crime and discover the criminal, I denounce him, even though he is my employer; for otherwise I should become an accessory. Whoever employs me as an investigator of crime does so at his own risk.

"Bear this in mind, Mayfield, before you go any further in this matter. I don't know what your relations are to these people, but I gather that they are your friends; and I want you to consider very seriously whether you are prepared to risk the possible consequences of employing me. It is actually possible that one or more of these persons may be indicted for the murder of Harold Monkhouse. That would, in any case, be extremely painful for you. But if it happened through the action of the police, you would be, after all, but a passive spectator of the catastrophe. Very different would be the position if it were your own hand that had let the axe fall. Are you prepared to face the risk of such a possibility?"

I must confess that I was daunted by Thorndyke's blunt statement of the position. There was no doubt as to the view that he took of the case. He made no secret of it. And he clearly gauged my own state of mind correctly. He saw that it was not the crime that was concerning me; that I was not seeking justice against the murderer but that I was looking to secure the safety of my friends.

I turned the question over rapidly in my mind. The contingency that Thorndyke had suggested was horrible. I could not face such a risk. Rather, by far, would I have had the murderer remain unpunished than be, myself, the agent of vengeance on any of these suspects. Hideous as the crime was, I could not bring myself to accept the office of executioner if one of my own friends was to be the victim.

I had almost decided to abandon the project and leave the result to Fate or the police. But then came a sudden revulsion. From the grounds of suspicion my thoughts flew to the persons suspected; to gentle, sympathetic Madeline, so mindful of the dead man's comfort, so solicitous about his needs, so eager to render him the little services that mean so much to a sick man. Could I conceive of her as hiding under this appearance of tender sympathy the purposes of a cruel and callous murderess? The thing was absurd. My heart rejected it utterly. Nor could I entertain for a moment such a thought of the kindly, attentive housemaid; and even Wallingford, much as I disliked him, was obviously outside the area of possible suspicion. An intolerable coxcomb he certainly was; but a murderer – never!

"I will take the risk, Thorndyke," said I.

He looked at me with slightly raised eyebrows, and I continued: "I know these people pretty intimately and I find it impossible to entertain the idea that any of them could have committed this callous, deliberate crime. At the moment, I realize circumstances seem to involve them in suspicion; but I am certain that there is some fallacy – that there are some facts which did not transpire at the inquest but which might be brought to the surface if you took the case in hand."

"Why not let the police disinter those facts?"

"Because the police evidently suspect the members of the household and they will certainly pursue the obvious probabilities."

"So should I, for that matter," said he; "and in any case, we can't prevent the police from bringing a charge if they are satisfied that they can support it. And your own experience will tell you that they will certainly not take a case into the Central Criminal Court unless they have enough evidence to make a conviction a virtual certainty. But I remind you, Mayfield, that they have got it all to do. There is grave suspicion in respect of a number of persons, but there is not, at present, a particle of positive evidence against any one person. It looks to me as if it might turn out to be a very elusive case."

"Precisely," said I. "That is why I am anxious that the actual perpetrator should be discovered. Until he is, all these people will be under suspicion, with the peril of a possible arrest constantly hanging over them. I might even say, 'hanging over us'; for you, yourself, have included me in the group of possible suspects."

He reflected for a few moments. At length he replied: "You are quite right, Mayfield. Until the perpetrator of a crime is discovered and his guilt established, it is always possible for suspicion to rest upon the innocent and even for a miscarriage of justice to occur. In all cases it is most desirable that the crime should be brought home to the actual perpetrator without delay for that reason, to say nothing of the importance, on grounds of public policy, of exposing and punishing wrong-doers. You know these people and I do not. If you are sufficiently confident of their innocence to take the risk of associating yourself with the agencies of detection, I have no more to say on that point. I am quite willing to go into the case so far as I can, though, at present, I see no prospect of success."

"It seems to you a difficult case, then?"

"Very. it is extraordinarily obscure and confused. Whoever poisoned that unfortunate man, seems to have managed most skilfully to confuse all the issues. Whatever may have been the medium through which the poison was given, that medium is associated equally with a number of different persons. If the medicine was the vehicle, then the responsibility is divided between Dimsdale, who prepared it, and the various persons who administered it. If the poison was mixed with the food, it may have been introduced by any of the persons who prepared it or had access to it on its passage from the kitchen to the patient's bedroom. There is no one person of whom we can say that he or she had any special opportunity that others had not. And it is the same with the motive. No one had any really, adequate motive for killing Monkhouse; but all the possible suspects benefited by his death, though they were apparently not aware of it."

"They all knew, in general terms, that they had been mentioned in the will though the actual provisions and amounts were not disclosed. But I should hardly describe Mrs Monkhouse as benefiting by her husband's death. She will not be as well off now as she was when he was alive and the whole of his income was available."

"No. But we were not including her in the group since she was not in the house when the poison was being administered We were speaking of those who actually had the opportunity to administer the poison; and we see that the opportunity was approximately equal in all. And you see, Mayfield, the trouble is that any evidence incriminating any one person would be in events which are past and beyond recall. The depositions contain all that we know and all that we are likely to know, unless the police are able to ascertain that some one of the parties has purchased arsenic from a chemist; which is extremely unlikely considering the caution and judgment that the poisoner has shown. The truth is that, if no new evidence is forthcoming, the murder of Harold Monkhouse will take its place among the unsolved and insoluble mysteries."

"Then, I take it that you will endeavour to find some new evidence? But I don't see, at all, how you will go about it."

"Nor do I," said he. "There seems to be nothing to investigate. However, I shall study the depositions and see if a careful consideration of the evidence offers any suggestion for a new line of research. And as the whole case now lies in the past, I shall try to learn as much as possible about everything and everybody concerned. Perhaps I had better begin with you. I don't quite understand what your position is in this household."

"I will tell you with pleasure all about my relations with the Monkhouses, but it is a rather long story, and I don't see that it will help you in any way."

"Now, Mayfield," said Thorndyke, "don't begin by considering what knowledge may or may not be helpful. We don't know. The most trivial or seemingly irrelevant fact may offer a most illuminating suggestion. My rule is, when I am gravelled for lack of evidence, to collect, indiscriminately, all the information that I can obtain that is in the remotest way connected with the problem that I am dealing with. Bear that in mind. I want to know all that you can tell me, and don't be afraid of irrelevant details. They may not be irrelevant, after all; and if they are, I can sift them out afterwards. Now, begin at the beginning and tell me the whole of the long story."

He provided himself with a note-book, uncapped his fountain pen and prepared himself to listen to what I felt to be a perfectly useless recital of facts that could have no possible bearing on the case.

"I will take you at your word," said I, "and begin at the very beginning, when I was quite a small boy. At that time, my father, who was a widower, lived at Highgate and kept the chambers in the Temple which I now occupy. A few doors away from us lived a certain Mr Keene, an old friend of my father's – his only really intimate friend, in fact – and, of course, I used to see a good deal of him. Mr Keene, who was getting on in years, had married a very charming woman, considerably younger than himself, and at this time there was one child, a little girl about two years old. Unfortunately, Mrs Keene was very delicate, and soon after the child's birth she developed symptoms of consumption Once started, the disease progressed rapidly inspite of the most careful treatment, and in about two years from the outset of the symptoms, she died.

"Her death was a great grief to Mr Keene, and indeed, to us all, for she was a most lovable woman; and the poor little motherless child made the strongest appeal to our sympathies She was the loveliest little creature imaginable and as sweet and winning in nature as she was charming in appearance On her mother's death, I adopted her as my little sister, and devoted myself to her service. In fact, I became her slave; but a very willing slave; for she was so quick and intelligent, so affectionate and so amiable that, in spite of the difference in our ages – some eight or nine years – I found her a perfectly satisfying companion. She entered quite competently into all my boyish sports and amusements, so that our companionship really involved very little sacrifice on my part but rather was a source of constant pleasure.

"But her motherless condition caused Mr Keene a good deal of anxiety. As I have said, he was getting on in life and was by no means a strong man, and he viewed with some alarm the, not very remote, possibility of her becoming an orphan with no suitable guardian, for my father was now an elderly man, and I was, as yet, too young to undertake the charge. Eventually, he decided, for the child's sake, to marry again; and about two years after his first wife's death he proposed to and was accepted by a lady named Ainsworth whom he had known for many years, who had been left a widow with one child, a girl some two years younger than myself.

"Naturally, I viewed the advent of the new Mrs Keene with some jealousy. But there was no occasion. She was a good, kindly woman who showed from the first that she meant to do her duty by her little stepdaughter. And her own child, Barbara, equally disarmed our jealousy. A quiet, rather reserved little girl, but very clever and quick-witted, she not only accepted me at once with the frankest friendliness but, with a curious tactfulness for such a young girl, devoted herself to my little friend, Stella Keene, without in the least attempting to oust me from my position. In effect, we three young people became a most united and harmonious little coterie in which our respective positions were duly recognized. I was the head of the firm, so to speak, Stella was my adopted sister, and Barbara was the ally of us both.

"So our relations continued as the years passed; but presently the passing years began to take toll of our seniors. My father was the first to go. Then followed Mr Keene, and after a few more years, Barbara's mother. By the time my twenty-fifth birthday came round, we were all orphans."

"What were your respective ages then?" Thorndyke asked.

Rather surprised at the question, I paused to make a calculation.

"My own age," I replied, "was, as I have said, twenty-five. Barbara would then be twenty-two and Stella sixteen."

Thorndyke made a note of my answer and I proceeded: "The death of our elders made no appreciable difference in our way of living. My father had left me a modest competence and the two girls were fairly provided for. The houses that we occupied were beyond our needs, reduced as we were in numbers and we discussed the question of sharing a house. But, of course, the girls were not really my sisters and the scheme was eventually rejected as rather too unconventional; so we continued to live in our respective houses."

"Was there any trustee for the girls?" Thorndyke asked.

"Yes, Mr Brodribb. The bulk of the property was, I believe, vested in Stella, but, for reasons which I shall come to in a moment, there was a provision that, in the event of her death, it should revert to Barbara."

"On account, I presume, of the tendency to consumption?"

"Exactly. For some time before Mr Keene's death there had been signs that Stella inherited her mother's delicacy of health. Hence the provisions for Barbara. But no definite manifestations of disease appeared until Stella was about eighteen. Then she developed a cough and began to lose weight; but, for a couple of years the disease made no very marked progress, in fact, there were times when she seemed to be in a fair way to recovery. Then, rather suddenly, her health took a turn for the worse. Soon she became almost completely bed-ridden. She wasted rapidly, and, in fact, was now the typical consumptive, hectic, emaciated, but always bright, cheerful and full of plans for the future and enthusiasm for the little hobbies that I devised to keep her amused.

"But all the time, she was going down the hill steadily, although, as I have said, there were remissions and fluctuations; and, in short, after about a year's definite illness, she went the way of her mother. Her death was immediately caused, I understand, by an attack of hemorrhage."

"You understand?" Thorndyke repeated, interrogatively.

"Yes. To my lasting grief, I was away from home when she died. I had been recently called to the bar and was offered a brief for the Chelmsford Assizes, which I felt I ought not to refuse, especially as Stella seemed, just then, to be better than usual. What made it worse was that the telegram which was sent to recall me went astray. I had moved on to Ipswich and had only just written to give my new address, so that I did not get home until just before the funeral. It was a fearful shock, for no one had the least suspicion that the end was so near. If I had supposed that there was the slightest immediate danger, nothing on earth would have induced me to go away from home."

Thorndyke had listened to my story not only with close attention but with an expression of sympathy which I noted gratefully and perhaps with a little surprise. But he was a strange man; as impersonal as Fate when he was occupied in actual research and yet showing at times unexpected gleams of warm human feeling and the most sympathetic understanding. He now preserved a thoughtful silence for some time after I had finished. Presently he said: "I suppose this poor girl's death caused a considerable change in your way of living?"

"Yes, indeed! Its effects were devastating both on Barbara and me. Neither of us felt that we could go on with the old ways of life. Barbara let her house and went into rooms in London, where I used to visit her as often as I could; and I sold my house, furniture and all and took up residence in the Temple. But even that I could not endure for long. Stella's death had broken me up completely. Right on from my boyhood, she had been the very hub of my life. All my thoughts and interests had revolved around her. She had been to me friend and sister in one. Now that she was gone, the world seemed to be a great, chilly void, haunted everywhere by memories of her. She had pervaded my whole life, and everything about me was constantly reminding me of her. At last I found that I could bear it no longer. The familiar things and places became intolerable to my eyes. I did not want to forget her; on the contrary, I loved to cherish her memory. But it was harrowing to have my loss thrust upon me at every turn. I yearned for new surroundings in which I could begin a new life; and in the end, I decided to go to Canada and settle down there to practise at the Bar.

"My decision came as a fearful blow to Barbara, and indeed, I felt not a little ashamed of my disloyalty to her; for she, too, had been like a sister to me and, next to Stella, had been my dearest friend. But it could not be helped. An intolerable unrest had possession of me. I felt that I must go; and go I did, leaving poor Barbara to console her loneliness with her political friends.

"I stayed in Canada nearly two years and meant to stay there for good. Then, one day, I got a letter from Barbara telling me that she was married. The news rather surprised me, for I had taken Barbara for an inveterate spinster with a tendency to avoid male friends other than myself. But the news had another, rather curious effect. It set my thoughts rambling amidst the old surroundings. And now I found that they repelled me no longer; that, on the contrary, they aroused a certain feeling of home-sickness, a yearning for the fuller, richer life of London and a sight of the English countryside. In not much more than a month, I had wound up my Canadian affairs and was back in my old chambers in the Temple, which I had never given up, ready to start practice afresh."

"That," said Thorndyke, "would be a little less than three years ago. Now we come to your relations with the Monkhouse establishment."

"Yes; and I drifted into them almost at once. Barbara received me with open arms, and of course, Monkhouse knew all about me and accepted me as an old friend. Very soon I found myself, in a way, a member of the household. A bedroom was set apart for my use, whenever I cared to occupy it, and I came and went as if I were one of the family. I was appointed a trustee, with Brodribb, and dropped into the position of general family counsellor."

"And what were your relations with Monkhouse?"

"We were never very intimate. I liked the man and I think he liked me. But he was not very approachable; a self-contained, aloof, undemonstrative man, and an inveterate book-worm. But he was a good man and I respected him profoundly, though I could never understand why Barbara married him, or why he married Barbara. I couldn't imagine him in love. On the other hand I cannot conceive any motive that anyone could have had for doing him any harm. He seemed to me to be universally liked in a rather lukewarm fashion."

"It is of no use, I suppose," said Thorndyke, "to ask you if these reminiscences have brought anything to your mind that would throw any light on the means, the motive or the person connected with the crime?"

"No," I answered; "nor can I imagine that they will bring anything to yours. In fact, I am astonished that you have let me go on so long dribbling out all these trivial and irrelevant details. Your patience is monumental."

"Not at all," he replied. "Your story has interested me deeply. It enables me to visualize very clearly at least a part of the setting of this crime, and it has introduced me to the personalities of some of the principal actors, including yourself. The details are not in the least trivial; and whether they are or are not irrelevant we cannot judge. Perhaps, when we have solved the mystery – if ever we do – we may find connections between events that had seemed to be totally unrelated."

"It is, I suppose, conceivable as a mere, speculative possibility. But what I have been telling you is mainly concerned with my own rather remote past, which can hardly have any possible bearing on comparatively recent events."

"That is perfectly true," Thorndyke agreed. "Your little autobiography has made perfectly clear your own relation to these people, but it has left most of them – and those in whom I am most interested – outside the picture. I was just wondering whether it would be possible for you to amplify your sketch of the course of events after Barbara's marriage – I am, like you, using the Christian name, for convenience. What I really want is an account of the happenings in that household during the last three years, and especially during the last year. Do you think that, if you were to turn out the garrets of your memory, you could draw up a history of the house in Hilborough Square and its inmates from the time when you first made its acquaintance? Have you any sort of notes that would help you?"

"By Jove!" I exclaimed. "Of course I have. There is my diary."

"Oh," said Thorndyke, with obviously awakened interest. "You keep a diary. What sort of diary is it? Just brief jottings, or a full record?"

"It is a pretty full diary. I began it more than twenty years ago as a sort of schoolboy hobby. But it turned out so useful and entertaining to refer to that I encouraged myself to persevere. Now, I am a confirmed diarist; and I write down not only facts and events, but also comments, which may be quite illuminating to study by the light of what has happened. I will read over the last three years and make an abstract of everything that has happened in that household. And I hope the reading of that abstract will entertain you; for I can't believe that it will help you to unravel the mystery of Harold Monkhouse's death."

"Well," Thorndyke replied, as I rose to take my leave, "don't let your scepticism influence you. Keep in your mind the actual position.

In that house a man was poisoned, and almost certainly feloniously poisoned. He must have been poisoned either by someone who was an inmate of that house or by someone who had some sort of access to the dead man from without. It is conceivable that the entries in your diary may bring one or other such person into view. Keep that possibility constantly before you; and fill your abstract with irrelevancies rather than risk omitting anything from which we could gather even the most shadowy hint."

CHAPTER NINE

Superintendent Miller is Puzzled

On arriving at my chambers after my conference with Thorndyke, I found awaiting me a letter from a Maidstone solicitor offering me a brief for a case of some importance that was to be tried at the forthcoming assizes. At first, I read it almost impatiently, so preoccupied was my mind with the tragedy in which I was involved. It seemed inopportune, almost impertinent. But, in fact it was most opportune, as I presently realized, in that it recalled me to the realities of normal life. My duties to my friends I did, indeed, take very seriously. But I was not an idle man. I had my way to make in my profession and could not afford to drop out of the race, to sacrifice my ambitions entirely, even on the altar of friendship.

I sat down and glanced through the instructions. It was a case of alleged fraud, an intricate case which interested me at once and in which I thought I could do myself credit; which was also the opinion of the solicitor, who was evidently anxious for me to undertake it. Eventually, I decided to accept the brief, and having written a letter to that effect, I set myself to spend the remainder of the evening in studying the instructions and mastering the rather involved details. For time was short, since the case was down for hearing in a couple of days' time and the morrow would be taken up by my engagements at Hilborough Square.

I pass over the incidents of the funeral. It was a dismal and unpleasant affair, lacking all the dignity and pathos that relieve the dreariness of an ordinary funeral. None of us could forget, as we sat back in the mourning coach as far out of sight as possible, that the corpse in the hearse ahead was the corpse of a murdered man, and that most of the bystanders knew it. Even in the chapel, the majestic service was marred and almost vulgarized by the self-consciousness of the mourners and at the grave-side we found one another peering furtively around for signs of recognition. To all of us it was a profound relief, when we were once more gathered together in the drawing room, to hear the street door close finally and the mourning carriage rumble away down the square.

I took an early opportunity of mentioning the brief and I could see that to both the women the prospect of my departure came as a disagreeable surprise.

"How soon will you have to leave us?" Madeline asked, anxiously.

"I must start for Maidstone tomorrow morning," I replied.

"Oh, dear!" she exclaimed. "How empty the place will seem and how lost we shall be without you to advise us."

"I hope," said I, "that the occasions for advice are past, and I shall not be so very far away, if you should want to consult me."

"No," said Barbara, "and I suppose you will not be away for very long. Shall you come back when your case is finished or shall you stay for the rest of the assizes?"

"I shall probably have some other briefs offered, which will detain me until the assizes are over. My solicitor hinted at some other cases, and of course there is the usual casual work that turns up on circuit."

"Well," she rejoined, "we can only wish you good luck and plenty of work, though we shall be glad when it is time for you to come back; and we must be thankful that you were here to help us through the worst of our troubles."

The general tenor of this conversation, which took place at the lunch table, was not, apparently, to Wallingford's taste; for he sat glumly consuming his food and rather ostentatiously abstaining from taking any part in the discussion. Nor was I surprised; for the obvious way in which both women leant on me was a reproach to his capacity, which ought to have made my advice and guidance unnecessary. But though

I sympathized in a way with his displeasure, it nevertheless made me a little uneasy. For there was another matter that I wanted to broach; one in which he might consider himself concerned; namely, my commission to Thorndyke. I had, indeed, debated with myself whether I should not be wiser to keep my own counsel on the subject; but I had decided that they were all interested parties and that it would seem unfriendly and uncandid to keep them in the dark. But, for obvious reasons, I did not propose to acquaint them with Thorndyke's views on the case.

The announcement, when I made it, was received without enthusiasm, and Wallingford, as I had feared, was inclined to be resentful.

"Don't you think, Mayfield," said he, "that you ought to have consulted the rest of us before putting this private inquiry agent, or whatever he is, on the case?"

"Perhaps I ought," I admitted. "But it is important to us all that the mystery should be cleared up."

"That is quite true," said Barbara, "and for my part, I shall never rest until the wretch who made away with poor Harold is dragged out into the light of day – that is, if there is really such a person; I mean, if Harold's death was not, after all, the result of some ghastly accident. But is it wise for us to meddle? The police have the case in hand. Surely, with all their experience and their machinery of detection, they are more likely to be successful than a private individual, no matter how clever he may be."

"That," I replied, "is, in fact, Dr Thorndyke's own view. He wished to leave the inquiry to the police; and I may say that he will not come into the case unless it should turn out that the police are unable to solve the mystery."

"In which case," said Wallingford, "it is extremely unlikely that an outsider, without their special opportunities, will be able to solve it. And if he should happen to find a mare's nest, we shall share the glory and the publicity of his discovery."

"I don't think," said I, "that you need have any anxiety on that score. Dr Thorndyke is not at all addicted to finding mare's nests and still less to publicity. If he makes any discovery he will probably keep it to himself until he has the whole case cut and dried. Then he will communicate the facts to the police; and the first news we shall have on the subject will be the announcement that an arrest has been made. And when the police make an arrest on Thorndyke's information, you can take it that a conviction will follow inevitably."

"I don't think I quite understand Dr Thorndyke's position," said Madeline. "What is he? You seem to refer to him as a sort of superior private detective."

"Thorndyke," I replied, "is a unique figure in the legal world. He is a barrister and a doctor of medicine. In the one capacity he is probably the greatest criminal lawyer of our time. In the other he is, among other things, the leading authority on poisons and on crimes connected with them; and so far as I know, he has never made a mistake."

"He must be a very remarkable man," Wallingford remarked, drily.

"He is," I replied; and in justification of my statement, I gave a sketch of one or two of the cases in which Thorndyke had cleared up what had seemed to be a completely and helplessly insoluble mystery. They all listened with keen interest and were evidently so far impressed that any doubts as to Thorndyke's capacity were set at rest. But yet I was conscious, in all three, of a certain distrust and uneasiness. The truth was, as it seemed to me, that none of them had yet recovered from the ordeal of the inquest. In their secret hearts, what they all wanted – even Barbara, as I suspected – was to bury the whole dreadful episode in oblivion. And seeing this, I had not the courage to remind them of their – of our position as the actual suspected parties whose innocence it was Thorndyke's function to make clear.

In view of my impending departure from London, I stayed until the evening was well advanced, though sensible of a certain impatience to be gone; and when, at length, I took my leave and set forth homeward, I was conscious of the same sense of relief that I had felt on the previous day. Now, for a time, I could dismiss this horror from my mind and let my thoughts occupy themselves with the activities that awaited me at Maidstone; which they did so effectually that by the time I reached my chambers, I felt that I had my case at my fingers' ends.

I had just set to work making my preparations for the morrow when my glance happened to light on the glazed bookcase in which the long series of my diaries was kept; and then I suddenly bethought me of the abstract which I had promised to make for Thorndyke. There would be no time for that now; and yet, since he had seemed to attach some importance to it, I could not leave my promise unfulfilled. The only thing to be done was to let him have the diary, itself. I was a little reluctant to do this for I had never yet allowed anyone to read it. But there seemed to be no alternative; and, after all, Thorndyke was a responsible person; and if the diary did contain a certain amount of confidential matter, there was nothing in it that was really secret or that I need object to anyone reading. Accordingly, I took out the current volume, and, dropping it into my pocket, made my way round to King's Bench Walk.

My knock at the door was answered by Thorndyke, himself, and as I entered the room, I was a little disconcerted at finding a large man seated in an easy chair by the fire with his back to me; and still more so when, on hearing me enter, he rose and turned to confront me. For the stranger was none other than Mr Superintendent Miller.

His gratification at the meeting seemed to be no greater than mine, though he greeted me quite courteously and even cordially. I had the uncomfortable feeling that I had broken in on a conference and began to make polite preparations for a strategic retreat. But Thorndyke would have none of it.

"Not at all, Mayfield," said he. "The superintendent is here on the same business as you are, and when I tell him that you have commissioned me to investigate this case, he will realize that we are colleagues."

I am not sure that the superintendent realized this so very vividly, but it was evident that Thorndyke's information interested him. Nevertheless he waited for me and Thorndyke to make the opening moves and only relaxed his caution by slow degrees.

"We were remarking when you came in," he said, at length, "what a curiously baffling case this is, and how very disappointing. At first it looked all plain sailing. There was the lady who used to prepare the special diet for the unfortunate man and actually take it up to him and watch him eat it. It seemed as if we had her in the hollow of our hand. And then she slipped out. The arsenic that was found in the stomach seemed to connect the death with the food; but then there was that confounded bottle of medicine that seemed to put the food outside the case. And when we came to reckon up the evidence furnished by the medicine, it proved nothing. Somebody put the poison in. All of them had the opportunity, more or less, and all about equally. Nothing pointed to one more than another. And that is how it is all through. There is any amount of suspicion; but the suspicion falls on a group of people, not on anyone in particular."

"Yes," said Thorndyke, "the issues are most strangely confused."

"Extraordinarily," said Miller. "This queer confusion runs all through the case. You are constantly thinking that you have got the solution, and just as you are perfectly sure, it slips through your fingers. There are lots of clues – fine ones; but as soon as you follow one up it breaks off in the middle and leaves you gaping. You saw what happened at the search, Mr Mayfield."

"I saw the beginning – the actual search; but I don't know what came of it."

"Then I can tell you in one word. Nothing. And yet we seemed to be right on the track every time. There was that secret drawer of Mr Wallingford's. When I saw that packet of white powder in it, I thought it was going to be a walk-over. I didn't believe for a moment that the stuff was cocaine. But it was. I went straight to our analyst to have it tested."

As the superintendent was speaking I caught Thorndyke's eye, fixed on me with an expression of reproachful inquiry. But he made no remark and Miller continued: "Then there were those two empty bottles. The one that I found in the library yielded definite traces of arsenic. But then, whose bottle was it? The place was accessible to the entire household. It was impossible to connect it with any one person.

On the other hand, the bottle that I found in Miss Norris' cupboard, and that was presumably hers – though she didn't admit it – contained no arsenic; at least the analyst said it didn't, though as it smelt of lavender and had a red stain at the bottom, I feel convinced that it had had Fowler's Solution in it. What do you think, Doctor? Don't you think the analyst may have been mistaken?"

"No," Thorndyke replied, decidedly. "If the red stain had been due to Fowler's Solution there would have been an appreciable quantity of arsenic present; probably a fiftieth of a grain at least. But Marsh's test would detect a much smaller quantity than that. If no arsenic was found by a competent chemist who was expressly testing for it, you can take it that no arsenic was there."

"Well," Miller rejoined, "you know best. But you must admit that it is a most remarkable thing that one bottle which smelt of lavender and had a red stain at the bottom, should contain arsenic, and that another bottle, exactly similar in appearance and smelling of lavender and having a red stain at the bottom, should contain no arsenic."

"I am entirely with you, Miller," Thorndyke agreed. "It is a most remarkable circumstance."

"And you see my point," said Miller. "Every discovery turns out a sell. I find a concealed packet of powder – with the owner lying like Ananias – but the powder turns out not to be arsenic. I find a bottle that did contain arsenic, and there is no owner. I find another, similar bottle, which has an owner, and there is no arsenic in it. Rum, isn't it? I feel like the donkey with the bunch of carrots tied to his nose. The carrots are there all right, but he can never get a bite at 'em."

Thorndyke had listened with the closest attention to the superintendent's observations and he now began a cautious cross-examination – cautious because Miller was taking it for granted that I had told him all about the search; and I could not but admire his discretion in suppressing the fact that I had not. For, while Thorndyke, himself, would not suspect me of any intentional concealment, Miller undoubtedly would, and what little confidence he had in me would have been destroyed. Accordingly, he managed the superintendent so adroitly that the latter described, piecemeal, all the incidents of the search.

"Did Wallingford say how he came to be in possession of all this cocaine and morphine?" he asked.

"No," replied Miller. "I asked him, but he refused to say where he had got it."

"But he could be made to answer," said Thorndyke. "Both of these drugs are poisons. He could be made to account for having them in his possession and could be called upon to show that he came by them lawfully. They are not ordinarily purchasable by the public."

"No, that's true," Miller admitted. "But is there any object in going into the question? You see, the cocaine isn't really any affair of ours."

"It doesn't seem to be," Thorndyke agreed, "at least, not directly; but indirectly it may be of considerable importance. I think you ought to find out where he got that cocaine and morphine, Miller."

The superintendent reflected with the air of having seen a new light.

"I see what you mean, Doctor," said he. "You mean that if he got the stuff from some Chinaman or common dope merchant, there wouldn't be much in it; whereas, if he got it from someone who had a general stock of drugs, there might be a good deal in it. Is that the point?"

"Yes. He was able to obtain poisons from somebody, and we ought to know exactly what facilities he had for obtaining poisons and what poisons he obtained."

"Yes, that is so," said Miller. "Well, I will see about it at once. Fortunately he is a pretty easy chappie to frighten. I expect, if I give him a bit of a shake-up, he will give himself away; and if he won't, we must try other means. And now, as I think we have said all that we have to say at present, I will wish you two gentlemen good night."

He rose and took up his hat, and having shaken our hands, was duly escorted to the door by Thorndyke; who, when he had seen his visitor safely on to the stairs, returned and confronted me with a look of deep significance.

"You never told me about that cocaine," said he.

"No," I admitted. "It was stupid of me, but the fact is that I was so engrossed by your rather startling observations on the case that this detail slipped my memory.

"And it really had not impressed me as being of any importance. I accepted Wallingford's statement that the stuff was cocaine and that, consequently, it was no concern of ours."

"I don't find myself able to agree to that 'consequently,' Mayfield. How did you know that the cocaine was no concern of ours?"

"Well, I didn't see that it was, and I don't now. Do you?"

"No; I know very little about the case at present. But it seems to me that the fact that a person in this house had a considerable quantity of a highly poisonous substance in his possession is one that at least requires to be noted. The point is, Mayfield, that until we know all the facts of this case we cannot tell which of them is or is not relevant. Try to bear that in mind. Do not select particular facts as important and worthy of notice. Note everything in any way connected with our problem that comes under your observation and pass it on to me without sifting or selection."

"I ought not to need these exhortations," said I. "However, I will bear them in mind should I ever have anything more to communicate. Probably I never shall. But I will say that I think Miller is wasting his energies over Wallingford. The man is no favourite of mine. He is a neurotic ass. But I certainly do not think he has the makings of a murderer."

Thorndyke smiled a little drily. "If you are able," said he, "to diagnose at sight a potential murderer, your powers are a good deal beyond mine. I should have said that every man has the makings of a murderer, given the appropriate conditions."

"Should you really?" I exclaimed. "Can you, for instance, imagine either of us committing a murder?"

"I think I can," he replied. "Of course, the probabilities are very unequal in different cases. There are some men who may be said to be prone to murder. A man of low intelligence, of violent temper, deficient in ordinary self-control, may commit a murder in circumstances that would leave a man of a superior type unmoved.

But still, the determining factors are motive and opportunity. Given a sufficient motive and a real opportunity, I can think of no kind of man who might not commit a homicide which would, in a legal sense, be murder."

"But is there such a thing as a sufficient motive for murder?"

"That question can be answered only by the individual affected. If it seems to him sufficient, it is sufficient in practice."

"Can you mention a motive that would seem to you sufficient?"

"Yes, I can. Blackmail. Let us take an imaginary case. Suppose a man to be convicted of a crime of which he is innocent. As he has been convicted, the evidence, though fallacious, is overwhelming. He is sentenced to a term of imprisonment – say penal servitude. He serves his sentence and is in due course discharged. He is now free; but the conviction stands against him. He is a discharged convict. His name is in the prison books, his photograph and his fingerprints are in the Habitual Criminals' Register. He is a marked man for life.

"Now suppose that he manages to shed his identity and in some place where he is unknown begins life afresh. He acquires the excellent character and reputation to which he is, in fact, entitled. He marries and has a family; and he and his family prosper and enjoy the advantages that follow deservedly from his industry and excellent moral qualities.

"And now suppose that at this point his identity is discovered by a blackmailer who forthwith fastens on him, who determines to live on him in perpetuity, to devour the products of his industry, to impoverish his wife and children and to destroy his peace and security by holding over his head the constant menace of exposure. What is such a man to do? The law will help him so far as it can; but it cannot save him from exposure. He can obtain the protection of the law only on condition that he discloses the facts. But that disclosure is precisely the evil that he seeks to avoid. He is an innocent man, but his innocence is known only to himself. The fact, which must transpire if he prosecutes, is that he is a convicted criminal.

"I say, Mayfield, what can he do? What is his remedy? He has but one; and since the law cannot really help him, he is entitled to help himself. If I were in that man's position and the opportunity presented itself, I would put away that blackmailer with no more qualms than I should have in killing a wasp."

"Then I am not going to blackmail you, Thorndyke, for I have a strong conviction that an opportunity *would* present itself."

"I think it very probable," he replied with a smile. "At any rate, I know a good many methods that I should not adopt, and I think arsenic poisoning is one of them. But don't you agree with me?"

"I suppose I do, at least in the very extreme case that you have put. But it is the only case of justifiable premeditated homicide that I can imagine; and it obviously doesn't apply to Wallingford."

"My dear Mayfield," he exclaimed. "How do we know what does or does not apply to Wallingford? How do we know what he would regard as an adequate motive? We know virtually nothing about him or his affairs or about the crime itself. What we do know is that a man has apparently been murdered, and that, of the various persons who had the opportunity to commit the murder (of whom he is one) none had any intelligible motive at all. It is futile for us to argue back and forth on the insufficient knowledge that we possess. We can only docket and classify all the facts that we have and follow up each of them impartially with a perfectly open mind. But, above all, we must try to increase our stock of facts. I suppose you haven't had time to consider that abstract of which we spoke?"

"That is really what brought me round here this evening. I haven't had time, and I shan't have just at present as I am starting tomorrow to take up work on the Southeastern Circuit. But I have brought the current volume of the diary, itself, if you would care to wade through it."

"I should, certainly. The complete document is much preferable to an abstract which might leave me in the dark as to the context. But won't you want to have your diary with you?"

"No, I shall take a short-hand note-book to use while I am away. That is, in fact, what I usually do."

"And you don't mind putting this very confidential document into the hands of a stranger?"

"You are not a stranger, Thorndyke. I don't mind you, though I don't think I would hand it to anybody else. Not that it contains anything that the whole world might not see, for I am a fairly discreet diarist. But there are references to third parties with reflections and comments that I shouldn't care to have read by Thomas, Richard and Henry. My only fear is that you will find it rather garrulous and diffuse."

"Better that than overcondensed and sketchy," said he, as he took the volume from me. He turned the leaves over, and having glanced at one or two pages exclaimed: "This is something like a diary, Mayfield! Quite in the classical manner. The common, daily jottings such as most of us make, are invaluable if they are kept up regularly, but this of yours is immeasurably superior. In a hundred years' time it will be a priceless historical work. How many volumes of it have you got?"

"About twenty: and I must say that I find the older ones quite interesting reading. You may perhaps like to look at one or two of the more recent volumes."

"I should like to see those recording the events of the last three years."

"Well, they are all at your service. I have brought you my duplicate latchkey and you will find the volumes of the diary in the glazed book-case. It is usually kept locked, but as nobody but you will have access to the chambers while I am away, I shall leave the key in the lock."

"This is really very good of you, Mayfield," he said, as I rose to take my departure. "Let me have your address, wherever you may be for the time being, and I will keep you posted in any developments that may occur. And now, good-bye and good luck!" He shook my hand cordially and I betook myself to my chambers to complete my preparations for my start on the morrow.

CHAPTER TEN

A Greek Gift

The incidents of my life while I was following the Southeastern Circuit are no part of this history, and I refer to this period merely by way of marking the passage of time. Indeed, it was its separateness, its detachment from the other and more personal aspects of my life that specially commended it to me. In the cheerful surroundings of the Bar Mess I could forget the terrible experiences of the last few weeks, and even in the grimmer and more suggestive atmosphere of the courts, the close attention that the proceedings demanded kept my mind in a state of wholesome preoccupation.

Quite a considerable amount of work came my way, and though most of the briefs were small – so small, often, that I felt some compunction in taking them from the more needy juniors – yet it was all experience and what was more important just now, it was occupation that kept my mind employed.

That was the great thing. To keep my mind busy with matters that were not my personal concern. And the intensity of my yearning for distraction was the measure of the extent to which my waking thoughts tended to be pervaded by the sinister surroundings of Harold Monkhouse's death. That dreadful event and the mystery that encompassed it had shaken me more than I had at first realized. Nor need this be a matter for surprise. Harold Monkhouse had apparently been murdered; at any rate that was the accepted view. And who was the murderer? Evade the answer as I would, the fact remained that the finger of suspicion pointed at my own intimate friends – nay, even at me. It is no wonder, then, that the mystery haunted me. Murder has an ominous sound to any ears; but to a lawyer practising in criminal courts the word has connotations to which his daily experiences impart a peculiarly hideous vividness and realism. Once, I remember that, sitting in court, listening to the evidence in a trial for murder, as my glance strayed to the dock where the prisoner stood, watched and guarded like a captured wild beast, the thought suddenly flashed on me that it was actually possible – and to the police actually probable – that thus might yet stand Wallingford or Madeline, or even Barbara or myself.

It would have been possible for me to run home from time to time at weekends but I did not. There was nothing that called for my presence in London and it was better to stick close to my work. Still, I was not quite cut off from my friends, for Barbara wrote regularly and I had an occasional letter from Madeline. As to Thorndyke, he was too busy to write unnecessary letters and his peculiar circumstances made a secretary impossible, so that I had from him no more than one or two brief notes reporting the absence of any new developments. Nor had Barbara much to tell excepting that she had decided to let or sell the house in Hilborough Square and take up her residence in a flat. The decision did not surprise me. I should certainly have done the same in her place; and I was only faintly surprised when I learned that she proposed to live alone and that Madeline had taken a small flat near the school. The two women had always been on excellent terms, but they were not specially devoted to one another; and Barbara would now probably pursue her own special interests. Of Wallingford I learned only that, on the strength of his legacy he had taken a set of rooms in the neighbourhood of Jermyn Street and that his nerves did not seem to have benefited by the change.

Such was the position of affairs when the Autumn Assizes came to an end and I returned home. I remember the occasion very vividly, as I have good reason to do – indeed, I had better reason than I knew at the time. It was a cold, dark, foggy evening, though not densely foggy, and my taxicab was compelled to crawl at an almost funereal pace (to the exasperation of the driver) through the murky streets, though the traffic was now beginning to thin out. We approached the Temple from the east and eventually entered by the Tudor Street Gate whence we crept tentatively across King's Bench Walk to the end of Crown Office Row. As we passed Thorndyke's chambers I looked up and had a momentary glimpse of lighted windows glimmering through the fog; then they faded away and I looked out on the other side where the great shadowy mass of Paper Buildings loomed above us. A man was standing at the end of the narrow passage that leads to Fig Tree Court – a tallish man wearing a preposterous wide-brimmed hat and a long overcoat with its collar turned up above his ears. I glanced at him incuriously as we approached but had no opportunity to inspect him more closely, if I had wished – which I did not – for, as the cab stopped he turned abruptly and walked away up the passage. The suddenness of his retirement struck me as a little odd and, having alighted from the cab, I stood for a moment or two watching his receding figure. But he soon disappeared in the foggy darkness, and I saw him no more. By the time that I had paid my fare and carried my portmanteau to Fig Tree Court, he had probably passed out into Middle Temple Lane.

When I had let myself into my chambers, switched on the light and shut the door, I looked round my little domain with somewhat mixed feelings. It was very silent and solitary. After the jovial Bar Mess and the bright, frequented rooms of the hotels or the excellent lodgings which I had just left, these chambers struck me as just a shade desolate. But yet there were compensations. A sense of peace and quiet pervaded the place and all around were my household gods; my familiar and beloved pictures, the little friendly cabinet busts and statuettes, and, above all, the goodly fellowship of books. And at this moment my glance fell on the long range of my diaries and I noticed that one of the series was absent. Not that there was anything remarkable in that, since I had given Thorndyke express permission to take them away to read. What did surprise me a little was the date of the missing volume. It was that of the year before Stella's death. As I noted this I was conscious of a faint sense of annoyance. I had, it is true, given him the free use of the diary, but only for purposes of reference. I had hardly bargained for his perusal of the whole series for his entertainment. However, it was of no consequence. The diary enshrined no secrets. If I had, in a way, emulated Pepys in respect of fulness, I had taken warning from his indiscretions; nor, in fact, was I quite so rich in the material of indiscreet records as the vivacious Samuel.

I unpacked my portmanteau – the heavier impedimenta were coming on by rail – lit the gas fire in my bedroom, boiled a kettle of water, partly for a comfortable wash and partly to fill a hotwater bottle wherewith to warm the probably damp bed, and then, still feeling a little like a cat in a strange house, decided to walk along to Thorndyke's chambers and hear the news, if there were any.

The fog had grown appreciably denser when I turned out of my entry, and, crossing the little quadrangle, strode quickly along the narrow passage that leads to the Terrace and King's Bench Walk. I was approaching the end of the passage when there came suddenly into view a shadowy figure which I recognized at once as that of the man whom I had seen when I arrived. But again I had no opportunity for a close inspection, for he had already heard my footsteps and he now started to walk away rapidly in the direction of Mitre Court. For a moment I was disposed to follow him, and did, in fact, make a few quick steps towards him – which seemed to cause him to mend his pace; but it was not directly my business to deal with loiterers, and I could have done nothing even if I had overtaken him. Accordingly I changed my direction, and crossing King's Bench Walk, bore down on Thorndyke's entry.

As I approached the house I was a little disconcerted to observe that there were now no lights in his chambers, though the windows above were lighted. I ran up the stairs, and finding the oak closed, pressed the electric bell, which I could hear ringing on the floor above. Almost immediately footsteps became audible descending the stairs and were followed by the appearance of a small gentleman whom I recognized as Thorndyke's assistant, artificer or familiar spirit, Mr Polton. He recognized me at the same moment and greeted me with a smile that seemed to break out of the corners of his eyes and spread in a network of wrinkles over every part of his face; a sort of compound smile inasmuch as every wrinkle seemed to have a smile of its own.

"I hope, Mr Polton," said I, "that I haven't missed the doctor."

"No, Sir," he replied. "He is up in the laboratory. We are just about to make a little experiment."

"Well, I am in no hurry. Don't disturb him. I will wait until he is at liberty."

"Unless, Sir," he suggested, "you would like to come up. Perhaps you would like to see the experiment."

I closed with the offer gladly. I had never seen Thorndyke's laboratory and had often been somewhat mystified as to what he did in it. Accordingly I followed Mr Polton up the stairs, at the top of which I found Thorndyke waiting.

"I thought it was your voice, Mayfield," said he, shaking my hand. "You are just in time to see us locate a mare's nest. Come in and lend a hand."

He led me into a large room around which I glanced curiously and not without surprise. One side was occupied by a huge copying camera, the other by a joiner's bench. A powerful back-geared lathe stood against one window, a jeweller's bench against the other, and the walls were covered with shelves and tool-racks, filled with all sorts of strange implements. From this room we passed into another which I recognized as a chemical laboratory, although most of the apparatus in it was totally unfamiliar to me.

"I had no idea," said I, "that the practice of Medical Jurisprudence involved such an outfit as this. What do you do with it all? The place is like a factory."

"It is a factory," he replied with a smile; "a place where the raw material of scientific evidence is worked up into the finished product suitable for use in courts of law."

"I don't know that that conveys much to me," said I. "But you are going to perform some sort of experiment; perhaps that will enlighten me."

"Probably it will, to some extent," he replied, "though it is only a simple affair. We have a parcel here which came by post this evening and we are going to see what is in it before we open it."

"The devil you are!" I exclaimed. "How in the name of Fortune are you going to do that?"

"We shall examine it by means of the X-rays."

"But why? Why not open it and find out what is in it in a reasonable way?"

Thorndyke chuckled softly. "We have had our little experiences, Mayfield, and we have grown wary. We don't open strange parcels nowadays until we are sure that we are not dealing with a 'Greek gift' of some sort. That is what we are going to ascertain now in respect of this."

He picked up from the bench a parcel about the size of an ordinary cigar-box and held it out for my inspection. "The overwhelming probabilities are," he continued, "that this is a perfectly innocent package. But we don't know. I am not expecting any such parcel and there are certain peculiarities about this one that attract one's attention. You notice that the entire address is in rough Roman capitals-what are commonly called 'block letters.' That is probably for the sake of distinctness; but it might possibly be done to avoid a recognizable handwriting or a possibly traceable typewriter. Then you notice that it is addressed to 'Dr Thorndyke' and conspicuously endorsed 'personal.' Now, that is really a little odd. One understands the object of marking a letter 'personal' – to guard against its being opened and read by the wrong person. But what does it matter who opens a parcel?"

"I can't imagine why it should matter," I admitted without much conviction, "but I don't see anything in the unnecessary addition that need excite suspicion. Do you?"

"Perhaps not; but you observe that the sender was apparently anxious that the parcel should be opened by a particular person."

I shrugged my shoulders. The whole proceeding and the reasons given for it struck me as verging on farce. "Do you go through these formalities with every parcel that you receive?" I asked.

"No," he replied. "Only with those that are unexpected or offer no evidence as to their origin. But we are pretty careful. As I said just now, we have had our experiences. One of them was a box which, on being opened, discharged volumes of poisonous gas."

"The deuce!" I exclaimed, rather startled out of my scepticism and viewing the parcel with a new-born respect, not unmixed with apprehension. "Then this thing may actually be an infernal machine! Confound it all, Thorndyke! Supposing it should have a clockwork detonator, ticking away while we are talking. Hadn't you better get on with the X-rays?"

He chuckled at my sudden change of attitude. "It is all right, Mayfield. There is no clockwork. I tried it with the microphone as soon as it arrived. We always do that. And, of course, it is a thousand to one that it is just an innocent parcel. But we will just make sure and then I shall be at liberty for a chat with you."

He led the way to a staircase leading to the floor above where I was introduced to a large, bare room surrounded by long benches or tables occupied by various uncanny-looking apparatus. As soon as we entered, he placed the parcel on a raised stand while Polton turned a switch connected with a great coil; the immediate result of which was a peculiar, high-pitched, humming sound as if a gigantic mosquito had got into the room. At the same moment a glass globe that was supported on an arm behind the parcel became filled with green light and displayed a bright red spot in its interior.

"This is a necromantic sort of business, Thorndyke," said I, "only you and Mr Polton aren't dressed for the part. You ought to have tall pointed caps and gowns covered with cabalistic signs. What is that queer humming noise?"

"That is the interrupter," he replied. "The green bulb is the Crookes's tube and the little red-hot disc inside it is the anti-cathode. I will tell you about them presently. That framed plate that Polton has is the fluorescent screen. It intercepts the X-rays and makes them visible. You shall see, when Polton has finished his inspection."

I watched Polton – who had taken the opportunity to get the first innings – holding the screen between his face and the parcel. After a few moments' inspection he turned the parcel over on its side and once more raised the screen, gazing at it with an expression of the most intense interest. Suddenly he turned to Thorndyke with a smile of perfectly incredible wrinkliness and, without a word, handed him the screen; which he held up for a few seconds and then silently passed to me.

I had never used a fluorescent screen before and I must confess that I found the experience most uncanny. As I raised it before the parcel behind which was the glowing green bulb, the parcel became invisible but in its place appeared the shadow of a pistol the muzzle of which seemed to be inserted into a jar. There were some other, smaller shadows, of which I could make nothing, but which seemed to be floating in the air.

"Better not look too long, Mayfield," said Thorndyke. "X-rays are unwholesome things. We will take a photograph and then we can study the details at our leisure; though it is all pretty obvious."

"It isn't to me," said I. "There is a pistol and what looks like a jar. Do you take it that they are parts of an infernal machine?"

"I suppose," he replied, "we must dignify it with that name. What do you say, Polton?"

"I should call it a booby-trap, Sir," was the reply. "What you might expect from a mischievous boy of ten – rather backward for his age."

Thorndyke laughed. "Listen to the artificer," said he, "and observe how his mechanical soul is offended by an inefficient and unmechanical attempt to blow us all up. But we won't take the inefficiency too much for granted. Let us have a photograph and then we can get to work with safety."

It seemed that this part also of the procedure was already provided for in the form of a large black envelope which Polton produced from a drawer and began forthwith to adjust in contact with the parcel; in fact the appearance of preparedness was so striking that I remarked: "This looks like part of a regular routine. It must take up a lot of your time."

"As a matter of fact," he replied, "we don't often have to do this. I don't receive many parcels and of those that are delivered, the immense majority come from known sources and are accompanied by letters of advice. It is only the strange and questionable packages that we examine with the X-rays. Of course, this one was suspect at a glance with that disguised handwriting and the special direction as to who should open it."

"Yes, I see that now. But it must be rather uncomfortable to live in constant expectation of having bombs or poison-gas handed in by the postman."

"It isn't as bad as that," said he. "The thing has happened only three or four times in the whole of my experience. The first gift of the kind was a poisoned cigar, which I fortunately detected and which served as a very useful warning. Since then I have kept my weather eyelid lifting, as the mariners express it."

"But don't you find it rather wearing to be constantly on the look-out for some murderous attack?"

"Not at all," he answered with a laugh. "It rather adds to the zest of life. Besides, you see, Mayfield, that on the rare occasions when these trifles come my way, they are so extremely helpful."

"Helpful!" I repeated. "In the Lord's name, how?"

"In a number of ways. Consider my position, Mayfield. I am not like an Italian or Russian politician who may have scores of murderous enemies. I am a lawyer and an investigator of crime. Whoever wants to get rid of me has something to fear from me; but at any given time, there will not be more than one or two of such persons. Consequently, when I receive a gift such as the present one, it conveys to me certain items of information. Thus it informs me that some one is becoming alarmed by some proceedings on my part. That is a very valuable piece of information, for it tells me that some one of my inquiries is at least proceeding along the right lines. It is virtually an admission that I have made, or am in the way of making a point. A little consideration of the cases that I have in hand will probably suggest the identity of the sender. But on this question the thing itself will, in most cases yield quite useful information as well as telling us a good deal about the personality of the sender. Take the present case. You heard Polton's contemptuous observations on the crudity of the device. Evidently the person who sent this is not an engineer or mechanician of any kind. There is an obvious ignorance of mechanism; and yet there is a certain simple ingenuity. The thing is, in fact, as Polton said, on the level of a schoolboy's booby-trap. You must see that if we had in view two or more possible senders, these facts might enable us to exclude one and select another. But here is Polton with the photograph. Now we can consider the mechanism at our leisure."

As he spoke, Polton deposited on the bench a large porcelain dish or tray in which was a very odd-looking photograph; for the whole of it was jet-black excepting the pistol, the jar, the hinges, and a small, elongated spot, which all stood out in clear, white silhouette.

"Why," I exclaimed as I stooped over it, "that is a muzzle-loading pistol!"

"Yes," Thorndyke agreed, "and a pocket pistol, as you can tell by the absence of a trigger-guard. The trigger is probably hinged and folds forward into a recess. I daresay you know the kind of thing. They were usually rather pretty little weapons – and useful, too, for you could carry one easily in your waistcoat pocket. They had octagon barrels, which screwed off for loading, and the butts were often quite handsomely ornamented with silver mounts. They were usually sent out by the gunsmiths in little baize-lined mahogany cases with compartments for a little powder-flask and a supply of bullets."

"I wonder why he used a muzzle-loader?" said I.

"Probably because he had it. It answers the purpose as well as a modern weapon, and, as it was probably made more than a hundred years ago, it would be useless to go round the trade enquiring as to recent purchases"

"Yes, it was safer to use an old pistol than to buy a new one and leave possible tracks. But how does the thing work? I can see that the hammer is at full cock and that there is a cap on the nipple. But what fires the pistol?"

"Apparently a piece of string, which hasn't come out in the photograph except, faintly, just above that small mark – string is not dense enough to throw a shadow at the full exposure – but you see, about an inch behind the trigger, an elongated shadow. That is probably a screw-eye seen end-ways. The string is tied to the trigger, passed through the screw-eye and fastened to the lid of the box. I don't see how. There is no metal fastening, and you see that the lid is not screwed or nailed down. As to how it works; you open the lid firmly; that pulls the string tight; that pulls back the trigger and fires the pistol into the jar, which is presumably full of some explosive; the jar explodes and – up goes the donkey. There is a noble simplicity about the whole thing. How do you propose to open it, Polton?"

"I think, Sir," replied the latter, "we had better get the paper off and have a look at the box."

"Very well," said Thorndyke, "but don't take anything for granted. Make sure that the paper isn't part of the joke."

I watched Polton with intense – and far from impersonal – interest, wishing only that I could have observed him from a somewhat greater distance. But for all his contempt for the "booby-trap," he took no unnecessary risks. First, with a pair of scissors, he cut out a piece at the back and enlarged the opening so that he could peer in and inspect the top of the lid. When he had made sure that there were no pitfalls, he ran the scissors round the top and exposed the box, which he carefully lifted out of the remainder of the wrapping and laid down tenderly on the bench. It was a cigar-box of the flat type and presented nothing remarkable excepting that the lid, instead of being nailed or pinned down, was secured by a number of strips of stout adhesive paper, and bore, near the middle, a large spot of sealing-wax.

"That paper binding is quite a happy thought," remarked Thorndyke, "though it was probably put on because our friend was afraid to knock in nails. But it would be quite effective. An impatient man would cut through the front strips and then wrench the lid open. I think that blob of sealing-wax answers our question about the fastening of the string. The end of it was probably drawn through a bradawl hole in the lid and fixed with sealing wax. But it must have been an anxious business drawing it just tight enough and not too tight. I suggest, Polton, that an inch-and-a-half centre-bit hole just below and to the right of the sealing-wax would enable us to cut the string. But you had better try it with the photograph first."

Polton picked the wet photograph out of the dish and carefully laid it on the lid of the box, adjusting it so that the shadows of the hinges were opposite the actual hinges. Then with a marking-awl he pricked through the shadow of the screw-eye, and again about two inches to the right and below it.

"You are quite right, Sir," said he as he removed the photograph and inspected the lid of the box. "The middle of the wax is exactly over the screw-eye. I'll just get the centre-bit."

He bustled away down the stairs and returned in less than a minute with a brace and a large centre-bit, the point of which he inserted into the second awl-hole. Then, as Thorndyke grasped the box (and I stepped back a pace or two), he turned the brace lightly and steadily, stopping now and again to clear away the chips and examine the deepening hole. A dozen turns carried the bit through the thin lid and the remaining disc of wood was driven into the interior of the box. As soon as the hole was clear, he cautiously inserted a dentist's mirror, which he had brought up in his pocket, and with its aid examined the inside of the lid.

"I can see the string, Sir," he reported; "a bit of common white twine and it looks quite slack. I could reach it easily with a small pair of scissors."

He handed the mirror to Thorndyke, who, having confirmed his observations, produced a pair of surgical scissors from his pocket. These Polton cautiously inserted into the opening, and as he closed them there was an audible snip. Then he slowly withdrew them and again inserted the mirror.

"It's all right," said he. "The string is cut clean through. I think we can open the lid now." With a sharp penknife he cut through the paper binding-strips and then, grasping the front of the lid, continued: "Now for it. Perhaps you two gentlemen had better stand a bit farther back, in case of accidents."

I thought the suggestion an excellent one, but as Thorndyke made no move, I had not the moral courage to adopt it. Nevertheless, I watched Polton's proceedings with my heart in my mouth. Very slowly and gently did that cunning artificer raise the lid until it had opened some two inches, when he stooped and peered in. Then, with the cheerful announcement that it was "all clear," he boldly turned it right back.

Of course, the photograph had shown us, in general, what to expect, but there were certain details that had not been represented. For instance, both the pistol and the jar were securely wedged between pieces of cork – sections of wine-bottle corks, apparently – glued to the bottom of the box.

"How is it," I asked, "that those corks did not appear in the photograph?"

"I think there is a faint indication of them," Thorndyke replied; "but Polton gave a rather full exposure. If you want to show bodies of such low density as corks, you have to give a specially short exposure and cut short the development, too. But I expect Polton saw them when he was developing the picture, didn't you, Polton?"

"Yes," the latter replied; "they were quite distinct at one time, but then I developed up to get the pistol out clear."

While these explanations were being given, Polton proceeded methodically to "draw the teeth" of the infernal apparatus. First, he cut a little wedge of cork which he pushed in between the threatening hammer and the nipple and having thus fixed the former he quietly removed the percussion-cap from the latter; on which I drew a deep breath of relief. He next wrenched away one of the corks and was then able to withdraw the pistol from the jar and lift it out of the box. I took it from him and examined it curiously, not a little interested to note how completely it corresponded with Thorndyke's description. It had a blued octagon barrel, a folding trigger which fitted snugly into a recess, a richly-engraved lock-plate and an ebony butt, decorated with numbers of tiny silver studs and a little lozenge-shaped scutcheon-plate on which a monogram had been engraved in minute letters, which, however, had been so thoroughly scraped out that I was unable to make out or even to guess what the letters had been.

My investigations were cut short by Thorndyke, who, having slipped on a pair of rubber gloves now took the pistol from me, remarking: "You haven't touched the barrel, I think, Mayfield?"

"No," I answered; "but why do you ask?"

"Because we shall go over it and the jar for fingerprints. Not that they will be much use for tracing the sender of this present, but they will be valuable corroboration if we catch him by other means; for whoever sent this certainly had a guilty conscience."

With this he delicately lifted out the jar – a small, dark-brown stoneware vessel such as is used as a container for the choicer kinds of condiments – and inverted it over a sheet of paper, upon which its contents, some two or three tablespoonfuls of black powder, descended and formed a small heap.

"Not a very formidable charge," Thorndyke remarked, looking at it with a smile.

"Formidable!" repeated Polton. "Why, it wouldn't have hurt a fly! Common black powder such as old women use to blow out the copper flues. He must be an innocent, this fellow – if it is a he," he added reflectively.

Polton's proviso suddenly recalled to my mind the man whom I had seen lurking at the corner of Fig Tree Court. It was hardly possible to avoid connecting him with the mysterious parcel, as Thorndyke agreed when I had described the incident.

"Yes," exclaimed Polton, "of course. He was waiting to hear the explosion. It is a pity you didn't mention it sooner, Sir. But he may be waiting there still. Hadn't I better run across and see?"

"And suppose he is there still," said Thorndyke. "What would you propose to do?"

"I should just pop up to the lodge and tell the porter to bring a policeman down. Why we should have him red-handed."

Thorndyke regarded his henchman with an indulgent smile. "Your handicraft, Polton," said he, "is better than your law. You can't arrest a man without a warrant unless he is doing something unlawful. This man was simply standing at the corner of Fig Tree Court."

"But," protested Polton, "isn't it unlawful to send infernal machines by parcel post?"

"Undoubtedly it is," Thorndyke admitted, "but we haven't a particle of evidence that this man has any connection with the parcel or with us. He may have been waiting there to meet a friend."

"He may, of course," said I, "but seeing that he ran off like a lamplighter on both the occasions when I appeared on the scene, I should suspect that he was there for no good And I strongly suspect him of having some connection with this precious parcel."

"So do I," said Thorndyke. "As a matter of fact, I have once or twice, lately, met a man answering to your description, loitering about King's Bench Walk in the evening. But I think it much better not to appear to notice him. Let him think himself unobserved and presently he will do something definite that will enable us to take action. And remember that the more thoroughly he commits himself the more valuable his conduct will be as indirect evidence on certain other matters."

I was amused at the way in which Thorndyke sank all considerations of personal safety in the single purpose of pursuing his investigations to a successful issue. He was the typical enthusiast. The possibility that this unknown person might shoot at him from some ambush, he would, I suspected, have welcomed as offering the chance to seize the aggressor and compel him to disclose his motives. Also, I had a shrewd suspicion that he knew or guessed who the man was and was anxious to avoid alarming him.

"Well," he said when he had replaced the pistol and the empty jar in the box and closed the latter, "I think we have finished for the present. The further examination of these interesting trifles can be postponed until tomorrow. Shall we go downstairs and talk over the news?"

"It is getting rather late," said I, "but there is time for a little chat, though, as to news, they will have to come from you, for I have nothing to tell."

We went down to the sitting room where, when he had locked up the box, we took each an armchair and filled our pipes.

"So you have no news of any kind?" said he.

"No; excepting that the Hilborough Square household has been broken up and the inmates scattered into various flats."

"Then the house is now empty?" said he, with an appearance of some interest.

"Yes, and likely to remain so with this gruesome story attached to it. I suppose I shall have to make a survey of the premises with a view to having them put in repair."

"When you do," said he, "I should like to go with you and look over the house."

"But it is all dismantled. Everything has been cleared out. You will find nothing there but empty rooms and a litter of discarded rubbish."

"Never mind," said he. "I have occasionally picked up some quite useful information from empty rooms and discarded rubbish. Do you know if the police have examined the house?"

"I believe not. At any rate, nothing has been said to me to that effect."

"So much the better," said he. "Can we fix a time for our visit?"

"It can't be tomorrow," said I, "because I must see Barbara and get the keys if she has them. Would the day after tomorrow do, after lunch?"

"Perfectly," he replied. "Come and lunch with me; and, by the way, Mayfield, it would be best not to mention to anyone that I am coming with you, and I wouldn't say anything about this parcel."

I looked at him with sudden suspicion, recalling Wallingford's observations on the subject of mare's nests. "But, my dear Thorndyke!" I exclaimed, "you don't surely associate that parcel with any of the inmates of that house!"

"I don't associate it with any particular person," he replied. "I know only what you know; that it was sent by someone to whom my existence is, for some reason, undesirable, and whose personality is to some extent indicated by the peculiarities of the thing itself."

"What peculiarities do you mean?"

"Well," he replied, "there is the nature and purpose of the thing. It is an appliance for killing a human being. That purpose implies either a very strong motive or a very light estimate of the value of human life. Then, as we have said, the sender is fairly ingenious but yet quite unmechanical and apparently unprovided with the common tools which ordinary men possess and are more or less able to use. You notice that the combination of ingenuity with non-possession of tools is a rather unusual one."

"How do you infer that the sender possessed no tools?"

"From the fact that none were used, and that such materials were employed as required no tools, though these were not the most suitable materials. For instance, common twine was used to pull the trigger, though it is a bad material by reason of its tendency to stretch. But it can be cut with a knife or a pair of scissors, whereas wire, which was the really suitable material, requires cutting pliers to divide it. Again, there were the corks. They were really not very safe, for their weakness and their resiliency might have led to disaster in the event of a specially heavy jerk in transit. A man who possessed no more than a common keyhole saw, or a hand-saw and a chisel or two, would have roughly shaped up one or two blocks of wood to fit the pistol and jar, which would have made the thing perfectly secure. If he had possessed a glue-pot, he would not have used seccotine. But every one has waste corks, and they can be trimmed to shape with an ordinary dinner-knife; and seccotine can be bought at any stationer's. But, to return to what we were saying. I had no special precautions in my mind. I suggested that we should keep our own counsel merely on the general principle that it is always best to keep one's own counsel. One may make a confidence to an entirely suitable person; but who can say that that person may not, in his or her turn, make a confidence? If we keep our knowledge strictly to ourselves we know exactly how we stand, and that if there has been any leakage, it had been from some other source. But I need not platitudinize to an experienced and learned counsel."

I grinned appreciatively at the neat finish; for "experienced counsel" as I certainly was not, I was at least able to realize, with secret approval, how adroitly Thorndyke had eluded my leading question.

And at that I left it, enquiring in my turn: "I suppose nothing of interest has transpired since I have been away?"

"Very little. There is one item of news, but that can hardly be said to have 'transpired' unless you can associate the process of transpiration with a suction-pump. Superintendent Miller took my advice and applied the suctorial method to Wallingford with results of which he possibly exaggerates the importance. He tells me – this is, of course, in the strictest confidence – that under pressure, Wallingford made a clean breast of the cocaine and morphine business. He admitted that he had obtained those drugs fraudulently by forging an order in Dimsdale's name, written on Dimsdale's headed note-paper, to the wholesale druggists to deliver to bearer the drugs mentioned. He had possessed himself of the note-paper at the time when he was working at the account books in Dimsdale's surgery."

"But how was it that Dimsdale did not notice what had happened when the accounts were sent in?"

"No accounts were ever sent in. The druggists whom Wallingford patronized were not those with whom Dimsdale had an account. The order stated, in every case, that bearer would pay cash."

"Quite an ingenious little plan of Wallingford's," I remarked. "It is more than I should have given him credit for. And you say that Miller attaches undue importance to this discovery. I am not surprised at that. But why do you think he exaggerates its importance?"

Thorndyke regarded me with a quizzical smile. "Because," he answered, "Miller's previous experiences have been repeated. There has been another discovery. It has transpired that Miss Norris also had dealings with a wholesale druggist. But in her case there was no fraud or irregularity. The druggist with whom she dealt was the one who used to supply her father with materia medica and to whom she was well known."

"Then, in that case, I suppose she had an account with him?"

"No, she did not. She also paid cash. Her purchases were only occasional and on quite a small scale; too small to justify an account."

"Has she made any statement as to what she wanted the drugs for?"

"She denies that she ever purchased drugs, in the usual sense, that is substances having medicinal properties. Her purchases were, according to her statement, confined to such pharmaceutical and chemical materials as were required for purposes of instruction in her classes. Which is perfectly plausible, for, as you know, academic cookery is a rather different thing from the cookery of the kitchen."

"Yes, I know that she had some materials in her cupboard that I shouldn't have associated with cookery and I should accept her statement without hesitation. In fact, the discovery seems to me to be of no significance at all."

"Probably you are right," said he; "but the point is that, in a legal sense, it confuses the issues hopelessly. In her case, as in Wallingford's, materials have been purchased from a druggist, and, as no record of those purchases has been kept, it is impossible to say what those materials were. Probably they were harmless, but it cannot be proved that they were. The effect is that the evidential value of Wallingford's admission is discounted by the fact that there was another person who is known to have purchased materials some of which may have been poisons."

"Yes," said I, "that is obvious enough. But doesn't it strike you, Thorndyke, that all this is just a lot of futile logic-chopping such as you might hear at a debating club? I can't take it seriously. You don't imagine that either of these two persons murdered Harold Monkhouse, do you? I certainly don't; and I can't believe Miller does."

"It doesn't matter very much what he believes, or, for that matter, what any of us believe. 'He discovers who proves.' Up to the present, none of us has proved anything, and my impression is that Miller is becoming a little discouraged. He is a genius in following up clues. But where there are no clues to follow up, the best of detectives is rather stranded."

"By the way," said I, "did you pick up anything from my diary that threw any light on the mystery?"

"Very little," he replied; "in fact nothing that gets us any farther. I was able to confirm our belief that Monkhouse's attacks of severe illness coincided with his wife's absence from home. But that doesn't help us much. It merely indicates, as we had already observed, that the poisoner was so placed that his or her activities could not be carried on when the wife was at home. But I must compliment you on your diary, Mayfield. It is quite a fascinating work; so much so that I have been tempted to encroach a little on your kindness. The narrative of the last three years was so interesting that it lured me on to the antecedents that led up to them. It reads like a novel."

"How much of it have you read?" I asked, my faint resentment completely extinguished by his appreciation.

"Six volumes," he replied, "including the one that I have just borrowed. I began by reading the last three years for the purposes of our inquiry, and then I ventured to go back another three years for the interest of tracing the more remote causation of recent events. I hope I have not presumed too much on the liberty that you were kind enough to give me."

"Not at all," I replied, heartily. "I am only surprised that a man as much occupied as you are should have been willing to waste your time on the reading of what is, after all, but a trivial and diffuse autobiography."

"I have not wasted my time, Mayfield," said he. "If it is true that 'the proper study of mankind is man,' how much more true is it of that variety of mankind that wears the wig and gown and pleads in Court. It seems to me that to lawyers like ourselves whose professional lives are largely occupied with the study of motives of human actions and with the actions themselves viewed in the light of their antecedents and their consequences, nothing can be more instructive than a full, consecutive diary in which, over a period of years, events may be watched growing out of those that went before and in their turn developing their consequences and elucidating the motives of the actors Such a diary is a synopsis of human life."

I laughed as I rose to depart. "It seems," said I, "that I wrought better than I knew; in fact I am disposed, like Pendennis, to regard myself with respectful astonishment. But perhaps I had better not be too puffed up. It may be that I am, after all, no more than a sort of literary Strasburg goose; an unconscious provider of the food of the gods."

Thorndyke laughed in his turn and escorted me down the stairs to the entry where we stood for a few moments looking out into the fog.

"It seems thicker than ever," said he. "However, you can't miss your way. But keep a look-out as you go, in case our friend is still waiting at the corner. Good night!"

I returned his farewell and plunged into the fog, steering for the corner of the library, and was so fortunate as to strike the wall within a few yards of it. From thence I felt my way without difficulty to the Terrace where I halted for a moment to look about and listen; and as there was no sign, visible or audible of any loiterer at the corner, I groped my way into the passage and so home to my chambers without meeting a single human creature.

CHAPTER ELEVEN

The Rivals

The warmth with which Barbara greeted me when I made my first appearance at her flat struck me as rather pathetic, and for the first time I seemed to understand what it was that had induced her to marry Harold Monkhouse. She was not a solitary woman by nature and she had never been used to a solitary existence. When Stella's death had broken up her home and left her with no intimate friend in the world but me, I had been too much taken up with my own bereavement to give much consideration to her. But now, as she stood before me in her pretty sitting room, holding both my hands and smiling her welcome, it was suddenly borne in on me that her state was rather forlorn in spite of her really comfortable means. Indeed, my heart prompted me to some demonstrations of affection and I was restrained only by the caution of a confirmed bachelor. For Barbara was now a widow; and even while my sympathy with my almost life-long friend tempted me to pet her a little, some faint echoes of Mr Tony Weller's counsels bade me beware.

"You are quite an anchoress here, Barbara," I said, "though you have a mighty comfortable cell. I see you have a new maid, too. I should have thought you would have brought Mabel with you."

"She wouldn't come – naturally. She said she preferred to go and live among strangers and forget what had happened at Hilborough Square. Poor Mabel! She was very brave and good, but it was a terrible experience for her."

"Do you know what has become of her?"

"No. She has disappeared completely. Of course, she has never applied for a reference."

"Why 'of course'?"

"My dear Rupert," she replied a little bitterly, "do you suppose that she would want to advertise her connection with Mrs Harold Monkhouse?"

"No, I suppose she would be likely to exaggerate the publicity of the affair, as I think you do. And how is Madeline? I rather expected that you and she would have shared a flat. Why didn't you?"

Barbara was disposed to be evasive. "I don't know," she replied, "that the plan commended itself to either of us. We have our separate interests, you know. At any rate, she never made any such suggestion and neither did I."

"Do you ever see Wallingford now?" I asked.

"Indeed, I do," she replied; "in fact I have had to hint to him that he mustn't call too frequently. One must consider appearances, and, until I spoke, he was here nearly every day. But I hated doing it."

"Still, Barbara, it was very necessary. It would be so in the case of any young woman, but in your case – er – especially so."

I broke off awkwardly, not liking to say exactly what was in my mind. For, of course, in the atmosphere of suspicion which hung about him, his frequent visits would be a source of real danger. No motive for the murder had yet been suggested. It would be a disaster if his folly were to create the false appearance of one. But, as I have said, I shrank from pointing this out, though I think she understood what was in my mind, for she discreetly ignored the abrupt finish of my sentence and continued: "Poor Tony! He is so very self-centred and he seems so dependent on me. And really, Rupert, I am a good deal concerned about him."

"Why?" I asked, rather unsympathetically.

"He is getting so queer. He was always rather odd, as you know, but this trouble seems to be quite upsetting his balance. I am afraid he is getting delusions – and yet, in a way, I hope that he is."

"What do you mean? What sort of delusions?"

"He imagines that he is being followed and watched. It is a perfect obsession, especially since that superintendent man called on him and cross-questioned him. But I don't think I told you about that."

"No, you did not," said I, quite truthfully, but with an uncomfortable feeling that I was indirectly telling a lie.

"Well, it seems that this man, Miller, called at his rooms – so you see he knew where Tony was living – and, according to Tony's account, extracted by all sorts of dreadful threats, a full confession of the means by which he obtained that cocaine."

"And how did he obtain it?"

"Oh, he just bought it at a wholesale druggist's. Rather casual of the druggist to have supplied him, I think, but still, he needn't have made such a secret of it. However, since then he has been possessed by this obsession. He imagines that he is constantly under observation. He thinks that some man hangs about near his rooms and watches his comings and goings and follows him about whenever he goes abroad. I suppose there can't be anything in it?"

"Of course not. The police have something better to do than spend their time shadowing harmless idiots. Why on earth should they shadow him? If they have any suspicions of him, those suspicions relate to the past, not to the present."

"But I don't think Tony connects these watchers with the police. I fancy he suspects them of being agents of Dr Thorndyke. You remember that he was suspicious and uneasy about Dr Thorndyke from the first; and I know that he suspects him of having set the superintendent on him about the cocaine."

"The deuce he does!" I exclaimed, a little startled. "Have you any idea what makes him suspect Thorndyke of that?"

"He says that the superintendent accepted his statement at the time when the cocaine was found, or at least, did not seem disposed to press him on the question as to where he obtained it, and that this inquisition occurred only after you had put the case in Dr Thorndyke's hands."

I reflected on this statement with some surprise. Of course, Wallingford was quite right, as I knew from first-hand knowledge. But how had he arrived at this belief? Was it a mere guess, based on his evident prejudice against Thorndyke? or had he something to go on? And was it possible that his other suspicions might be correct? Could it be that Thorndyke was really keeping him under observation? I could imagine no object for such a proceeding. But Thorndyke's methods were so unlike those of the police or of anyone else that it was idle to speculate on what he might do; and his emphatic advice to Miller showed that he regarded Wallingford at least with some interest.

"Well, Barbara," I said, mentally postponing the problem for future consideration, "let us forget Wallingford and everybody else. What are we going to do this afternoon? Is there a matinée that we could go to, or shall we go and hear some music?"

"No, Rupert," she replied. "I don't want any theatres or music. I can have those when you are not here. Let us go and walk about Kensington Gardens and gossip as we used to in the old days. But we have a little business to discuss first. Let us get that finished and then we can put it away and be free. You were going to advise me about the house in Hilborough Square. My own feeling is that I should like to sell it and have done with it once for all."

"I shouldn't do that, Barbara," said I. "It is a valuable property, but just at present its value is depreciated. It would be difficult to dispose of at anything like a reasonable price until recent events have been forgotten. The better plan would be to let it at a low rent for a year or two."

"But would anybody take it?"

"Undoubtedly, if the rent were low enough. Leave it to Brodribb and me to manage. You needn't come into the matter at all beyond signing the lease. Is the house in fairly good repair?"

"Most of it is, but there are one or two rooms that will need redecorating, particularly poor Harold's. That had to be left when the other rooms were done because he refused to be disturbed. It is in a very dilapidated state. The paint is dreadfully shabby and the paper is positively dropping off the walls in places. I daresay you remember its condition."

"I do, very well, seeing that I helped Madeline to paste some of the loose pieces back in their places. But we needn't go into details now I will go and look over the house and see what is absolutely necessary to make the place presentable. Who has the keys?"

"I have the latch-keys. The other keys are inside the house."

"And I suppose you don't wish to inspect the place yourself?"

"No. I do not. I wish never to set eyes upon that house again."

She unlocked a little bureau, and taking a bunch of latch-keys from one of the drawers handed it to me. Then she went away to put on her outdoor clothes.

Left alone in the room, I sauntered round and inspected Barbara's new abode, noting how, already, it seemed to reflect in some indefinable way the personality of the tenant. It is this sympathetic quality in human dwelling-places which gives its special charm and interest to a room in which some person of character has lived and worked, and which, conversely, imparts such deadly dullness to the "best room" in which no one is suffered to distribute the friendly, humanizing litter, and which is jealously preserved, with all its lifeless ornamentation – its unenjoyed pictures and its unread books – intact and undefiled by any traces of human occupation. The furniture of this room was mostly familiar to me, for it was that of the old boudoir. There was the little piano, the two cosy armchairs, the open book-shelves with their array of well-used books, the water-colours on the walls, and above the chimney-piece, the little portrait of Stella with the thin plait of golden hair bordering the frame.

I halted before it and gazed at the beloved face which seemed to look out at me with such friendly recognition, and let my thoughts drift back into the pleasant old times and stray into those that might have been if death had mercifully passed by this sweet maid and left me the one companion that my heart yearned for. Now that time had softened my passionate grief into a tender regret, I could think of her with a sort of quiet detachment that was not without its bitter-sweet pleasure. I could let myself speculate on what my life might have been if she had lived, and what part she would have played in it; questions that, strangely enough, had never arisen while she was alive.

I was so immersed in my reverie that I did not hear Barbara come into the room, and the first intimation that I had of her presence was when I felt her hand slip quietly into mine. I turned to look at her and met her eyes, brimming with tears, fixed on me with an expression of such unutterable sadness that, in a moment, my heart leaped out to her, borne on a wave of sympathy and pity which swept away all my caution and reserve. Forgetful of everything but her loneliness and the grief which we shared, I drew her to me and kissed her. It seemed the natural thing to do and I felt that she understood, though she flushed warmly and the tears started from her eyes so that she must needs wipe them away. Then she looked at me with the faintest, most pathetic little smile and without a word, we turned together and walked out of the room.

Barbara was, as I have said, a rather inscrutable and extremely self-contained woman, but she could be, on occasions, a very delightful companion. And so I found her today. At first a little pensive and silent, she presently warmed up into a quite unwonted gaiety and chatted so pleasantly and made so evident her pleasure at having me back that I yearned no more for the Bar Mess but was able to forget the horrors and anxieties of the past and give myself up to the very agreeable present.

I have seldom spent a more enjoyable afternoon. Late autumn as it was, the day was mild and sunny, the sky of that wonderful tender, misty blue that is the peculiar glory of London. And the gardens, too, though they were beginning to take on their winter garb, had not yet quite lost their autumnal charm. Still, on the noble elms, thin as their raiment was growing, the golden and russet foliage lingered, and the leaves that they had already shed remained to clothe the earth with a many-coloured carpet.

We had crossed the gardens by some of the wider paths and had turned into one of the pleasant by-paths when Barbara, spying a seat set back between a couple of elms, suggested that we should rest for a few minutes before recrossing the gardens to go forth in search of tea. Accordingly we sat down, sheltered on either side by the great boles of the elms and warmed by the rays of the late afternoon sun;

but we had been seated hardly a minute when the peace and forgetfulness that had made our ramble so delightful were dissipated in a moment by an apparition on the wide path that we had just left.

I was the first to observe it. Glancing back through the interval between the elm on my left and another at a little distance, I noticed a man coming toward us. My attention was first drawn to him by his rather singular behaviour. He seemed to be dividing his attention between something that was ahead of him and something behind. But I had taken no special note of him until I saw him step, with a rather absurd air of secrecy and caution, behind a tree-trunk and peer round it along the way that he had come. After keeping a look-out in this fashion for nearly a minute, apparently without result, he backed away from the tree and came forward at a quick pace, peering eagerly ahead and on both sides and pausing now and again to cast a quick look back over his shoulder. I drew Barbara's attention to him, remarking: "There is a gentleman who seems to be afflicted with Wallingford's disease. He is trying to look all round the compass at once."

Barbara looked at the man, watching his movements for a time with a faint smile. But suddenly the smile faded and she exclaimed: "Why, I believe it *is* Tony! Yes, I am sure it is."

And Tony it was. I recognized him almost as soon as she spoke. He came on now at a quick pace and seemed in a hurry either to escape from what he supposed to be behind him or to overtake whatever was in front. He had apparently not seen us, for though we must have been visible to him – or we could not have seen him – we were rendered inconspicuous by the two trees between which we sat. Presently he disappeared as the nearer elm-trunk hid him from our view, and I waited with half-amused annoyance for him to reappear.

"What a nuisance he is!" said Barbara. "Disturbing our peaceful tête-à-tête. But he won't freeze on to us. He would rather forego my much desired society than put up with yours." She laughed softly and added in a thoughtful tone: "I wonder what he is doing here."

"I had been wondering that, myself. Kensington Gardens were quite near to Barbara's flat, but they were a long way from Jermyn Street. It was certainly odd that he should be here and on this day of all days. But at this point my reflections were interrupted by the appearance of their subject from behind the big elm-trunk.

He came on us suddenly and was quite close before he saw us. When he did see us, however, he stopped short within a few paces of us, regarding us with a wild stare. It was the first time that I had seen him since the funeral; and certainly his appearance had not improved in the interval. There was something neglected and dishevelled in his aspect that was distinctly suggestive of drink or drugs. But what principally struck me was the expression of furious hate with which he glared at me. There was no mistaking it. Whatever might be the cause, there could be no doubt that he regarded me with almost murderous animosity. He remained in this posture only for a few seconds. Then, as Barbara had begun to utter a few words of greeting, he raised his hat and strode away without a word.

Barbara looked at his retreating figure with a vexed smile.

"Silly fellow!" she exclaimed. "He is angry that I have come out to spend a few hours with my oldest friend, and shows it like a bad-mannered child. I wish he would behave more like an ordinary person."

"You can hardly expect him to behave like what he is not," I said. "Besides, a very ordinary man may feel jealous at seeing another man admitted to terms of intimacy, which are denied to him, with the woman to whom he is specially attached. For I suppose, Barbara, we may take it that that is the position?"

"I suppose so," she admitted. "He is certainly very devoted to me, and I am afraid he is rather jealous of you."

As she spoke, I looked at her and could not but feel a faint sympathy with Wallingford. She was really a very handsome woman; and today she was not only looking her best; she seemed, in some mysterious way to have grown younger, more girlish. The rather sombre gravity of the last few years seemed to be quite dissipated since we had left the flat, and much of the charm of her youth had come back to her.

"He looked more than rather jealous," said I. "Venomous hatred was what I read in his face. Do you think he has anything against me other than my position as his rival in your affections?"

"Yes, I do. He is mortally afraid of you. He believes that you suspect him of having at least had a hand in poor Harold's death and that you have set Dr Thorndyke to track him down and bring the crime home to him. And his terror of Dr Thorndyke is positively an insane obsession."

I was by no means so sure of this, but I said nothing, and she continued: "I suppose you don't know whether Dr Thorndyke does really look on him with. any suspicion? To me the idea is preposterous. Indeed, I find it impossible to believe that there was any crime at all. I am convinced that poor Harold was the victim of some strange accident."

"I quite agree with you, Barbara. That is exactly my own view. But I don't think it is Thorndyke's. As to whom he suspects – if he suspects anybody – I have not the faintest idea. He is a most extraordinarily close and secretive man. No one ever knows what is in his mind until the very moment when he strikes. And he never does strike until he has his case so complete that he can take it into court with the certainty of getting a conviction, or an acquittal, as the case may be."

"But I suppose there are mysteries that elude even his skill?"

"No doubt there are; and I am not sure that our mystery is not one of them. Even Thorndyke can't create evidence, and as he pointed out to me, the evidence in our case lies in the past and is mostly irrecoverable."

"I hope it is not entirely irrecoverable," said she; "for until some reasonable solution of the mystery is reached, an atmosphere of suspicion will continue to hang about all the inmates of that house. So let us wish Dr Thorndyke his usual success; and when he has proved that no one was guilty – which I am convinced is the fact – perhaps poor Tony will forgive him."

With this, we dismissed the subject, and, getting up from the seat, made our way out of the gardens just as the sun was setting behind the trees, and went in search of a suitable tea-shop. And there we lingered gossiping until the evening was well advanced and it was time for me to see Barbara home to her flat and betake myself to Fig Tree Court and make some pretence of doing an evening's work.

CHAPTER TWELVE

Thorndyke Challenges the Evidence

My relations with Thorndyke were rather peculiar and a little inconsistent. I had commissioned him, somewhat against his inclination, to investigate the circumstances connected with the death of Harold Monkhouse. I was, in fact, his employer. And yet, in a certain subtle sense, I was his antagonist. For I held certain beliefs which I, half-unconsciously, looked to him to confirm. But apparently he did not share those beliefs. As his employer, it was clearly my duty to communicate to him any information which he might think helpful or significant, even if I considered it irrelevant. He had, in fact, explicitly pointed this out to me; and he had specially warned me to refrain from sifting or selecting facts which might become known to me according to my view of their possible bearing on the case.

But yet this was precisely what I felt myself constantly tempted to do; and as we sat at lunch in his chambers on the day after my visit to Barbara, I found myself consciously suppressing certain facts which had then come to my knowledge. And it was not that those facts appeared to me insignificant. On the contrary, I found them rather surprising. Only I had the feeling that they would probably convey to Thorndyke a significance that would be erroneous and misleading.

There was, for instance, the appearance of Wallingford in Kensington Gardens. Could it have been sheer chance? If so, it was a most remarkable coincidence; and one naturally tends to look askance at remarkable coincidences. In fact, I did not believe it to be a coincidence at all. I felt little doubt that Wallingford had been lurking about the neighbourhood of Barbara's flat and had followed us, losing sight of us temporarily, when we turned into the by-path. But, knowing Wallingford as I did, I attached no importance to the incident. It was merely a freak of an unstable, emotional man impelled by jealousy to make a fool of himself. Again, there was Wallingford's terror of Thorndyke and his ridiculous delusions on the subject of the "shadowings." How easy it would be for a person unacquainted with Wallingford's personality to read into them a totally misleading significance! Those were the thoughts that drifted half-consciously through my mind as I sat opposite my friend at the table. So, not without some twinges of conscience, I held my peace.

But I had not allowed for Thorndyke's uncanny capacity for inferring what was passing in another person's mind. Very soon it became evident to me that he was fully alive to the possibility of some reservations on my part; and when one or two discreet questions had elicited some fact which I ought to have volunteered, he proceeded to something like definite cross-examination.

"So the household has broken up and the inmates scattered?" he began, when I had told him that I had obtained possession of the keys. "And Mabel Withers seems to have vanished, unless the police have kept her in view. Did you hear anything about Miss Norris?"

"Not very much. Barbara and she have exchanged visits once or twice, but they don't seem to see much of each other."

"And what about Wallingford? Does he seem to have been much disturbed by Miller's descent on him?"

I had to admit that he was in a state bordering on panic.

"And what did Mrs Monkhouse think of the forged orders on Dimsdale's headed paper?"

"He hadn't disclosed that. She thinks that he bought the cocaine at a druggist's in the ordinary way, and I didn't think it necessary to undeceive her."

"No. The least said the soonest mended. Did you gather that she sees much of Wallingford?"

"Yes, rather too much. He was haunting her flat almost daily until she gave him a hint not to make his visits too noticeable."

"Why do you suppose he was haunting her flat? So far as you can judge, Mayfield – that is in the strictest confidence, you understand – does there seem to be anything between them beyond ordinary friendliness?"

"Not on her side, certainly, but on his – yes, undoubtedly. His devotion to her amounts almost to infatuation, and has for a long time past. Of course, she realizes his condition, and though he is rather a nuisance to her, she takes a very kindly and indulgent view of his vagaries."

"Naturally, as any well-disposed woman would. I suppose you didn't see anything of him yesterday?"

Of course I had to relate the meeting in Kensington Gardens, and I could see by the way Thorndyke looked at me that he was wondering why I had not mentioned the matter before.

"It almost looks," said he, "as if he had followed you there. Was there anything in his manner of approach that seemed to support that idea?"

"I think there was, for I saw him at some distance," and here I felt bound to describe Wallingford's peculiar tactics.

"But," said Thorndyke, "why was he looking about behind him? He must have known that you were in front."

"It seems," I explained, feebly, "that he has some ridiculous idea that he is being watched and followed."

"Ha!" said Thorndyke. "Now I wonder who he supposes is watching and following him."

"I fancy he suspects you," I replied. And so the murder was out, with the additional fact that I had not been very ready with my information.

Thorndyke, however, made no comment on my reticence beyond a steady and significant look at me.

"So," said he, "he suspects me of suspecting him. Well, he is giving us every chance. But I think, Mayfield, you would do well to put Mrs Monkhouse on her guard. If Wallingford makes a public parade of his feelings towards her, he may put dangerous ideas into the head of Mr Superintendent Miller. You must realize that Miller is looking for a motive for the assumed murder. And if it comes to his knowledge that Harold Monkhouse's secretary was in love with Harold Monkhouse's wife, he will think that he has found a motive that is good enough."

"Yes, that had occurred to me; and in fact, I did give her a hint to that effect, but it was hardly necessary. She had seen it for herself."

As we now seemed to have exhausted this topic, I ventured to make a few enquiries about the rather farcical infernal machine.

"Did your further examination of it," I asked, "yield any new information?"

"Very little," Thorndyke replied, "but that little was rather curious. There were no finger-prints at all. I examined both the pistol and the jar most thoroughly, but there was not a trace of a finger-mark, to say nothing of a print. It is impossible to avoid the conclusion that the person who sent the machine wore gloves while he was putting it together."

"But isn't that a rather natural precaution in these days?" I asked.

"A perfectly natural precaution, in itself," he replied, "but not quite consistent with some other features. For instance, the wadding with which the pistol-barrel was plugged consisted of a little ball of knitting-wool of a rather characteristic green. I will show it to you, and you will see that it would be quite easy to match and therefore possible to trace. But you see that there are thus shown two contrary states of mind. The gloves suggest that the sender entertained the possibility that the machine might fail to explode, whereas the wool seems to indicate that no such possibility was considered."

He rose from the table – lunch being now finished – and brought from a locked cabinet a little ball of wool of a rather peculiar greenish blue. I took it to the window and examined it carefully, impressed by the curious inconsistency which he had pointed out.

"Yes," I agreed, "there could be no difficulty in matching this. But as to tracing it, that is a different matter. There must have been thousands of skeins of this sold to, at least, hundreds of different persons."

"Very true," said he. "But I was thinking of it rather as a corroborating item in a train of circumstantial evidence."

He put the "corroborating item" back in the cabinet and as, at this moment a taxi was heard to draw up at our entry, he picked up a large attaché case and preceded me down the stairs.

During the comparatively short journey I made a few not very successful efforts to discover what was Thorndyke's real purpose in making this visit of inspection to the dismantled house. But his reticence and mine were not quite similar. He answered all my questions freely. He gave me a wealth of instances illustrating the valuable evidence obtained by the inspection of empty houses. But none of them seemed to throw any light on his present proceedings. And when I pointed this out, he smilingly replied that I was in precisely the same position as himself.

"We are not looking for corroborative evidence," said he. "That belongs to a later stage of the inquiry. We are looking for some suggestive fact which may give us a hint where to begin. Naturally we cannot form any guess as to what kind of fact that might be."

It was not a very illuminating answer, but I had to accept it, although I had a strong suspicion that Thorndyke's purpose was not quite so vague as he represented it to be, and determined unobtrusively to keep an eye on his proceedings.

"Can I give you any assistance?" I enquired, craftily, when I had let him into the hall and shut the outer door.

"Yes," he replied, "there is one thing that you can do for me which will be very helpful. I have brought a packet of cards with me" – here he produced from his pocket a packet of stationer's postcards. "If you will write on each of them the description and particulars of one room with the name of the occupant in the case of bedrooms, and lay the card on the mantelpiece of the room which it describes, I shall be able to reconstitute the house as it was when it was inhabited. Then we can each go about our respective businesses without hindering one another."

"I took the cards – and the fairly broad hint – and together we made a preliminary tour of the house, which, now that the furniture, carpets and pictures were gone, looked very desolate and forlorn; and as it had not been cleaned since the removal, it had a depressingly dirty and squalid appearance. Moreover, in each room, a collection of rubbish and discarded odds and ends had been roughly swept up on the hearth, converting each fireplace into a sort of temporary dustbin.

After a glance around the rooms on the ground floor, I made my way up to the room in which Harold Monkhouse had died, which was my principal concern as well as Thorndyke's.

"Well, Mayfield," the latter remarked, running a disparaging eye round the faded, discoloured walls and the blackened ceiling, "you will have to do something here. It is a shocking spectacle. Would you mind roughly sketching out the position of the furniture? I see that the bedstead stood by this wall with the head, I presume, towards the window, and the bedside table about here, I suppose, at his right hand. By the way, what was there on that table? Did he keep a supply of food of any kind for use at night?"

"I think they usually put a little tin of sandwiches on the table when the night preparations were made."

"You say 'they.' Who put the box there?"

"I can't say whose duty it was in particular. I imagine Barbara would see to it when she was at home. In her absence it would be done by Madeline or Mabel."

"Not Wallingford?"

"No. I don't think Wallingford ever troubled himself about any of the domestic arrangements excepting those that concerned Barbara."

"Do you know who made the sandwiches?"

"I think Madeline did, as a rule. I know she did sometimes."

"And as to drink? I suppose he had a water-bottle, at any rate"

"Yes, that was always there, and a little decanter of whiskey. But he hardly ever touched that. Very often a small flagon of lemonade was put on the table with the sandwiches."

"And who made the lemonade?"

"Madeline. I know that, because it was a very special brand which no one else could make."

"And supposing the sandwiches and the lemonade were not consumed, do you happen to know what became of the remainder?"

"I have no idea. Possibly the servants consumed them, but more probably they were thrown away. Well-fed servants are not partial to remainders from a sick-room."

"You never heard of any attacks of illness among any of the servants?"

"Not to my knowledge. But I shouldn't be very likely to, you know."

"No. You notice, Mayfield, that you have mentioned one or two rather material facts that were not disclosed at the inquest?"

"Yes. I was observing that. And it is just as well that they were not disclosed. There were enough misleading facts without them."

Thorndyke smiled indulgently. "You seem to have made up your mind pretty definitely, on the negative side, at least," he remarked; and then, looking round once more at the walls with their faded, loosened paper, he continued: "I take it that Mr Monkhouse was not a fresh-air enthusiast."

"He was not," I replied. "He didn't much care for open windows, especially at night. But how did you arrive at that fact?"

"I was looking at the wallpaper. This is not a damp house, but yet the paper on the walls of this room is loosening and peeling off in all directions. And if you notice the distribution of this tendency you get the impression that the moisture which loosened the paper proceeded from the neighbourhood of the bed. The wall which is most affected is the one against which the bed stood; and the part of that wall that has suffered most is that which was nearest to the occupant of the bed, and especially to his head. That large piece, hanging down, is just where the main stream of his breath would have impinged."

"Yes, I see the connection now you mention it; and yet I am surprised that his breath alone should have made the air of the room so damp. All through the winter season, when the window would be shut most closely, the gas was burning; and at night, when the gas was out, he commonly had his candle-lamp alight. I should have thought that the gas and the candle together would have kept the air fairly dry."

"That," said Thorndyke, "is a common delusion. As a matter of fact they would have quite the opposite effect. You have only to hold an inverted tumbler over a burning candle to realize, from the moisture which immediately condenses on the inside of the tumbler, that the candle, as it burns, gives off quite a considerable volume of steam. But of course, the bulk of the moisture which has caused the paper to peel in this room came from the man's own breath. However, we didn't come here for debating purposes. Let us complete our preliminary tour, and when we have seen the whole house we can each make such more detailed inspection as seems necessary for our particular purposes."

We accordingly resumed our perambulation (but I noticed that Thorndyke deposited his attaché case in Monkhouse's room with the evident intention of returning thither), both of us looking about narrowly: Thorndyke, no doubt, in search of the mysterious "traces" of which he had spoken, and I with an inquisitive endeavour to ascertain what kind of objects or appearances he regarded as "traces."

We had not gone very far before we encountered an object that even I was able to recognize as significant. It was in a corner of the long corridor that we came upon a little heap of rubbish that had been swept up out of the way; and at the very moment when Thorndyke stopped short with his eyes fixed on it, I saw the object – a little wisp of knitting-wool of the well-remembered green colour. Thorndyke picked it up, and, having exhibited it to me, produced from his letter-case a little envelope such as seedsmen use, in which he put the treasure trove, and as he uncapped his fountain pen, he looked up and down the corridor.

"Which is the nearest room to this spot?" he asked.

"Madeline's," I replied. "That is the door of her bedroom, on the right. But all the principal bedrooms are on this floor and Barbara's boudoir as well. This heap of rubbish is probably the sweepings from all the rooms."

"That is what it looks like," he agreed as he wrote the particulars on the envelope and slipped the latter in his letter-case. "You notice that there are some other trifles in this heap – some broken glass, for instance. But I will go through it when we have finished our tour, though I may as well take this now."

As he spoke, he stooped and picked up a short piece of rather irregularly shaped glass rod with a swollen, rounded end.

"What is it?" I asked.

"It is a portion of a small glass pestle and it belongs to one of those little glass mortars such as chemists use in rubbing up powders into solutions or suspensions. You had better not touch it, though it has probably been handled pretty freely. But I shall test it on the chance of discovering what it was last used for."

He put it away carefully in another seed-envelope and then looked down thoughtfully at the miniature dust-heap; but he made no further investigations at the moment and we resumed the perambulation, I placing the identification card on the mantelpiece of each room while he looked sharply about him, opening all cupboards and receptacles and peering into their, usually empty, interiors.

When we had inspected the servants' bedrooms and the attics – leaving the indispensable cards – we went down to the basement and visited the kitchen, the scullery, the servants' parlour and the cellars; and this brought our tour to an end.

"Now," said Thorndyke, "we proceed from the general to the particular. While you are drawing up your schedule of dilapidations I will just browse about and see if I can pick up any stray crumbs in which inference can find nourishment. It isn't a very hopeful quest, but you observe that we have already lighted on two objects which may have a meaning for us."

"Yes, we have ascertained that someone in this house used a particular kind of wool and that someone possessed a glass mortar. Those do not seem to me very weighty facts."

"They are not," he agreed; "indeed, they are hardly facts at all. The actual fact is that we have found the things here. But trifles light as air sometimes serve to fill up the spaces in a train of circumstantial evidence. I think I will go and have another look at that rubbish-heap."

I was strongly tempted to follow him, but could hardly do so in face of his plainly expressed wish to make his inspection alone. Moreover, I had already seen that there was more to be done than I had supposed. The house was certainly not in bad repair, but neither did. it look very fresh nor attractive. Furniture and especially pictures have a way of marking indelibly the walls of a room, and the paintwork in several places showed disfiguring traces of wear. But I was anxious to let this house, even at a nominal rent, so that, by a few years' normal occupation its sinister reputation might be forgotten and its value restored.

As a result, I was committed to a detailed inspection of the whole house and the making of voluminous notes on the repairs and re-decorations which would be necessary to tempt even an impecunious tenant to forget that this was a house in which a murder had been committed. For that was the current view, erroneous as I believed it to be. Note-book in hand, I proceeded systematically from room to room and from floor to floor, and became so engrossed with my own business that I almost forgot Thorndyke; though I could hear him moving about the house, and once I met him – on the first floor, with a couple of empty medicine bottles and a small glass jar in his hands, apparently making his way to Harold's room, where, as I have said, he had left his attaché case.

That room I left to the last, as it was already entered in my list and I did not wish to appear to spy upon Thorndyke's proceedings. When, at length, I entered the room I found that he, like myself, had come to the end of his task. On the floor his attaché case lay open, crammed with various objects, several of which appeared to be bottles, wrapped in oddments of waste paper (including some pieces of wallpaper which he had apparently stripped off *ad hoc* when the other supplies failed) and among which I observed a crumpled fly-paper. Respecting this I remarked:"I don't see why you are burdening yourself with this. A fly-paper is in no sense an incriminating object, even though such things have, at times, been put to unlawful use."

"Very true," he replied as he peeled off the rubber gloves which he had been wearing during the search. "A fly-paper is a perfectly normal domestic object. But, as you say, it can on occasion be used as a source of arsenic for criminal purposes; and a paper that has been so used will be found to have had practically the whole of the arsenic soaked out of it. As I happened to find this in the servants' parlour, it seemed worth while to take it to see whether its charge of arsenic had or had not been extracted."

"But," I objected, "why on earth should the poisoner – if there really is such a person – have been at the trouble of soaking out fly-papers when, apparently he was able to command an unlimited supply of Fowler's Solution?"

"Quite a pertinent question, Mayfield," he rejoined. "But may I ask my learned friend whether he found the evidence relating to the Fowler's Solution perfectly satisfactory?"

"But surely!" I exclaimed. "You had the evidence of two expert witnesses on the point. What more would you require? What is the difficulty?"

"The difficulty is this. There were several witnesses who testified that when they saw the bottle of medicine, the Fowler's Solution had not yet been added; but there was none who saw the bottle after the addition had been made."

"But it must have been added before Mabel gave the patient the last dose."

"That is the inference. But Mabel said nothing to that effect. She was not asked what colour the medicine was when she gave the patient that dose."

"But what of the analysts and the post mortem?"

"As to the post mortem, the arsenic which was found in the stomach was not recognized as being in the form of Fowler's Solution; and as to the analysts, they made their examination three days after the man died."

"Still, the medicine that they analysed was the medicine that deceased had taken. You don't deny that, do you?"

"I neither deny it nor affirm it. I merely say that no evidence was given that proved the presence of Fowler's Solution in that bottle before the man died; and that the bottle which was handed to the analysts was one that had been exposed for three days in a room which had been visited by a number of persons, including Mrs Monkhouse, Wallingford, Miss Norris, Mabel Withers, Amos Monkhouse, Dr Dimsdale and yourself."

"You mean to suggest that the bottle might have been tampered with or changed for another? But, my dear Thorndyke, why in the name of God should anyone want to change the bottle?"

"I am not suggesting that the bottle actually was changed. I am merely pointing out that the evidence of the analysts is material only subject to the conditions that the bottle which they examined was the bottle from which the last dose of medicine was given and that its contents were the same as on that occasion; and that no conclusive proof exists that it was the same bottle or that the contents were unchanged."

"But what reason could there be for supposing that it might have been changed?"

"There is no need to advance any reason. The burden of proof lies on those who affirm that it was the same bottle with the same contents. It is for them to prove that no change was possible. But obviously a change was possible."

"But still," I persisted, "there seems to be no point in this suggestion. Who could have had any motive for making a change? And what could the motive have been? It looks to me like mere logic-chopping and hair-splitting."

"You wouldn't say that if you were for the defence," chuckled Thorndyke. "You would not let a point of first-rate importance pass on a mere assumption, no matter how probable. And as to a possible motive, surely a most obvious one is staring us in the face. Supposing some person in this household had been administering arsenic in the food. If it could be arranged that a poisonous dose could be discovered in the medicine, you must see that the issue would be at once transferred from the food to the medicine, and from those who controlled the food to those who controlled the medicine. Which is, in fact, what happened. As soon as the jury heard about the medicine, their interest in the food became extinct."

I listened to this exposition with a slightly sceptical smile. It was all very ingenious but I found it utterly unconvincing.

"You ought to be pleading in court, Thorndyke," I said, "instead of grubbing about in empty houses and raking over rubbish-heaps. By the way, have you found anything that seems likely to yield any suggestions?"

"It is a little difficult to say," he replied. "I have taken possession of a number of bottles and small jars for examination as to their contents, but I have no great expectation in respect of them. I also found some fragments of the glass mortar – an eight-ounce mortar it appears to have been."

"Where did you find those?" I asked.

"In Miss Norris' bedroom, in a little pile of rubbish under the grate. They are only tiny fragments, but the curvature enables one to reconstruct the vessel pretty accurately."

It seemed to me a rather futile proceeding, but I made no comment. Nor did I give utterance to a suspicion which had just flashed into my mind, that it was the discovery of these ridiculous fragments of glass that had set my learned friend splitting straws on the subject of the medicine bottle. I had not much liked his suggestion as to the possible motive of that hypothetical substitution, and I liked it less now that he had discovered the remains of the mortar in Madeline's room. There was no doubt that Thorndyke had a remarkable constructive imagination; and, as I followed him down the stairs and out into the square, I found myself faintly uneasy lest that lively imagination should carry him into deeper waters than I was prepared to navigate in his company.

CHAPTER THIRTEEN

Rupert Makes Some Discoveries

By a sort of tacit understanding Thorndyke and I parted in the vicinity of South Kensington Station, to which he had made a bee line on leaving the square. As he had made no suggestion that I should go back with him, I inferred that he had planned a busy evening examining and testing the odds and ends that he had picked up in the empty house; while I had suddenly conceived the idea that I might as well take the opportunity of calling on Madeline, who might feel neglected if I failed to put in an appearance within a reasonable time after my return to town. Our researches had taken up most of the afternoon and it was getting on for the hour at which Madeline usually left the school; and as the latter was less than half-an-hour's walk from the station, I could reach it in good time without hurrying.

As I walked at an easy pace through the busily populated streets, I turned over the events of the afternoon with rather mixed feelings. In spite of my great confidence in Thorndyke, I was sensible of a chill of disappointment in respect alike of his words and his deeds. In this rather farcical grubbing about in the dismantled house there was a faint suggestion of charlatanism; of the vulgar, melodramatic sleuth, nosing out a trail; while, as to his hair-splitting objections to a piece of straightforward evidence, they seemed to me to be of the kind at which the usual hard-headed judge would shake his hard head while grudgingly allowing them as technically admissible.

But whither was Thorndyke drifting? Evidently he had turned a dubious eye on Wallingford; and that egregious ass seemed to be doing all that he could to attract further notice. But today I had seemed to detect a note of suspicion in regard to Madeline; and even making allowance for the fact that he had not my knowledge of her gentle, gracious personality, I could not but feel a little resentful. Once more, Wallingford's remarks concerning a possible mare's nest and a public scandal recurred to me, and, not for the first time, I was aware of faint misgivings as to my wisdom in having set Thorndyke to stir up these troubled waters. He had, indeed, given me fair warning, and I was half-inclined to regret that I had not allowed myself to be warned off. Of course, Thorndyke was much too old a hand to launch a half-prepared prosecution into the air. But still, I could not but ask myself uneasily whither his overacute inferences were leading him.

These reflections brought me to the gate of the school, where I learned from the porter that Madeline had not yet left and accordingly sent up my card. In less than a minute she appeared, dressed in her out-of-door clothes and wreathed in smiles, looking, I thought, very charming.

"How nice of you, Rupert!" she exclaimed, "to come and take me home. I was wondering how soon you would come to see my little spinster lair. It is only a few minutes' walk from here. But I am sorry I didn't know you were coming, for I have arranged to make a call – a business call – and I am due in about ten minutes. Isn't it a nuisance?"

"How long will you have to stay?"

"Oh, a quarter of an hour, at least. Perhaps a little more."

"Very well. I will wait outside for you and do sentry-go."

"No, you won't. I shall let you into my flat – I should have to pass it – and you can have a wash and brush-up, and then you can prowl about and see how you like my little mansion – I haven't quite settled down in it yet, but you must overlook that. By the time you have inspected everything, I shall be back and then we can consider whether we will have a late tea or an early supper. This is the way."

She led me into a quiet by-street, one side of which was occupied by a range of tall, rather forbidding buildings whose barrack-like aspect was to some extent mitigated by signs of civilized humanity in the tastefully curtained windows. Madeline's residence was on the second floor, and when she had let me in by the diminutive outer door and switched on the light, she turned back to the staircase with a wave of her hand.

"I will be back as soon as I can," she said. "Meanwhile go in and make yourself at home."

I stood at the door and watched her trip lightly down the stairs until she disappeared round the angle, when I shut the door and proceeded to follow her injunctions to the letter by taking possession of the bathroom, in which I was gratified to find a constant supply of hot water. When I had refreshed myself by a wash, I went forth and made a leisurely survey of the little flat. It was all very characteristic of Madeline, the professional exponent of Domestic Economy, in its orderly arrangement and its evidences of considered convenience. The tiny kitchen reminded one of a chemical laboratory or a doctor's dispensary with its labelled jars of the cook's materials set out in ordered rows on their shelves, and the two little mortars, one of Wedgewood ware and the other of glass. I grinned as my eye lighted on this latter and I thought of the fragments carefully collected by Thorndyke and solemnly transported to the Temple for examination. Here, if he could have seen it, was evidence that proved the ownership of that other mortar and at the same time demolished the significance of that discovery.

I ventured to inspect the bedroom, and a very trim, pleasant little room it was; but the feature which principally attracted my attention was an arrangement for switching the electric light off and on from the bed — an arrangement suspiciously correlated to a small set of bookshelves also within easy reach of the bed. What interested me in it was what Thorndyke would have called its "unmechanical ingenuity"; for it consisted of no more than a couple of lengths of stout string, of each of which one end was tied to the light-switch and the other end led by a pair of screw-eyes to the head of the bed. No doubt the simple device worked well enough in spite of the friction at each screw-eye, but a man of less intelligence than Madeline would probably have used levers or bell-cranks, or at least pulleys to diminish the friction in changing the direction of the pull.

There was a second bedroom, at present unoccupied and only partially furnished and serving, apparently, as a receptacle for such of Madeline's possessions as had not yet had a permanent place assigned to them. Here were one or two chairs, some piles of books, a number of pictures and several polished wood boxes and cases of various sizes; evidently the residue of the goods and chattels that Madeline had brought from her home and stored somewhere while she was living at Hilborough Square. I ran my eye along the range of boxes, which were set out on the top of a chest of drawers. One was an old-fashioned tea-caddy, another an obvious folding desk of the same period, while a third, which I opened, turned out to be a work-box of mid-Victorian age. Beside it was a little flat rosewood case which looked like a small case of mathematical instruments. Observing that the key was in the lock, I turned it and lifted the lid, not with any conscious curiosity as to what was inside it, but in the mere idleness of a man who has nothing in particular to do. But the instant that the lid was up my attention awoke with a bound and I stood with dropped jaw staring at the interior in utter consternation.

There could be not an instant's doubt as to what this case was, for its green-baize-lined interior showed a shaped recess of the exact form of a pocket pistol; and, if that were not enough, there, in its own compartment was a little copper powder-flask, and in another compartment about a dozen globular bullets.

I snapped down the lid and turned the key and walked guiltily out of the room. My interest in Madeline's flat was dead. I could think of nothing but this amazing discovery And the more I thought, the more overpowering did it become. The pistol that fitted that case was the exact counterpart of the pistol that I had seen in Thorndyke's laboratory; and the case, itself, corresponded, exactly to his description of the case from which that pistol had probably been taken. It was astounding; and it was profoundly disturbing. For it admitted of no explanation that I could bring myself to accept other than that of a coincidence. And coincidences are unsatisfactory things; and you can't do with too many of them at once.

Yet, on reflection, this was the view that I adopted. Indeed, there was no thinkable alternative. And really, when I came to turn the matter over, it was not quite so extraordinary as it had seemed at the first glance. For what, after all, was this pistol with its case? It was not a unique thing. It was not even a rare thing. Thorndyke had spoken of these pistols and cases as comparatively common things with which he expected me to be familiar. Thousands of them must have been made in their time, and since they were far from perishable, thousands of them must still exist. The singularity of the coincidence was not in the facts; it was the product of my own state of mind.

Thus I sought – none too successfully – to rid myself of the effects of the shock that I had received on raising the lid of the case; and I was still moodily gazing out of the sitting room window and arguing away my perturbation when I heard the outer door shut and a moment later Madeline looked into the room.

"I haven't been so very long, have I?" she said, cheerily. "Now I will slip off my cloak and hat and we will consider what sort of meal we will have; or perhaps you will consider the question while I am gone."

With this she flitted away; and my thoughts, passing by the problem submitted, involuntarily reverted to the little rosewood case in the spare room. But her absence was of a brevity suggesting the performance of the professional quick-change artist. In a minute or two I heard her approach and open the door; and I turned – to receive a real knock-out blow.

I was so astonished and dismayed that I suppose I must have stood staring like a fool, for she asked in a rather disconcerted tone: "What is the matter, Rupert? Why are you looking at my jumper like that? Don't you like it?"

"Yes," I stammered, "of course I do. Most certainly. Very charming. Very – er – becoming. I like it – er – exceedingly."

"I don't believe you do," she said, doubtfully, "you looked so surprised when I first came in. You don't think the colour too startling, do you? Women wear brighter colours than they used to, you know, and I do think this particular shade of green is rather nice. And it is rather unusual, too."

"It is," I agreed, recovering myself by an effort. "Quite distinctive." And then, noting that I had unconsciously adopted Thorndyke's own expression, I added, hastily, "And I shouldn't describe it as startling, at all. It is in perfectly good taste."

"I am glad you think that," she said, "for you certainly did look rather startled at first, and I had some slight misgivings about it myself when I had finished it. It looked more brilliant in colour as a garment than it did in the form of mere skeins."

"You made it yourself, then?"

"Yes. But I don't think I would ever knit another. It took me months to do, and I could have bought one for very little more than the cost of the wool, though, of course, I shouldn't have been able to select the exact tint that I wanted. But what about our meal? Shall we call it tea or supper?"

She could have called it breakfast for all I cared, so completely had this final shock extinguished my interest in food. But I had to make some response to her eager hospitality.

"Let us split the difference or strike an average," I replied. "We will call it a 'swarry' – tea and unusual trimmings."

"Very well," said she, "then you shall come to the kitchen and help. I will show you the raw material of the feast and you shall dictate the bill of fare."

We accordingly adjourned to the kitchen where she fell to work on the preparations with the unhurried quickness that is characteristic of genuine efficiency, babbling pleasantly and pausing now and then to ask my advice (which was usually foolish and had to be blandly rejected) and treating the whole business with a sort of playful seriousness that was very delightful. And all the time I looked on in a state of mental chaos and bewilderment for which I can find no words. There she was, my friend, Madeline, sweet, gentle, feminine – the very type of gracious womanhood, and the more sweet and gracious by reason of these homely surroundings. For it is an appalling reflection, in these days of lady professors and women legislators, that to masculine eyes a woman never looks so dignified, so worshipful, so entirely desirable, as when she is occupied in the traditional activities that millenniums of human experience have associated with her sex. To me, Madeline, flitting about the immaculate little kitchen, neat-handed, perfect in the knowledge of her homely craft; smiling, dainty, fragile, with her gracefully flowing hair and the little apron that she had slipped on as a sort of ceremonial garment, was a veritable epitome of feminine charm. And yet, but a few feet away was a rosewood case that had once held a pistol; and even now, in Thorndyke's locked cabinet – but my mind staggered under the effort of thought and refused the attempt to combine and collate a set of images so discordant.

"You are very quiet, Rupert," she said, presently, pausing to look at me. "What is it? I hope you haven't any special worries."

"We all have our little worries, Madeline," I replied, vaguely.

"Yes, indeed," said she, still regarding me thoughtfully; and for the first time I noticed that she seemed to have aged a little since I had last seen her and that her face, in repose, showed traces of strain and anxiety. "We all have our troubles and we all try to put them on you. How did you think Barbara was looking?"

"Extraordinarily well. I was agreeably surprised."

"Yes. She is wonderful. I am full of admiration of the way she has put away everything connected with – with that dreadful affair. I couldn't have done it if I had been in her place. I couldn't have let things rest. I should have wanted to know."

"I have no doubt that she does. We all want to know. But she can do no more than the rest of us. Do you ever see Wallingford now?"

"Oh, dear, yes. He was inclined to be rather too attentive at first, but Barbara gave him a hint that spinsters who live alone don't want too many visits from their male friends, so now he usually comes with her."

"I must bear Barbara's words of wisdom in mind," said I.

"Indeed you won't!" she exclaimed. "Don't be ridiculous, Rupert. You know her hint doesn't apply to you. And I shouldn't have troubled about the proprieties in Tony's case if I had really wanted him. But I didn't, though I am awfully sorry for him."

"Yes, he seems to be in a bad way mentally, poor devil. Of course you have heard about his delusions?"

"If they really are delusions, but I am not at all sure that they are. Now help me to carry these things into the sitting room and then I will do the omelette and bring it in."

I obediently took up the tray and followed her into the sitting room, where I completed the arrangement of the table while she returned to the kitchen to perform the crowning culinary feat. In a minute or two she came in with the product under a heated cover and we took our seats at the table.

"You were speaking of Wallingford," said I. "Apparently you know more about him than I do. It seemed to me that he was stark mad."

"He is queer enough, I must admit – don't let your omelette get cold – but I think you and Barbara are mistaken about his delusions. I suspect that somebody is really keeping him under observation; and if that is so, one can easily understand why his nerves are so upset."

"Yes, indeed. But when you say you suspect that we are mistaken, what does that mean? Is it just a pious opinion or have you something to go upon?"

"Oh, I shouldn't offer a mere pious opinion to a learned counsel," she replied, with a smile. "I have something to go upon, and I will tell you about it, though I expect you will think I am stark mad, too. The fact is that I have been under observation, too."

"Nonsense, Madeline," I exclaimed. "The thing is absurd. You have let Wallingford infect you."

"There!" she retorted. "What did I say? You think I am qualifying for an asylum now. But I am not. Absurd as the thing seems – and I quite agree with you on that point – it is an actual fact. I haven't the slightest doubt about it."

"Well," I said, "I am open to conviction. But let us have your actual facts. How long do you think it has been going on?"

"That I can't say; and I don't think it is going on now at all. At any rate, I have seen no signs of any watcher for more than a week, and I keep a pretty sharp lookout. The way I first became aware of it was this: I happened one day at lunch time to be looking out of this window through the chink in the curtains when I saw a man pass along slowly on the other side of the street and glance up, as it seemed, at this window. I didn't notice him particularly, but still I did look at him when he glanced up, and of course, his face was then directly towards me. Now it happened that, a few minutes afterwards, I looked out again; and then I saw what looked like the same man pass along again, at the same slow pace and in the same direction. And again he looked up at the window, though he couldn't have seen me because I was hidden by the curtain. But this time I looked at him very closely and made careful mental notes of his clothing, his hat and his features, because, you see, I remembered what Tony had said and I hadn't forgotten the way I was treated at the inquest or the way in which that detective man had turned out my cupboard when he came to search the house. So I looked this man over very carefully indeed so that I should recognize him without any doubt if I should see him again.

"Well, before I went out after lunch I had a good look out of the window, but I couldn't see anything of him; nor did I see him on my way to the school, though I stopped once or twice and looked back. When I got to the school I stopped at the gate and looked along the street both ways, but still there was no sign of him. Then I ran up to a class-room window from which I could see up and down the street; and presently I saw him coming along slowly on the school side and I was able to check him off point by point, and though he didn't look up this time, I could see his face and check that off, too. There was no doubt whatever that it was the same man.

"When I came out of school that afternoon I looked round but could not see him, so I walked away quickly in the direction that I usually take when going home, but suddenly turned a corner and slipped into a shop. I stayed there a few minutes buying some things, then I came out, and, seeing no one, slipped round the corner and took my usual way home but kept carefully behind a man and a woman who were going the same way. I hadn't gone very far before I saw my man standing before a shop window but evidently looking up and down the street. I was quite close to him before he saw me and of course I did not appear to notice him; but I hurried home without looking round and ran straight up to this window to watch for him. And sure enough, in about a couple of minutes I saw him come down the street and walk slowly past."

"And did you see him again after that?"

"Yes, I saw him twice more that same day. I went out for a walk in the evening on purpose to give him a lead. And I saw him from time to time every day for about ten days. Then I missed him, and I haven't seen a sign of him for more than a week. I suppose he found me too monotonous and gave me up."

"It is very extraordinary," I said, convinced against my will by her very circumstantial description. "What possible object could anyone have in keeping a watch on you?"

"That is what I have wondered," said she. "But I suppose the police have to do something for their pay."

"But this doesn't quite look like a police proceeding. There is something rather feeble and amateurish about the affair. With all due respect to your powers of observation, Madeline, I don't think a Scotland Yard man would have let himself be spotted quite so easily."

"But who else could it be?" she objected; and then, after a pause, she added with a mischievous smile, "unless it should be your friend, Dr Thorndyke. That would really be a quaint situation – if I should, after all, be indebted to you, Rupert, for these polite attentions."

I brushed the suggestion aside hastily but with no conviction. And once more I recalled Wallingford's observations on mare's nests. Obviously this clumsy booby was not a professional detective. And if not, what could he be but some hired agent of Thorndyke's. It was one more perplexity, and added to those with which my mind was already charged, it reduced me to moody silence which must have made me the very reverse of an exhilarating companion. Indeed, when Madeline had rallied me once or twice on my gloomy preoccupation, I felt that the position was becoming untenable. I wanted to be alone and think things out; but as it would have been hardly decent to break up our little party and take my departure, I determined, if possible, to escape from this oppressive tête-à-tête. Fortunately, I remembered that a famous pianist was giving a course of recitals at a hall within easy walking distance and ventured to suggest that we might go and hear him.

"I would rather stay here and gossip with you," she replied, "but as you don't seem to be in a gossiping humour, perhaps the music might be rather nice. Yes, let us go. I don't often hear any good music nowadays."

Accordingly we went, and on the way to the hall Madeline gave me a few further details of her experiences with her follower; and I was not a little impressed by her wariness and the ingenuity with which she had lured that guileless sleuth into exposed and well-lighted situations.

"By the way," said I, "what was the fellow like? Give me a few particulars of his appearance in case I should happen to run across him."

"Good Heavens, Rupert!" she exclaimed, laughing mischievously, "you don't suppose he will take to haunting you, do you? That would really be the last straw, especially if he should happen to be employed by Dr Thorndyke."

"It would," I admitted with a faint grin, "though Thorndyke is extremely thorough and he plumes himself on keeping an open mind. At any rate, let us have a few details."

"There was nothing particularly startling about him. He was a medium-sized man, rather fair, with a longish, sharp, turned-up nose and a sandy moustache, rather bigger than men usually have nowadays. He was dressed in a blue serge suit, without an overcoat and he wore a brown soft felt hat, a turn-down collar and a dark green necktie with white spots. He had no gloves but he carried a walking-stick – a thickish yellow cane with a crooked handle."

"Not very distinctive," I remarked, disparagingly.

"Don't you think so?" said she. "I thought he was rather easy to recognize with that brown hat and the blue suit and the big moustache and pointed nose. Of course, if he had worn a scarlet hat and emerald-green trousers and carried a brass fire-shovel instead of a walking-stick he would have been still easier to recognize; but you mustn't expect too much, even from a detective."

I looked with dim surprise into her smiling face and was more bewildered than ever. If she were haunted by any gnawing anxieties, she had a wonderful way of throwing them off. Nothing could be less suggestive of a guilty conscience than this quiet gaiety and placid humour. However, there was no opportunity for moralizing, for her little retort had brought us to the door of the hall; and we had barely time to find desirable seats before the principal musician took his place at the instrument.

It was a delightful entertainment; and if the music did not "soothe my savage breast" into complete forgetfulness, it occupied my attention sufficiently to hinder consecutive thought on any other subject. Indeed, it was not until I had said "good night" to Madeline outside her flat and turned my face towards the neighbouring station that I was able to attempt a connected review of the recent startling discoveries.

What could they possibly mean? The pistol alone could have been argued away as a curious coincidence, and the same might have been possible even in the case of the wool. But the two together! The long arm of coincidence was not long enough for that. The wisp of wool that we had found in the empty house was certainly – admittedly – Madeline's. But that wisp matched identically the ball of wool from the pistol; and here was a missing pistol which was certainly the exact counterpart of that which had contained the wool plug. The facts could not be disputed. Was it possible to escape from the inferences which they yielded?

The infernal machine, feeble as it was, gave evidence of a diabolical intention – an intention that my mind utterly refused to associate with Madeline. And yet, even in the moment of rejection, my memory suddenly recalled the arrangement connected with the electric light switch in Madeline's bedroom. Its mechanism was practically identical with that of the infernal machine, and the materials used – string and screw-eyes – were actually the same. It seemed impossible to escape from this proof piled on proof.

But if the machine itself declared an abominable intention, what of that which lay behind the machine? The sending of that abomination was not an isolated or independent act. It was related to some antecedent act, as Thorndyke had implied. Whoever sent it, had a guilty conscience.

But guilty of what?

As I asked myself this question, and the horrid, inevitable answer framed itself in my mind, I turned automatically from Middle Temple Lane and passed into the deep shadow of the arch that gives entrance to Elm Court.

CHAPTER FOURTEEN

Rupert Confides in Thorndyke

Although few of its buildings (excepting the Halls) are of really great antiquity, the precinct of the Temples shares with the older parts of London at least one medieval characteristic: it abounds in those queer little passages and alleys which, burrowing in all directions under the dwelling-houses, are a source of endless confusion and bewilderment to the stranger, though to the accustomed denizen they offer an equally great convenience. For by their use the seasoned Templar makes his way from any one part of the precinct to any other, if not in an actual bee-line, at least in an abbreviated zig-zag that cuts across the regular thoroughfares as though they were mere paths traversing an open meadow. Some of these alleys do, indeed, announce themselves even to unaccustomed eyes, as public passage-ways, by recognizable entrance arches; but many of them scorn even this degree of publicity, artfully concealing their existence from the uninitiated by an ordinary doorway, which they share with a pair of houses. Whereby the unsuspecting stranger, entering what, in his innocence, he supposes to be the front doorway of a house, walks along the hall and is presently astonished to find himself walking out of another front door into another thoroughfare.

The neighbourhood of Fig Tree Court is peculiarly rich in these deceptive burrows, indeed, excepting from the Terrace, it has no other avenue of approach. On the present occasion I had the choice of two, and was proceeding along the narrow lane of Elm Court to take the farther one, which led to the entry of my chambers, when I caught sight of a man approaching hurriedly from the direction of the Cloisters. At the first glance, I thought I recognized him – though he was a mere silhouette in the dim light – as the loiterer whom I had seen on the night of my return. And his behaviour confirmed my suspicion; for as he came in sight of me, he hesitated for a moment and then, quickening his pace forward, disappeared suddenly through what appeared to be a hole in the wall but was, in fact, the passage for which I was making.

Instantly, I turned back and swiftly crossing the square of Elm Court, dived into the burrow at its farther corner and came out into the little square of Fig Tree Court at the very moment when the mysterious stranger emerged from the burrow at the other side, so that we met face to face in the full light of the central lamp.

Naturally, I was the better prepared for the encounter and I pursued my leisurely way towards my chambers with the air of not having observed him; while he, stopping short for a moment with a wild stare at me, dashed across the square and plunged into the passage from which I had just emerged.

I did not follow him. I had seen him and had thereby confirmed a suspicion that had been growing upon me, and that was enough. For I need hardly say that the man was Anthony Wallingford. But though I was prepared for the identification, I was none the less puzzled and worried by it. Here was yet another perplexity; and I was just stepping into my entry to reflect upon it at my leisure when I became aware of hurrying footsteps in the passage through which Wallingford had come. Quickly drawing back into the deep shadow of the vestibule, I waited to see who this new-comer might be. In a few seconds he rushed out of the passage and came to a halt in the middle of the square, nearly under the lamp, where he stood for a few moments, looking to right and left and listening intently. And now I realized the justice of what Madeline had said; for, commonplace as the man was, I recognized him in an instant. Brown hat, blue serge suit, big, sandy moustache and concave, pointed nose; they were not sensational characteristics, but they identified him beyond a moment's doubt.

Apparently, his ear must have caught the echoes of Wallingford's footsteps, for, after a very brief pause, he started off at something approaching a trot and disappeared into the passage by which I had come and Wallingford had gone. A sudden, foolish curiosity impelled me to follow and observe the methods of this singular and artless sleuth. But I did not follow directly. Instead, I turned and ran up the other passage, which leads into the narrow part of Elm Court; and as I came flying out of the farther end of it I ran full tilt into a man who was running along the court towards the Cloisters. Of course the man was Wallingford. Who else would be running like a lunatic through the Temple at night, unless it were his pursuer?

With muttered curses but no word of recognition, he disengaged himself and pursued his way, disappearing at length round the sharp turn in the lane which leads towards the Cloisters. I did not follow him, but drew back into the dark passage and waited. Very soon another figure became visible, approaching rapidly along the dimly lighted lane. I drew farther back and presently from my hiding-place I saw the brown-hatted shadower steal past with a ridiculous air of secrecy and caution; and when he had passed, I peered out and watched his receding figure until it disappeared round the angle of the lane.

I felt half-tempted to join the absurd procession and see what eventually became of these two idiots. But I had really seen enough. I now knew that Wallingford's "delusions" were no delusions at all and that Madeline's story set forth nothing but the genuine, indisputable truth. And with these new facts to add to my unwelcome store of data, I walked slowly back to my chambers, cogitating as I went.

In truth, I had abundant material for reflection. The more I turned over my discoveries in Madeline's flat the more did the incriminating evidence seem to pile up. I recalled Polton's plainly expressed suspicion that the sender of the infernal machine was a woman; and I recalled Thorndyke's analysis of the peculiarities of the thing with the inferences which those peculiarities suggested, and read into them a more definite meaning. I now saw what the machine had conveyed to him, and what he had been trying to make it convey to me. The unmechanical outlook combined with evident ingenuity, the unfamiliarity with ordinary mechanical appliances, the ignorance concerning the different kinds of gun-powder, the lack of those common tools which nearly every man, but hardly any woman, possesses and can use: all these peculiarities of the unknown person were feminine peculiarities. And finally, there had been the plug of knitting-wool: a most unlikely material for a man to use for such a purpose, or, indeed, to possess at all.

So my thoughts went over and over the same ground, and every time finding escape from the obvious conclusion more and more impossible. The evidence of Madeline's complicity – at the very least – in the sending of the infernal machine appeared overwhelming. I could not reject it. Nor could I deny what the sending of it implied. It was virtually a confession of guilt. And yet, even as I admitted this to myself, I was strangely enough aware that my feelings towards Madeline remained unaltered. The rational, legal side of me condemned her. But somehow, in some incomprehensible way, that condemnation had a purely technical, academic quality. It left my loyalty and affection for her untouched.

But what of Thorndyke? Had his reasoning travelled along the same lines? If it had, there would be nothing sentimental in *his* attitude. He had warned me, and I knew well enough that whenever there should be evidence enough to put before a court, the law would be set in motion. What, then, was his present position? And even as I asked myself the question, there echoed uncomfortably in my mind the significant suggestion that he had thrown out only a few hours ago concerning the bottle of medicine. Evidently, he at least entertained the possibility that the Fowler's Solution had been put into that bottle after Monkhouse's death, and that for the express purpose of diverting suspicion from the food. The manifest implication was that he entertained the possibility that the poison had been administered in the food. But to suspect this was to suspect the person who prepared the food of being the poisoner. And the person who prepared the food was Madeline.

The question, therefore, as to Thorndyke's state of mind was a vital one. He had expressed no suspicion of Madeline. But then he had expressed no suspicion of anybody. On the other hand, he had exonerated nobody. He was frankly observant of every member of that household. Then there was the undeniable fact that Madeline had been watched and followed. Somebody suspected her. But who? The watcher was certainly not a detective. Amateur was writ large all over him. Then it was not the police who suspected her. Apparently there remained only Thorndyke, though one would have expected him to employ a more efficient agent.

But Wallingford was also under observation, and more persistently. Then he, too, was suspected. But here there was some show of reason. For what was Wallingford doing in the Temple? Evidently he had been lurking about, apparently keeping a watch on Thorndyke, though for what purpose I could not imagine. Still, it was a suspicious proceeding and justified some watch being kept on him. But the shadowing of Madeline was incomprehensible.

I paced up and down my sitting room turning these questions over in my mind and all the time conscious of a curious sense of unreality in the whole affair; in all this watching and following and dodging which looked so grotesque and purposeless. I felt myself utterly bewildered. But I was also profoundly unhappy and, indeed, overshadowed by a terrible dread. For out of this chaos one fact emerged clearly: there was a formidable body of evidence implicating Madeline. If Thorndyke had known what I knew, her position would have been one of the gravest peril. My conscience told me that it was my duty to tell him; and I knew that I had no intention of doing anything of the kind. But still the alarming question haunted me: how much did he really know? How much did he suspect?

In the course of my perambulations I passed and repassed a smallish deed box which stood on a lower book-shelf and which was to me what the Ark of the Covenant was to the ancient Israelites: the repository of my most sacred possessions. Its lid bore the name "Stella," painted on it by me, and its contents were a miscellany of trifles, worthless intrinsically, but to me precious beyond all price as relics of the dear friend who had been all in all to me during her short life and who, though she had been lying in her grave for four long years, was all in all to me still. Often, in the long, solitary evenings, had I taken the relics out of their abiding-place and let the sight of them carry my thoughts back to the golden days of our happy companionship, filling in the pleasant pictures with the aid of my diary – but that was unnecessary now, since I knew the entries by heart – and painting other, more shadowy pictures of a future that might have been. It was a melancholy pleasure, perhaps, but yet, as the years rolled on, the bitterness of those memories grew less bitter and still the sweet remained.

Presently, as for the hundredth time the beloved name met my eye, there came upon me a yearning to creep back with her into the sunny past; to forget, if only for a short hour, the hideous anxieties of the present and in memory to walk with her once more "along the meads of asphodel."

Halting before the box, I stood and lifted it tenderly to the table and having unlocked it, raised the lid and looked thoughtfully into the interior. Then, one by one, I lifted out my treasures, set them out in order on the table. and sat down to look at them and let them speak to me their message of peace and consolation.

To a stranger's eye they were a mere collection of odds and ends. Some would have been recognizable as relics of the more conventional type. There were several photographs of the dead girl, some taken by myself, and a tress of red-gold hair – such hair as I had been told often glorifies the victims whom consumption had marked for its own. It had been cut off for me by Barbara when she took her own tress, and tied up with a blue ribbon. But it was not these orthodox relics that spoke to me most intimately. I had no need of their aid to call up the vision of her person. The things that set my memory working were the records of actions and experiences; the sketch-books, the loose sketches and the little plaster plaques and medallions that she had made with my help after she had become bed-ridden and could go no more abroad to sketch. Every one of these had its story to tell, its vision to call up.

I turned over the sketches – simple but careful pencil drawings for the most part, for Stella, like me, had more feeling for form than for colour – and recalled the making of them; the delightful rambles across the sunny meadows or through the cool woodlands, the solemn planting of sketching-stools and earnest consultation on the selection and composition of the subjects. These were the happiest days, before the chilly hand of the destroyer had been laid on its chosen victim and there was still a long and sunny future to be vaguely envisaged.

And then I turned to the little plaques and medallions which she had modelled under my supervision and of which I had made the plaster moulds and casts. These called up sadder memories, but yet they spoke of an even closer and more loving companionship; for each work was, in a way, a joint achievement over which we had triumphed and rejoiced together. So it happened that, although the shadow of sickness, and at last of death, brooded over them, it was on these relics that I tended to linger most lovingly.

Here was the slate that I had got for her to stick the clay on and which she used to hold propped up against her knees as she worked with never-failing enthusiasm through the long, monotonous days, and even, when she was well enough, far into the night by the light of the shaded candle. Here were the simple modelling-tools and the little sponge and the Camelhair brush with which she loved to put the final finish on the damp clay reliefs. Here was Lanterri's priceless text-book over which we used to pore together and laud that incomparable teacher. Here were the plaques, medals and medallions that we had prised out, with bated breath, from their too-adherent moulds. And here – the last and saddest relic – was the wax mould from which no cast had ever been made, the final, crowning work of those deft, sensitive fingers.

For the thousandth time, I picked it up and let the light fall obliquely across its hollows. The work was a medal some three inches across, a portrait of Stella, herself, modelled from a profile photograph that I had taken for the purpose. It was an excellent likeness and unquestionably the best piece of modelling that she had ever done.

Often, I had intended to take the cast from it, but always had been restrained by a vague reluctance to disturb the mould. Now, as I looked at the delicate, sunken impression, I had again the feeling that this, her last work, ought to be finished; and I was still debating the matter with the mould in my hand when I heard a quick step upon the stair, followed by a characteristic knock on my door.

My first impulse was to hustle my treasures back into their box before answering the summons. But this was almost instantly followed by a revulsion. I recognized the knock as Thorndyke's; and somehow there came upon me a desire to share my memories with him. He had shown a strangely sympathetic insight into my feelings towards Stella. He had read my diary. He now knew the whole story; and he was the kindest, the most loyal and most discreet of friends. Gently laying down the mould I went to the door and threw it open.

"I saw your light burning as I passed just now," said Thorndyke as he entered and shook my hand warmly, "so I thought I would take the opportunity to drop in and return your diary. I hope I am not disturbing you. If I am, you must treat me as a friend and eject me."

"Not at all, Thorndyke," I replied. "On the contrary, you would be doing me a charity if you would stay and smoke a companionable pipe."

"Good," said he, "then I will give myself the pleasure of a quiet gossip. But what is amiss, Mayfield?" he continued, laying a friendly hand on my shoulder and looking me over critically. "You look worn, and worried and depressed. You are not letting your mind dwell too much, I hope, on the tragedy that has come unbidden into your life?"

"I am afraid I am," I replied. "The horrible affair haunts me. Suspicion and mystery are in the very air I breathe. A constant menace seems to hang over all my friends, so that I am in continual dread of some new catastrophe. I have just ascertained that Wallingford is really being watched and shadowed; and not only Wallingford but even Miss Norris."

He did not appear surprised or seek for further information. He merely nodded and looked into my face with grave sympathy.

"Put it away, Mayfield," said he. "That is my counsel to you. Try to forget it. You have put the investigation into my hands. Leave it there and wash your own of it. You did not kill Harold Monkhouse. Whoever did must pay the penalty if ever the crime should be brought home to the perpetrator. And if it never can be, it were better that you and all of us should let it sink into oblivion rather than allow it to remain to poison the lives of innocent persons. Let us forget it now. I see you were trying to."

I had noticed that when he first entered the room, he cast a single, swift glance at the table which, I was sure, had comprehended every object on it. Then he had looked away and never again let his eyes stray in that direction. But now, as he finished speaking, he glanced once more at the table, and this time with undisguised interest.

"Yes," I admitted. "I was trying to find in the memories of the past an antidote for the present. These are the relics of that past. I daresay you have read of them in the diary and probably have written me down a mawkish sentimentalist."

"I pray you, my friend, not to do me that injustice!" he exclaimed. "Faithful friendship that even survives the grave, is not a thing that any man can afford to despise. But for the disaster of untimely death, your faithfulness and hers would have created for two persons the perfect life. I assure you, Mayfield, that I have been deeply moved by the story of your delightful friendship and your irreparable loss. But don't let us dwell too much on the sad aspects of the story. Show me your relics. I see some very charming little plaques among them."

He picked up one with reassuring daintiness of touch and examined it through a reading-glass that I handed to him.

"It really is a most admirable little work," said he. "Not in the least amateurish. She had the makings of a first-class medallist; the appreciation of the essential qualities of a miniature relief. And she had a fine feeling for composition and spacing."

Deeply gratified by his appreciation and a little surprised by his evident knowledge of the medallist's art, I presented the little works, one after another, and we discussed their merits with the keenest interest. Presently he asked: "Has it never occurred to you, Mayfield, that these charming little works ought to be finished?"

"Finished?" I repeated. "But, aren't they finished?"

"Certainly not. They are only in the plaster. But a plaster cast is an intermediate form, just a mere working model. It is due to the merits of these plaques and medals that they should be put into permanent material – silver or copper or bronze. I'll tell you what, Mayfield," he continued, enthusiastically. "You shall let Polton make replicas of some of them – he could do it with perfect safety to the originals. Then we could hand the casts to an electrotyper or a founder – I should favour the electrotype process for such small works – and have them executed in whichever metal you preferred. Then you would be able to see, for the first time, the real quality of the modelling."

I caught eagerly at the idea, but yet I was a little nervous.

"You think it would be perfectly safe?" I asked.

"Absolutely safe. Polton would make gelatine moulds which couldn't possibly injure the originals."

That decided me. I fell in with the suggestion enthusiastically, and forthwith we began an anxious consultation as to the most suitable pieces with which to make a beginning. We had selected half a dozen casts when my glance fell on the wax mould. That was Stella's masterpiece and it certainly ought to be finished; but I was loath to part with the mould for fear of an accident. Very dubiously, I handed it to Thorndyke and asked: "What do you think of this? Could it be cast without any risk of breaking it?"

He laid the mould on the table before him so that the light fell obliquely across it and looked down on it reflectively.

"So," said he, "this is the wax mould. I was reading about it only yesterday and admiring your resourcefulness and ingenuity. I must read the entry again with the actual object before me."

He opened the diary, which he had laid on the table, and when he had found the entry, read it to himself in an undertone.

"Dropped in to have tea with Stella and found her bubbling with excitement and triumph. She had just finished the portrait medal and though her eyes were red and painful from the strain of the close work, in spite of her new spectacles, she was quite happy and as proud as a little peacock. And well she might be. I should like Lanterri to see his unknown pupil's work. We decided to make the mould of it at once, but when I got out the plaster tin, I found it empty. Most unfortunate, for the clay was beginning to dry and I didn't dare to damp it. But something had to be done to protect it. Suddenly I had a brilliant idea. There was nearly a whole candle in Stella's candlestick, quite enough for a mould, and good, hard wax that wouldn't warp. I took off the reflector and lighted the candle, which I took out of the candlestick and held almost upside down over the clay medal and let the wax drip on to it. Soon the medal was covered by a film of wax which grew thicker and thicker, until, by the time I had used up practically the whole of the candle, there was a good, solid crust of wax, quite strong enough to cast from. When I went home, I took the slate with me with the wax mould sticking to it, intending to cover it with a plaster shell for extra safety. But my plaster tin was empty, too, so I put the slate away in a safe place until I should get some fresh plaster to make the cast; which will not happen until I get back from Chelmsford.

"Busy evening getting ready for tomorrow; hope I shall feel less cheap then than I do now."

As Thorndyke finished reading he looked up and remarked: "That was an excellent plan of yours. I have seen Polton use the same method. But how was it that you never made the cast?"

"I was afraid of damaging the mould. As you know, when I came back from Ipswich, Stella was dead, and as the medal was her last work and her best, I hardly dared to risk the chance of destroying it."

"Still," Thorndyke urged, "it was the medal that was her work. The mould was your own; and the medal exists only potentially in the mould. It will come into actual existence only when the cast is made."

I saw the force of this, but I was still a little uneasy, and said so.

"There is no occasion," said he. "The mould is amply strong enough to cast from. It might possibly break in separating the cast, but that would be of no consequence, as you would then have the cast, which would be the medal, itself. And it could then be put into bronze or silver."

"Very well," I said, "if you guarantee the safety of the operation, I am satisfied. I should love to see it in silver; or perhaps it might look even better in gold."

Having disposed of the works, themselves, we fell to discussing the question of suitable settings or frames; and this led us to the subject of the portraits. Thorndyke glanced over the collection, and picking up one, which happened to be my own favourite, looked at it thoughtfully.

"It is a beautiful face," said he, "and this seems to have been a singularly happy portrait. In red chalk autotype, it would make a charming little picture. Did you take it?"

"Yes; and as I have the negative I am inclined to adopt your suggestion. I am surprised that I never thought of it myself, for red chalk is exactly the right medium."

"Then let Polton have the negative. He is quite an expert in autotype work."

I accepted the offer gladly and we then came back to the question of framing. Thorndyke's suggestion was that the portrait should be treated as a medallion and enclosed in a frame to match that of the medal. The idea appealed to me rather strongly, and presently a further one occurred to me, though it was suggested indirectly by Thorndyke, who had taken up the tress of Stella's hair and was looking at it admiringly as he drew it softly between his fingers

"Human hair," he remarked, "and particularly a woman's hair, is always a beautiful material, no matter what its colour may be; but this red-gold variety is one of the most gorgeous of Nature's productions."

"Yes," I agreed, "it is extremely decorative. Barbara had her tress made up into a thin plait and worked into the frame of a miniature of Stella. I liked the idea, but somehow the effect is not so very pleasing. But it is an oblong frame."

"I don't think," said Thorndyke, "that a plait was quite the best form. A little cable would look better, especially for a medallion portrait; indeed I think that if you had a plain square black frame with a circular opening, a little golden cable, carried round concentrically with the opening would have a rather fine effect."

"So it would," I exclaimed. "I think it would look charming. I had no idea, Thorndyke, that you were a designer. Do you think Polton could make the cable?"

"Polton," he replied, impressively, "can do anything that can be done with a single pair of human hands. Let him have the hair, and he will make the cable and the frame, too; and he will see that the glass cover is an airtight fit – for, of course, the cable would have to be under the glass."

To this also I agreed with a readiness that surprised myself. And yet it was not surprising. Hitherto I had been accustomed secretly and in solitude to pore over these pathetic little relics of happier days and lock up my sorrows and my sense of bereavement in my own breast. Now, for the first time, I had a confidant who shared the knowledge of my shattered hopes and vanished happiness; and so wholeheartedly, with such delicate sympathy and perfect understanding had Thorndyke entered into the story of my troubled life that I found in his companionship not only a relief from my old self-repression but a sort of subdued happiness. Almost cheerfully I fetched an empty cigar-box and a supply of cotton wool and tissue paper and helped him tenderly and delicately to pack my treasures for their first exodus from under my roof. And it was with only a faint twinge of regret that I saw him, at length, depart with the box under his arm.

"You needn't be uneasy, Mayfield," he said, pausing on the stairs to look back. "Nothing will be injured; and as soon as the casting is successfully carried through, I shall drop a note in your letter-box to set your mind at rest. Good night."

I watched him as he descended the stairs, and listened to his quick foot-falls, fading away up the court. Then I went back to my room with a faint sense of desolation to repack the depleted deed-box and thereafter to betake myself to bed.

CHAPTER FIFTEEN

A Pursuit and a Discovery

More than a week had passed since that eventful evening – how eventful I did not then realize – when I had delivered my simple treasures into Thorndyke's hands. But I was not uneasy; for, within twenty-four hours, I had found in my letter-box the promised note, assuring me that the preliminary operations had been safely carried through and that nothing had been damaged. Nor was I impatient. I realized that Polton had other work than mine on hand and that there was a good deal to do. Moreover, a little rush of business had kept me employed and helped me to follow Thorndyke's counsel and forget, as well as I could, the shadow of mystery and peril that hung over my friends, and, by implication, over me.

But on the evening of which I am now speaking I was free. I had cleared off the last of the day's work, and, after dining reposefully at my club, found myself with an hour or two to spare before bed-time; and it occurred to me to look in on Thorndyke to smoke a friendly pipe and perchance get a glimpse of the works in progress.

I entered the Temple from the west, and, threading my way through the familiar labyrinth, crossed Tanfield Court, and passing down the narrow alley at its eastern side, came out into King's Bench Walk. I crossed the Walk at once and was sauntering down the pavement towards Thorndyke's house when I noticed a large, closed car drawn up at its entry, and, standing on the pavement by the car, a tall man whom I recognized by the lamp light as Mr Superintendent Miller.

Now I did not much want to meet the superintendent, and in any case it was pretty clear to me that my visit to Thorndyke was not very opportune. The presence of Miller suggested business, and the size of the car suggested other visitors. Accordingly I slowed down and was about to turn back when my eye caught another phenomenon. In the entry next to Thorndyke's a man was standing, well back in the shadow, but not so far that he could not get a view of the car; on which he was quite obviously keeping a watchful eye. Indeed, he was so preoccupied with his observation of it that he had not noticed my approach, his back being turned towards me.

Naturally, the watchful attitude and the object of his watchfulness aroused my suspicions as to his identity But a movement backward on his part which brought him within range of the entry lamp, settled matter. He was Anthony Wallingford.

I turned and walked quietly back a few paces. What, was this idiot doing here within a few yards of Thorndyke's threshold? Was he merely spying fatuously and without purpose? Or was it possible that he might be up to some kind of mischief? As I framed the question my steps brought me opposite another entry. The walk was in darkness save for the few lamps and the place was practically deserted. After a moment's reflection, I stepped into the entry and decided thence to keep a watch upon the watcher.

I had not long to wait. Hardly had I taken up my rather undignified position when three men emerged from the house and walked slowly to the car. By the light of the lamp above Thorndyke's entry, I could see them quite plainly and I recognized them all. One was Thorndyke, himself, another was Dr Jervis, Thorndyke's colleague, now in the employ of the Home Office, and the third was Dr Barnwell, well-known to me as the analyst and toxicologist to the Home Office. All three carried substantial bags and Dr Barnwell was encumbered with a large case, like an out-size suit-case, suggestive of chemical apparatus. While they were depositing themselves and their impedimenta in the car, Superintendent Miller gave directions to the driver. He spoke in clear, audible tones, but though (I have to confess) I listened intently, I caught only the question: "Do you know the way?" The words which preceded and followed it were just audible but not intelligible to me. It appeared, however, that they were intelligible to Wallingford, for, as soon as they were spoken and while the superintendent still held the open door of the car, he stepped forth from his lurking-place and walked boldly and rapidly across to the narrow passage by which I had come.

Realizing instantly what his intention was, I came out of the entry and started in pursuit. As I reached the entrance to the passage, my ear caught the already faint sound of his receding footsteps; by which I learned that he was running swiftly and as silently as he could. Since I did not intend to lose him, I had no choice but to follow his example, and I raced across Tanfield Court, past the Cloisters and round by the church as if the Devil were after me instead of before. Half-way up Inner Temple Lane he slowed down to a walk – very wisely, for otherwise the night porter would certainly have stopped him – and was duly let out into Fleet Street, whither I followed him at a short interval.

When I stepped out of the gate I saw him some little distance away to the west, giving directions to the driver of a taxi. I looked round desperately, and, to my intense relief, perceived an apparently empty taxi approaching from the east. I walked quickly towards it, signalling as I went, and the driver at once drew in to the kerb and stopped. I approached him, and, leaning forward, said in a low voice – though there was no one within earshot: "There is a taxi just in front. It will probably follow a big car which is coming up Middle Temple Lane. I want you to keep that taxi in sight, wherever it may go. Do you understand?"

The man broke into a cynical grin – the nearest approach to geniality of which a taxi-driver is capable – and replied that he understood; and as, at this moment, the nose of the car appeared coming through the arched entrance gate of Middle Temple Lane, I sprang into the taxi and shut the door. From the off-side window, but keeping well back out of sight, I saw the car creep across Fleet Street, turn eastward and then sweep round into Chancery Lane. Almost immediately, Wallingford's taxi moved off and followed; and then, after a short interval, my own vehicle started, and, crossing directly to Chancery Lane, went ahead in the wake of the others.

It was an absurd affair. Now that the pursuit was started and its conduct delegated for the time to the driver, I leaned back in the shadow and was disposed to grin a little sheepishly at my own proceedings. I had embarked on them in obedience to a sudden impulse without reflection – for which, indeed, there had been no time. But was there anything to justify me in keeping this watch on Wallingford? I debated the question at some length and finally decided that, although he was probably only playing the fool, still it was proper that I should see what he was really up to. Thorndyke was my friend and it was only right that I should stand between him and any possible danger. Well as he was able to take care of himself, he could not be always on his guard. And I could not forget the infernal machine. Someone at least had the will to do him an injury.

But what about the brown-hatted man? Why had he not joined in this novel sport? Or had he? I put my head out of the window and looked along the street in our rear, but there was no sign of any pursuing taxi. The ridiculous procession was limited to three vehicles; which was just as well, since we did not want a police cyclist bringing up the rear.

From my own proceedings my thoughts turned to those of Thorndyke and his companions, though they were no affair of mine, or of Wallingford's either, for that matter. Apparently the three men were going somewhere to make a post mortem examination. The presence of Dr Barnwell suggested an analysis in addition; and the presence of Miller hinted at a criminal case of some kind. But it was not my case or Wallingford's. For both of us the analyst had already done his worst.

While I reflected, I kept an eye on the passing landmarks, checking our route and idly trying to forecast our destination. From Chancery Lane we crossed Holborn and entered Gray's Inn Road, at the bottom of which we swept round by King's Cross into Pancras Road. At the end of this we turned up Great College Street, crossed Camden Road and presently passed along the Kentish Town Road. So far I had noted our progress with no more than a languid interest. It did not matter to me whither we were going. But when, at the Bull and Gate, we swept round into Highgate Road, my attention awoke; and when the taxi turned sharply at the Duke of St Albans and entered Swain's Lane, I sat up with a start. In a moment of sudden enlightenment, I realized what our destination must be; and the realization came upon me with the effect of a palpable blow. This lane, with its precipitous ascent at the upper end, was no ordinary thoroughfare. It was little more than an approach to the great cemetery whose crowded areas extended on either side of it; its traffic was almost completely limited to the mournful processions that crept up to the wide gates by the mortuary chapel. Indeed, on the very last occasion when I had ridden up this lane, my conveyance had been the mourning carriage which followed poor little Stella to her last home.

Before I had recovered from the shock of this discovery sufficiently to consider what it might mean, the taxi came to a sudden halt. I stepped out, and, looking up the lane, made out the shadowy form of Wallingford's vehicle, already backing and manoeuvring to turn round.

"Bloke in front has got out," my driver announced in a hoarse whisper, and as he spoke, I caught sight of Wallingford – or at least of a human figure – lurking in the shadow of the trees by the railings on the right-hand side of the road. I paid off my driver (who, thereupon, backed on to the footway, turned and retired down the hill) and having waited for the other taxi to pass down, began slowly to ascend the lane, keeping in the shadow of the trees. Now that the two taxis were gone, Wallingford and I had the lane to ourselves, excepting where, in the distance ahead, the reflected light from the headlamps of the car made a dim halo and the shape of the gothic chapel loomed indistinctly against the murky sky. I could see him quite plainly, and no doubt he was aware of my presence; at any rate, I did not propose to attempt any concealment, so far as he was concerned. His movements had ceased to be of any interest to me. My entire concern was with the party ahead and with the question as to what Thorndyke was doing at this time of night in Highgate Cemetery.

The burial ground is divided, as I have said, into two parts, which lie on either side of the lane; the old cemetery with its great gates and the large mortuary chapel, on the left or west side and the newer part on the right. To which of these two parts was Thorndyke bound? That was the question that I had to settle.

I continued to advance up the lane, keeping in the shadow, though it was a dark night and the precaution was hardly necessary. Presently I overtook Wallingford and passed him without either concealment or recognition on either side. I could now clearly make out the gable and pinnacles of the chapel and saw the car turn in the wide sweep and then extinguish its headlights. Presently, from the gate-house there emerged a party of men of whom some carried lanterns, by the light of which I could recognize Thorndyke and his three companions; and I noted that they appeared to have left their cases either in the car or elsewhere for they now carried nothing. They lingered for a minute or two at the wicket by the great gates; then, accompanied by a man whom I took to be the gate-keeper, they crossed the road to the gate of the eastern cemetery and were at once followed by another party of men, who trundled two wheel-barrows, loaded with some bulky objects the nature of which I could not make out. I watched them with growing anxiety and suspicion as they passed in at the gate; and when they had all entered and moved away along the main path, I came forth from the shadow and began to walk quickly up the lane.

The eastern cemetery adjoins Waterlow Park, from which it is separated by a low wall surmounted by tall railings, and this was my objective. The park was now, of course, closed for the night, locked up and deserted. So much the better. Locks and bars were no hindrance to me. I knew the neighbourhood of old. Every foot of the lane was familiar to me, though the houses that had grown up at the lower end had changed its aspect from that which I remembered when as a boy I had rambled through its leafy shades. On I strode, past the great gates on the left and the waiting car, within which I could see the driver dozing, past the white gatehouse on the right, up the steep hill until I came to the place where a tall oak fence encloses the park from the lane. Here I halted and took off my overcoat, for the six-foot fence is guarded at the top by a row of vicious hooks. Laying the folded overcoat across the top of the fence, I sprang up, sat for a moment astride and then dropped down into the enclosure.

I now stood in a sort of dry ditch between the fence and a steep bank, covered with bushes which rose to the level of the park. I had just taken down my overcoat and was putting it on before climbing the bank when its place was taken by another overcoat cast over from without. Then a pair of hands appeared, followed by the clatter of feet against the fence and the next moment I saw Wallingford astride of the top and looking down at me.

I still affected to be unaware of him, and, turning away, began to scramble up the bank, at the summit of which I pushed my way through the bushes, and, stepping over a three-foot fence, came out upon a by-path overshadowed by trees. Pausing for a moment to get my bearings and to mark out a route by which I could cross the park without coming into the open, where I might be seen by some watchful keeper, I started off towards a belt of trees just as Wallingford stepped over the dwarf fence and came out upon the path behind me.

The position was becoming absurd, though I was too agitated to appreciate its humour. I could not protest against his following me seeing that I had come in the first place to spy upon him, and was now, like himself, engaged in spying upon Thorndyke. However, he soon solved the difficulty by quickening his pace and overtaking me, when he asked in a quite matter-of-fact tone: "What is Thorndyke up to, Mayfield?"

"That is what I want to find out," I replied.

"He is not acting on your instructions, then?"

"No; and the probability is that what he is doing is no concern of mine or of yours either. But I don't know; and I have come here to make sure. Keep in the shadow. We don't want the keeper to see us prowling about here."

He stepped back into the shade and we pursued our way in silence; and even then, troubled and agitated as I was, I noted that he asked me no question as to what was in my mind. He was leaving the initiative entirely to me.

When we had crossed the park in the shelter of the trees and descended into the hollow by the little lake where we were out of sight of the gate-house, I led the way towards the boundary between the park and the cemetery. The two enclosures were separated, as I have said, by a low wall surmounted by a range of high, massive railings; and the wall and the cemetery beyond were partially concealed by an irregular hedge of large bushes. Pushing through the bushes, I moved along the wall until I came to the place which I intended to watch; and here I halted in the shade of a tall mass of bushes, and resting my arms on the broad coping of the wall, took up my post of observation with Wallingford, silently attentive at my side.

The great burial ground was enveloped in darkness so profound that the crowded headstones and monuments conveyed to the eye no more than a confused glimmer of ghostly pallor that was barely distinguishable from the general obscurity. One monument only could be separately identified: a solitary stone cross that rose above a half-seen grave some sixty yards from the wall. But already the mysterious procession could be seen threading its way in and out by the intricate, winding paths, the gleam of the lanterns lighting up now a marble figure and now a staring head-stone or urn or broken column; and as it drew ever nearer, the glare of the lanterns, the rumble of the barrow-wheels on the hard paths and the spectral figures of the men grew more and more distinct. And still Wallingford watched and spoke never a word.

At length, a turn of the path brought the procession into full view, and as it approached I could make out a man – evidently by his uniform, the cemetery keeper – leading, lantern in hand and showing the way. Nearer and nearer the procession drew until at last, close by the stone cross, the leader halted. Then, as Thorndyke and his companions – now clearly visible – came up, he lifted his lantern and let its light fall full on the cross. And even at this distance I could read with ease – though it was unnecessary – the single name STELLA.

As that name – to me so sacred – flashed out of the darkness, Wallingford gripped my arm. "Great God!" he exclaimed. "It is Stella Keene's grave! I came here once with Barbara to plant flowers on it."

He paused, breathing hard and still clutching my arm. Then, in a hoarse whisper, he demanded: "What can that devil be going to do?"

There was little need to ask. Even as he spoke, the labourers began to unload from the first barrow its lading of picks, shovels and coils of rope. And when these were laid on the ground, the second barrow yielded up its cargo; a set of rough canvas screens which the men began to set up around the grave. And even as the screens were being erected, another lantern slowly approaching along the path, revealed two men carrying a long, bedstead-like object – a bier – which they at length set down upon its stunted legs just outside the screens.

With set teeth I stared incredulously between the railings at these awful preparations while Wallingford, breathing noisily, held fast to my arm with a hand that I could feel shaking violently. The lanterns inside the screens threw a weird, uncertain light on the canvas, and monstrous, distorted shadows moved to and fro. Presently, amidst these flitting, spectral shapes, appeared one like an enormous gnome, huge, hideous and deformed, holding an up-raised pick. The shadowy implement fell with an audible impact, followed by the ring of a shovel.

At the sight and the sound – so dreadfully conclusive – Wallingford sprang up with a stifled cry.

"God Almighty! That devil is going to dig her up!"

He stood motionless and rigid for a few moments. Then, turning suddenly, without another word, he burst through the bushes, and I heard him racing madly across the park.

I had half a mind to follow him. I had seen enough. I now knew the shocking truth. Why stay and let my soul be harrowed by the sight of these ghouls. Every stroke of pick or shovel seemed to knock at my heart. Why not go and leave them to their work of desecration? But I could not go. I could not tear myself away. There was the empty bier. Presently she would be lying on it. I could not go until I had seen her borne away.

So I stayed there gazing between the railings, watching the elfin shapes that flitted to and fro on the screen, listening to the thud of pick and the ring and scrape of shovel and letting my confused thoughts wander obscurely through a maze of half-realized pain and anger. I try in vain to recall clearly what was my state of mind. Out of the confusion and bewilderment little emerges but a dull indignation and especially a feeling of surprised resentment against Thorndyke.

The horrible business went on methodically. By degrees a shadowy mound grew up at the bottom of the screen. And then other movements and other sounds; a hollow, woody sound that seemed to bring my heart into my mouth. At last, the screens were opened at the end and then the coffin was borne out and laid on the bier. By the light of the lanterns I could see it distinctly. I was even able to recognize it, shabby and earth-stained as it now was. I saw Thorndyke help the keeper to spread over it some kind of pall, and then two men stepped between the handles of the bier, stooped and picked it up; and then the grim procession re-formed and began slowly to move away.

I watched it until it had passed round a turn of the path and was hidden from my view. Then I stood up, pushed my way through the bushes and stole away across the park by the way I had come. In the ditch inside the fence I stood for a few moments listening, but the silence was as profound as the darkness. As quietly as I could I climbed over the fence and dropped down into the lane. There seemed to be not a soul moving anywhere near; nevertheless, when I had slipped on my overcoat, instead of retracing my steps down the lane past the entrance-gates of the cemetery, I turned to the right and toiled up the steep hill to its termination in South Grove, where I bore away westward and descending the long slope of West Hill, passed the Duke of St Albans and re-entered the Highgate Road.

It did not occur to me to look out for any conveyance. My mind was in a whirl that seemed to communicate itself to my body and I walked on and on like one in a dream.

The dreary miles of deserted streets were consumed unreckoned – though still, without conscious purpose, I followed the direct road home as a well-constructed automaton might have done. But I saw nothing. Nor, for a time, could I be said to think coherently. My thoughts seethed and eddied in such confusion that no product emerged. I was conscious only of an indignant sense of shocked decency and a loathing of Thorndyke and all his works.

Presently, however, I grew somewhat more reasonable and my thoughts began to take more coherent shape. As a lawyer, I could not but perceive that Thorndyke must have something definite in his mind. He could not have done what I had seen him do without a formal authority from the Home Secretary; and before any such authority would have been given he would have been called upon to show cause why the exhumation should be carried out. And such licences are not lightly granted. Nor, I had to admit, was Thorndyke likely to have made the application without due consideration. He must have had reasons for this outrageous proceeding which not only appeared sufficient to him but which must have appeared sufficient to the Home Secretary.

All this became by degrees clear enough to me. But yet I had not a moment's doubt that he had made some monstrous mistake. Probably he had been misled by something in my diary. That seemed to be the only possible explanation. Presently he would discover his error – by means which I shudderingly put aside. But when the error was discovered, the scandal would remain. It is impossible to maintain secrecy in a case like this. In twenty-four hours or less, all the world would know that the body of Mrs Monkhouse's step-sister had been exhumed; and no subsequent explanation would serve to destroy the effect of that announcement. Wallingford's dismal prophecy was about to be fulfilled.

Moreover, Thorndyke's action amounted in effect to an open accusation – not of Madeline or Wallingford but of Barbara, herself. And this indignity she would suffer at my hands – at the hands of her oldest friend! The thought was maddening. But for the outrageous lateness of the hour, I would have gone to her at once to put her on her guard and crave her pardon. It was the least that I could do. But it could not be done tonight, for she would have been in bed hours ago and her flat locked up for the night. However, I would go in the morning at the earliest possible hour. I knew that Barbara was an early riser and it would not be amiss if I arrived at the flat before the maid.

She must be warned at the earliest possible moment and by me, who was the author of the mischief.

Thus, by the time that I reached my chambers I had decided clearly what was to be done. At first, I was disposed to reject altogether the idea of sleep. But presently, more reasonable thoughts prevailing, I decided at least to lie down and sleep a little if I could. But first I made a few indispensable preparations for the morning; filled the kettle and placed it on the gas-ring, set out the materials for a hasty breakfast, and cleaned my shoes. Then, when I had wound the alarm clock and set it for five, I partially undressed and crept into bed.

CHAPTER SIXTEEN

Barbara's Message

The routine of modern life creates the habit of dividing the day into a series of definite phases which we feel impelled to recognize even in circumstances to which they have no real application. Normally, the day is brought formally to an end by retirement to bed, a process that – also normally – leads to a lapse into unconsciousness the emergence from which marks the beginning of another day. So, in mere obedience to the call of habit, I had gone to bed, though, in spite of bodily fatigue, there had been no hint of any tendency to sleep. But I might have saved myself the trouble. True, my tired limbs stretch themselves out restfully and mere muscular fatigue slowly wore off; but my brain continued, uselessly and chaotically to pursue its activities only the more feverishly when the darkness and the silence closed the avenues of impressions from without.

Hour after hour crept by with incredible slowness, marked at each quarter by the gentle undertone of the Treasury clock, voicing its announcement, as it seemed, in polite protest (surely there was never a clock that hinted so delicately and unobtrusively at the passage of the irrevocable minutes "that perish for us and are reckoned"). Other sound there was none to break the weary silence of the night; but by the soft, mellow chime I was kept informed of the birth of another day and the progress of its infancy, which crawled so tardily in the wake of my impatience.

At last, when half-past four had struck, I threw back the bed-clothes, and, stepping out, switched on the light and put a match to the gas under the kettle. I had no occasion to hurry, but rather sought to make my preparations with studied deliberation; in spite of which I had shaved, washed and dressed and was sitting down to my frugal breakfast when the alarm clock startled me by blurting out with preposterous urgency its unnecessary reminder.

It had just turned a quarter-past five when I set forth to take my way on foot towards Kensington. No conveyance was necessary, nor would it have been acceptable; for though throughout the wearisome hours that I had spent in bed my thoughts had never ceased to revolve around the problem that Thorndyke had set, I still seemed to have the whole matter to debate afresh.

What should I say to Barbara? How should I break to her the news that my own appointed agent had made an undissembled accusation and was holding over her an unconcealed menace? I knew well enough what her attitude would be. She would hold me blameless and she would confront the threat against her reputation – even against her liberty – calmly and unafraid. I had no fear for her either of panic or recrimination. But how could I excuse myself? What could I say in extenuation of Thorndyke's secret, hostile manoeuvre?

The hands of the church clock were approaching half-past six when I turned the corner and came in sight of the entrance to her flat. And at the same moment I was made to realize the imminence and the actuality of the danger which threatened her. In a narrow street nearly opposite to the flat, a closed car was drawn up in such a position that it could move out into the main road either to the right or left without turning round; and a glance at the alert driver and a watchful figure inside – both of whom looked at me attentively as I passed – at once aroused my suspicions. And when, as I crossed to the flat, I observed a tall man perambulating the pavement, those suspicions were confirmed. For this was no brown-hatted neophyte. The hard, athletic figure and the calm, observant face were unmistakable. I had seen too many plain-clothes policemen to miss the professional characteristics. And this man also took unobtrusive note of me as my destination became apparent.

The church clock was chiming half-past six as I pressed the button of the electric bell by Barbara's front door. In the silence that still wrapped the building, I could hear the bell ring noisily, though far away, and I listened intently for some sounds of movement within. The maid would not arrive for another half hour, but I knew that Barbara was usually up at this hour. But I could hear no sign of any one stirring in the flat. Then I rang again, and yet again; and as there was still no sound from within, a vague uneasiness began to creep over me. Could Barbara be away from home? That might be as well in some respects. It might give time for the discovery of the error and save some unpleasantness. On the other hand – but at this moment I made a singular discovery myself. The latch-key was in the door! That was a most remarkable circumstance. It was so very unlike the methodical, self-possessed Barbara. But probably it had been left there by the maid. At any rate, there it was; and as I had now rung four times without result, I turned the key, pushed open the door and entered.

When I had closed the door behind me, I stood for some seconds in the dark hall, listening. There was not a sound. I was astonished that the noise of the bell had not aroused Barbara; indeed, I was surprised that she was not already up and about. Still vaguely uneasy, I felt for the light-switch, and when I had turned it on, stole along the hall and peered into the sitting room. Of course there was no one in it; nor was there any one in the kitchen, or in the spare bedroom. Finally, I went to Barbara's bedroom and knocked loudly, at the same time calling her by name. But still there was no response or sound of movement.

At last, after one or two more trials, I turned the handle and opening the door a few inches, looked in. The room was nearly dark, but the cold, wan light of the early morning was beginning to show on the blind; and in that dim twilight I could just make out a figure lying on the bed. With a sudden thrill of alarm, I stepped into the room and switched on the light. And then I stood, rooted to the spot, as if I had been turned into stone.

She was there, lying half-dressed upon the bed and as still as a bronze effigy upon a tomb. From where I stood I could see that her right hand, resting on the bed, lightly held a hypodermic syringe, and that her left sleeve was rolled up nearly to the shoulder. And when, approaching stealthily on tip-toe, I drew near, I saw upon the bare arm a plainly visible puncture and close by it a little blister-like swelling.

The first glance had made plain the dreadful truth. I had realized instantly that she was dead. Yet still, instinctively, I put my fingers to her wrist in the forlorn hope of detecting some lingering trace of life; and then any possible doubt was instantly dispelled; for the surface was stone-cold and the arm as rigid as that of a marble statue. Not only was she dead; she had been lying here dead while I, in my bed in the Temple, had lain listening to the chimes and waiting for the hour when I could come to her.

For quite a long time I stood by the bed looking down on her in utter stupefaction. So overwhelming was the catastrophe that for the moment my faculties seemed to be paralysed, my power of thought suspended. In a trance of amazement I gazed at her, and, with the idle irrelevancy of a dreamer, noted how young, how beautiful she looked; how lissom and graceful was the pose of the figure, how into the waxen face with its drowsy eyes and parted lips, there had come a something soft and youthful, almost girlish, that had not been there during life. Dimly and dreamily I wondered what the difference could be.

Suddenly my glance fell on the syringe that still rested in her hand. And with that my faculties awoke. She had killed herself! But why? Even as I asked myself the question, the terrible, the incredible answer stole into my mind only to be indignantly cast out. But yet – I lifted my eyes from the calm, pallid face, so familiar and yet so strange, and cast a scared glance round the room; and then I observed for the first time a small table near the bed on which beside a flat candle-stick containing the remains of a burnt-out candle, lay two unstamped letters. Stepping over to the table, I read their superscriptions. One was addressed to me, the other to Superintendent Miller, CID, and both were in Barbara's handwriting.

With a shaking hand I snatched up the one addressed to me, tore open the envelope and drew out the letter; and this is what I read: –

"Thursday, 1 a.m.

My dearest Rupert,

This letter is to bid you farewell. When you receive it you will curse and revile me, but I shall not hear those curses. Now, as I write, you are my darling Rupert and I am your dear friend, Barbara. With what will be when I am gone, I have no concern. It would be futile to hope that any empty words of mine could win your forgiveness. I have no such thought and do not even ask for pardon. When you think of me in the future it will be with hatred and loathing. It cannot be otherwise. But I have no part in the future. In the present – which runs out with every word that I write – I love you, and you, at least, are fond of me. And so it will be to the end, which is now drawing near.

But though this which I write to you in love will be read by you in hatred, yet I have a mind to let you know the whole truth. And that truth can be summed up in three words. I love you. I have always loved you, even when I was a little girl and you were a boy. My desire for you has been the constant, consuming passion of my life, and to possess you for my own has been the settled purpose from which I have never deviated but once – when I married Harold.

As I grew up from girlhood to womanhood, my love grew from a girl's to a woman's passion and my resolution became more fixed. I meant to have you for my own. But there was Stella. I could see that you worshipped her, and I knew that I should never have you while she lived. I was fond of poor Stella. But she stood as an insuperable obstacle between you and me. And – I suppose I am not quite as other women. I am a woman of a single purpose. Stella stood in the way of that purpose. It was a terrible necessity. But it had to be.

And after all, I seemed to have failed. When Stella was gone, you went away and I thought I had lost you for ever. For I could

209

not follow you. I knew that you had understood me, at least partly, and that you had fled from me.

Then I was in despair. It seemed that I had dismissed poor Stella to no purpose. For once, I lost courage, and, in my loneliness, committed myself to a marriage with poor Harold. It was a foolish lapse. I ought to have kept my courage and lived in hope, as I realized almost as soon as I had married him.

But when you came back, I could have killed myself. For I could see that you were still the same old Rupert and my love flamed up more intensely than ever. And once more I resolved that you should be my own; and so you would have been in the end but for Dr Thorndyke. That was the fatal error that I fell into; the error of under-valuing him. If I had only realized the subtlety of that man, I would have made a serious effort to deal with him. He should have had something very different from the frivolous make-believe that I sent him.

Well, Rupert, my darling, I have played my hand and I have lost. But I have lost only by the merest mischance. As I sit here with the ready-filled syringe on the table at my side, I am as confident as ever that it was worth while. I regret nothing but the bad luck that defeated skilful play, and the fact that you, my dear one, have had to pay so large a proportion of my losings.

I will say no more. You know everything now; and it has been a melancholy pleasure to me to have this little talk with you before making my exit.

Your loving friend,

BARBARA.

I have just slipped the key into the latch on the chance that you may come to me early. From what Tony said and what I know of you, I think it just possible. I hope you may. I like to think that we may meet, for the last time, alone."

To say that this astounding letter left me numb and stupefied with amazement would be to express but feebly its effect on me. The whole episode presented itself to me as a frightful dream from which I should presently awaken and come back to understandable and believable realities. For I know not how long I stood, dazed by the shock, with my eyes riveted on that calm, comely figure on the bed, trying to grasp the incredible truth that this dead woman was Barbara, that she had killed herself and that she had murdered Stella – murdered her callously, deliberately and with considered intent.

Suddenly, the deathly silence of the flat was broken by the sound of an opening, and then of a closing door. Then a strong masculine voice was borne to my ear saying, in a not unkindly tone, "Now, my girl, you had better run off to the kitchen and shut yourself in."

On this I roused, and, walking across to the door, which was still ajar, went out into the hall, where I confronted Superintendent Miller and Barbara's maid. Both stared at me in astonishment and the maid uttered a little cry of alarm as she turned and hurried into the kitchen. The superintendent looked at me steadily and with obvious suspicion, and, after a moment or two, asked, gruffly, nodding at the bedroom door, "Is Mrs Monkhouse in there?"

"Mrs Monkhouse is dead," I answered.

"Dead!" he repeated, incredulously. Then, pushing past me, he strode into the room, and as I followed, I could hear him cursing furiously in a not very low undertone. For a few moments he stood looking down on the corpse, gently touching the bare arm and apparently becoming aware of its rigidity. Suddenly he turned, and, glaring fiercely at me, demanded: "What is the meaning of this, Mr Mayfield?"

"The meaning?" I repeated, looking at him inquiringly.

"Yes. How came you to let her do this – that is, if she did it herself?"

"I found her dead when I arrived here," I explained.

"And when did you arrive here?"

"About half an hour ago."

He shook his head and rejoined in an ominously quiet tone: "That won't do, Sir. The maid has only just come and the dead woman couldn't have let you in."

I explained that I had found the key in the outer door but he made no pretence of accepting the explanation.

"That is well enough," said he, "if you can prove that the key was in the door. Otherwise it is a mere statement which may or may not be true. The actual position is that I have found you alone in this flat with the body of a woman who has died a violent death. You will have to account satisfactorily for your presence here at this time in the morning, and for your movements up to the time of your arrival here."

The very equivocal, not to say perilous, position in which I suddenly found myself served to steady my wits. I realized instantly how profoundly suspicious the appearances really were and that if I could not produce evidence of my recent arrival I should quite probably have to meet the charge of being an accessory to the suicide. And an accessory to suicide is an accessory to murder. It was a very serious position.

"Have you seen your man yet?" I asked. "The men, I mean, who were on observation duty outside."

"I have seen them, but I haven't spoken to them. They are waiting out on the landing now. Why do you ask?"

"Because I think they saw me come in here."

"Ah, well, we can see about that presently. Is that letter that you have in your hand from Mrs Monkhouse? Because, if it is, I shall want to see it."

"I don't want to show it unless it is necessary; and I don't think it will be. There is a letter addressed to you which will probably tell you all that you need know."

He snatched up the letter, and, tearing it open, glanced through it rapidly. Then, without comment, he handed it to me. It was quite short and ran as follows:

"Thursday, 1.35 a.m.

Mr Superintendent Miller, CID

This is to inform you that I alone am responsible for the death of my late husband, Harold Monkhouse, and also for that of the late Miss Stella Keene. I had no confidants or accomplices and no one was aware of what I had done.

As my own death will occur in about ten minutes (from an injection of morphine which I shall administer to myself) this statement may be taken as my dying declaration.

I may add that no one is aware of my intention to take my life.

Yours very truly
BARBARA MONKHOUSE."

"Well," said Miller, as I returned the letter to him, "that supports your statement, and if my men saw you enter the flat, that will dispose of the matter so far as the suicide is concerned. But there is another question. It is evident that she knew that a discovery had been made. Now, who told her? Was it you, Mr Mayfield?"

"No," I replied, "it was not. I found her dead when I arrived, as I have told you."

"Do you know who did tell her?"

"I do not; and I am not disposed to make any guesses."

"No, it's no use guessing. Still, you know, Mr Mayfield, *you* knew, and you came here to tell her; and you know who knew besides yourself. But there," he added, as we moved out into the hall, "it is no use going into that now. I've acted like a fool – too punctilious by half. I oughtn't to have let her slip through my fingers. I should have acted at once on Dr Thorndyke's hint without waiting for confirmation."

He was still speaking in an angry, reproachful tone; but suddenly his manner changed. Looking at me critically but with something of kindly sympathy, he said: "It has been a trying business for you, Mr Mayfield – the whole scandalous affair; and this must have given you a frightful shock, though I expect you would rather have it as it is than as it ought to have been. But you don't look any the better for it."

He escorted me politely but definitely to the outer door, and when he opened it I saw his two subordinates waiting on the landing; to both of whom collectively Miller addressed the inquiry: "Did you see Mr Mayfield enter this flat?"

"Yes, Sir," was the reply of one, confirmed by the other. "He went up the stairs at exactly half-past six."

Miller nodded, and wishing me "good morning," beckoned to the two officers; and as I turned to descend the stairs, I saw the three enter and heard the door shut.

Once more in the outer world, walking the grey, half-lighted streets, to which the yet unextinguished lamps seemed only to impart an added chill, my confused thoughts took up the tangled threads at the point at which the superintendent's appearance had broken them off. But I could not get my ideas arranged into any intelligible form. Each aspect of the complex tragedy conflicted with all the others. The pitiful figure that I had left lying on the bed made its appeal in spite of the protest of reason; for the friendship of a lifetime cannot easily be extinguished in a moment. I knew now that she was a wretch, a monster; and when I reminded myself of what she had done, I grudged the easy, painless death by which she had slipped away so quietly from the wreckage that her incredible wickedness had created. When I contrasted that death – a more gentle lapsing into oblivion – with the long, cheerfully endured sufferings of brave, innocent little Stella, I could have cursed the faithful friendship of Wallingford which had let her escape from the payment to the uttermost farthing of her hideous debt. And yet the face that haunted me – the calm, peaceful, waxen face – was the face of Barbara, my friend, almost my sister, who had been so much to me, who had loved me with that strange, tenacious, terrible passion.

It was very confusing And the same inconsistency pervaded my thoughts of Thorndyke. Unreasonably, I found myself thinking of him with a certain repulsion, almost of dislike, as the cause of this catastrophe. Yet my reason told me that he had acted with the highest motives of justice; that he had but sought retribution for Stella's sufferings and death and those of poor, harmless Harold Monkhouse; that as a barrister, even as a citizen, he could do no less than denounce the wrong-doer. But my feelings were too lacerated, my emotions too excited to allow my reason to deal with the conflicting elements of this tragedy.

In this confused state of mind, I walked on, hardly conscious of direction, until I found myself at the entry of my chambers. I went in and made a futile attempt to do some work. Then I paced the room for an hour or more, alternately raging against Barbara and recalling the lonely figure that I had seen in the twilight of that darkened room, until my unrest drove me forth again to wander through the streets, away into the squalid east, among the docks and the rookeries from Whitechapel to Limehouse.

It was evening when, once more, I dragged myself up my stairs, and, spent with fatigue and exhausted by lack of food – for during the whole day I had taken but a few cups of tea, hastily snatched in the course of my wanderings – re-entered my chamber. As I closed the door, I noticed a letter in the box, and taking it out, listlessly opened the envelope. It was from Thorndyke; a short note, but very cordially worded, begging me "like a good fellow" to go round to have a talk with him.

I flung the note down impatiently on the table, with an immediate resurgence of my unreasonable sense of resentment. But in a few minutes I experienced a sudden revulsion of feeling. A sense of profound loneliness came upon me; a yearning for human companionship, and especially for the companionship of Thorndyke, from whom I had no secrets, and who knew the whole dreadful story even to its final culmination.

Once more, foot-sore as I was, I descended my stairs and a couple of minutes later was ascending the "pair" that led up to Thorndyke's chambers.

CHAPTER SEVENTEEN

Thorndyke Retraces the Trail

Apparently Thorndyke had seen me from the window as I crossed the Walk, for, when I reached the landing, I found him standing in the open doorway of his chambers; and at the sight of him, whatever traces of unreasonable resentment may have lingered in my mind, melted away instantly. He grasped my hand with almost affectionate warmth, and looking at me earnestly and with the most kindly solicitude, said: "I am glad you have come, Mayfield. I couldn't bear to think of you alone in your chambers, haunted by this horrible tragedy."

"You have heard, then – about Barbara, I mean?"

"Yes. Miller called and told me. Of course, he is righteously angry that she has escaped, and I sympathize with him. But for us – for you and me – it is a great deliverance. I was profoundly relieved when I heard that she was gone; that the axe had fallen once for all."

"Yes," I admitted, "it was better than the frightful alternative of a trial and what would have followed. But still, it was terrible to see her, lying dead, and to know that it was my hand – the hand of her oldest and dearest friend – that had struck the blow."

"It was my hand, Mayfield, not yours that actually struck the blow. But even if it had been yours instead of your agent's, what could have been more just and proper than that retribution should have come through the hand of the friend and guardian of that poor murdered girl?"

216

I assented with a shudder to the truth of what he had said, but still my mind was too confused to allow me to see things in their true perspective. Barbara, my friend, was still more real to me than Barbara the murdress. He nodded sympathetically enough when I explained this, but rejoined, firmly: "You must try, my dear fellow, to see things as they really are. Shocking as this tragedy is, it would have been immeasurably worse if that terrible woman had not received timely warning. As it is, the horrible affair has run its course swiftly and is at an end. And do not forget that if the axe has fallen on the guilty its menace has been lifted from the innocent. Madeline Norris and Anthony Wallingford will sleep in peace tonight, free from the spectre of suspicion that has haunted them ever since Harold Monkhouse died. As to the woman whose body you found this morning, she was a monster. She could not have been permitted to live. Her very existence was a menace to the lives of all who came into contact with her."

Again, I could not but assent to his stern indictment and his impartial statement of the facts.

"Very well, Mayfield," said he. "Then try to put it to yourself that, for you, the worst has happened and is done with. Try to put it away as a thing that now belongs to the past and is, in so far as it is possible, to be forgotten."

"As far as is possible," I repeated. "Yes, of course, you are quite right, Thorndyke. But forgetfulness is not a thing which we can command at will."

"Very true," he replied. "But yet we can control to a large extent the direction of our thoughts. We can find interests and occupations. And, speaking of occupations, let me show you some of Polton's productions."

He rose, and putting a small table by the side of my chair, placed on it one or two small copper plaques and a silver medallion which he had taken from a drawer. The medallion was the self-portrait of Stella which had lain dormant in the wax mould through all the years which had passed since her death, and as I took it in my hand and gazed at the beloved face, I found it beautiful beyond my expectations.

"It is a most charming little work," I said, holding it so that the lamp light fell most favourably on the relic, "I am infinitely obliged to you, Thorndyke."

"Don't thank me," said he. "The whole credit is due to Polton. Not that he wants any thanks, for the work has yielded him hours of perfect happiness. But here he is with the products of another kind of work."

As he spoke, Polton entered with a tray and began in his neat, noiseless way, to lay the table. I don't know how much he knew, but when I caught his eye and his smile of greeting, it seemed to me that friendliness and kindly sympathy exuded from every line of his quaint, crinkly face. I thanked him for his skilful treatment of my treasures and then, observing that he was apparently laying the table for supper, would have excused myself. But Thorndyke would hear of no excuses.

"My dear fellow," said he, "you are the very picture of physical exhaustion. I suspect that you have had practically no food today. A meal will help you to begin to get back to the normal. And, in any case, you mustn't disappoint Polton, who has been expecting you to supper and has probably made a special effort to do credit to the establishment."

I could only repeat my acknowledgments of Polton's goodness (noting that he certainly must have made a special effort, to judge by the results which began to make themselves evident) and, conquering my repugnance to the idea of eating, take my place at the table.

It is perhaps somewhat humiliating to reflect that our emotional states, which we are apt to consider on a lofty spiritual plane, are controlled by matters so grossly material as the mere contents of our stomachs. But such is the degrading truth, as I now realized. For no sooner had I commenced a reluctant attack on the products of Polton's efforts and drunk a glass of Burgundy – delicately warmed by that versatile artist to the exact optimum temperature – than my mental and physical unrest began to subside and allow a reasonable, normal outlook to develop, with a corresponding bodily state. In effect, I made quite a good meal and found myself listening with lively interest to Thorndyke's account of the technical processes involved in converting my little plaster plaques and the wax mould into their final states in copper and silver.

Nevertheless, in the intervals of conversation the unforgettable events of the morning and the preceding night tended to creep back into my consciousness; and now a question which I had hitherto hardly considered began to clamour for an answer. Towards the end of the meal, I put it into words. Apropos of nothing in our previous conversation, I asked: "How did you know; Thorndyke?" and as he looked up inquiringly, I added: "I mean, how were you able to make so confident a guess, for, of course, you couldn't actually know?"

"When do you mean?" he asked.

"I mean that when you applied for a Home Office authority you must have had something to go on beyond a mere guess."

"Certainly I had," he replied. "It was not a guess at all. It was a certainty. When I made the application I was able to say that I had positive knowledge that Stella Keene had been poisoned with arsenic. The examination of the poor child's body was not for my information. I would have avoided it if that had been possible. But it was not. As soon as my declaration was made, the exhumation became inevitable. The Crown could not have prosecuted on a charge of poisoning without an examination of the victim's body."

"But, Thorndyke," I expostulated, "how could you have been certain – I mean certain in a legal sense? Surely it could have been no more than a matter of inference."

"It was not," he replied. "It was a matter of demonstrated fact. I could have taken the case into court and proved the fact of arsenical poisoning. But, of course, the jury would have demanded evidence from an examination of the body, and quite properly, too. Every possible corroboration should be obtained in a criminal trial."

"Certainly," I agreed. "But still I find your statement incomprehensible. You speak of demonstrated fact. But what means of demonstration had you? There was my diary. I take it that that was the principal source of your information; in fact I can't think of any other. But the diary could only have yielded documentary evidence, which is quite a different thing from demonstrated fact."

"Quite," he agreed. "The diary contributed handsomely to the train of circumstantial evidence that I had constructed. But the demonstration – the final, positive proof – came from another source. A very curious and unexpected source."

"I suppose," said I, "as the case is finished and dealt with, there would be no harm in my asking how you arrived at your conclusion?"

"Not at all," he replied. "The whole investigation is a rather long story, but I will give you a summary of it if you like."

"Why a summary?" I objected. "I would rather have it *in extenso* if it will not weary you to relate it."

"It will be more likely to weary you," he replied. "But if you are equal to a lengthy exposition, let us take to our easy chairs and combine bodily comfort with forensic discourse."

We drew up the two arm-chairs before the hearth, and when Polton had made up the fire and placed between us a small table furnished with a decanter and glasses, Thorndyke began his exposition.

"This case is in some respects one of the most curious and interesting that I have met with in the whole of my experience of medico-legal practice. At the first glance, as I told you at the time, the problem that it presented seemed hopelessly beyond solution. All the evidence appeared to be in the past and utterly irrecoverable. The vital questions were concerned with events that had passed unrecorded and of which there seemed to be no possibility that they could ever be disinterred from the oblivion in which they were buried. Looking back now on the body of evidence that has gradually accumulated, I am astonished at the way in which the apparently forgotten past has given up its secrets, one after another, until it has carried its revelation from surmise to probability and from probability at last to incontestible proof.

"The inquiry divides itself into certain definite stages, each of which added new matter to that which had gone before. We begin, naturally, with the inquest on Harold Monkhouse, and we may consider this in three aspects: the ascertained condition of the body;

the evidence of the witnesses; and the state of affairs disclosed by the proceedings viewed as a whole.

"First, as to the body: there appeared to be no doubt that Monkhouse died from arsenical poisoning, but there was no clear evidence as to how the poison had been administered. It was assumed that it had been taken in food or in medicine – that it had been swallowed – and no alternative method of administration was suggested or considered. But on studying the medical witnesses' evidence, and comparing it with the descriptions of the patient's symptoms, I was disposed to doubt whether the poison had actually been taken by the mouth at all."

"Why," I exclaimed, "how else could it have been taken?"

"There are quite a number of different ways in which poisonous doses of arsenic can be taken. Finely powdered arsenic is readily absorbed by the skin. There have been several deaths from the use of 'violet powder' contaminated with arsenic, and clothing containing powdered arsenic would produce poisonous effects. Then there are certain arsenical gases – notably arsine, or arseniureted hydrogen – which are intensely poisonous and which possibly account for a part of the symptoms in poisoning from arsenical wallpapers. There seemed to me to be some suggestion of arsenical gas in Monkhouse's case, but it was obviously not pure gas-poisoning. The impression conveyed to me was that of a mixed poisoning; that the arsenic had been partly inhaled and partly applied to the skin, but very little, if any, taken by the mouth."

"You are not forgetting that arsenic was actually found in the stomach?"

"No. But the quantity was very minute; and a minute quantity is of no significance. One of the many odd and misleading facts about arsenic poisoning is that, in whatever way the drug is taken, a small quantity is always found in the stomach and there are always some signs of gastric irritation The explanation seems to be that arsenic which has got into the blood in any way – through the skin, the lungs or otherwise – tends to be eliminated in part through the stomach. At any rate, the fact is that the presence of minute quantities of arsenic in the stomach affords no evidence that the poison was swallowed."

"But," I objected, "what of the Fowler's Solution which was found in the medicine?"

"Exactly," said he. "That was the discrepancy that attracted my attention. The assumption was that deceased had taken in his medicine a quantity of Fowler's Solution representing about a grain and a half of arsenious acid. If that had been so we should have expected to find a very appreciable quantity in the stomach: much more than was actually found. The condition of the body did not agree with the dose that was assumed to have been taken; and when one came to examine the evidence of the various witnesses there was further room for doubt. Two of them had noticed the medicine at the time when the Fowler's Solution had not been added; but no witness had noticed it after the alleged change and before the death of deceased. The presence of the Fowler's Solution was not observed until several days after his death. Taking all the facts together, there was a distinct suggestion that the solution had been added to the medicine at some time after Monkhouse's death. But this suggestion tended to confirm my suspicion that the poison had not been swallowed. For the discovery of the Fowler's Solution in the medicine would tend to divert inquiry – and did, in fact, divert it – from any other method of administering the poison.

"To finish with the depositions: not only was there a complete lack of evidence even suggesting any one person as the probable delinquent; there was not the faintest suggestion of any motive that one could consider seriously. The paltry pecuniary motive applied to all the parties and could not be entertained in respect of any of them. The only person who could have had a motive was Barbara. She was a young, attractive woman, married to an elderly, unattractive husband. If she had been attached to another man, she would have had the strongest and commonest of all motives. But there was nothing in the depositions to hint at any other man; and since she was absent from home when the poisoning occurred, she appeared to be outside the area of possible suspicion.

"And now to look at the evidence as a whole: you remember Miller's comment. There was something queer about the case; something very oddly elusive. At the first glance it seemed to bristle with suspicious facts. But when those facts were scrutinized they meant nothing. There were plenty of clues but they led nowhere. There was Madeline Norris who prepared the victim's food – an obvious suspect. But then it appeared that the poison was in the medicine, not in the food. There was Wallingford who actually had poison in his possession. But it was the wrong poison. There was the bottle that had undoubtedly contained arsenic. But it was nobody's bottle. There was the bottle that smelled of lavender and had red stains in it and was found in Miss Norris' possession; but it contained no arsenic. And so on.

"Now all this was very strange. The strongest suspicion was thrown on a number of people collectively. But it failed every time to connect itself with any one individually. I don't know precisely what Miller thought of it, but to me it conveyed the strong impression of a scheme – of something arranged, and arranged with extraordinary skill and ingenuity. I had the feeling that, behind all these confusing and inconsistent appearances, was a something quite different, with which they had no real connection; that all these apparent clues were a sort of smoke-screen thrown up to conceal the actual mechanism of the murder.

"What could the mechanism of the murder have been? That was what I asked myself. And by whom could the arrangements have been made and carried out? Here the question of motive became paramount. What motive could be imagined? And who could have been affected by it? That seemed to be the essential part of the problem, and the only one that offered the possibility of investigation.

"Now, as I have said, the most obvious motive in cases of this kind is that of getting rid of a husband or wife to make room for another. And ignoring moral considerations, it is a perfectly rational motive; for the murder of the unwanted spouse is the only possible means of obtaining the desired release. The question was, could such a motive have existed in the present case; and the answer was that, on inspection, it appeared to be a possible motive, although there was no evidence that it actually existed. But, assuming its possibility for the sake of argument, who could have been affected by it? At once, one saw that Madeline Norris was excluded. The death of Harold Monkhouse did not affect her, in this respect, at all. There remained only Barbara and Wallingford. To take the latter first: he was a young man, and the wife was a young, attractive woman; he had lived in the same house with her, appeared to be her social equal and was apparently on terms of pleasant intimacy with her. If he had any warmer feelings towards her, her husband's existence formed an insuperable obstacle to the realization of his wishes. There was no evidence that he had any such feelings, but the possibility had to be borne in mind. And there were the further facts that he evidently had some means of obtaining poisons and that he had ample opportunities for administering them to the deceased. All things considered, Wallingford appeared, prima facie, to be the most likely person to have committed the murder.

"Now to take the case of Barbara. In the first place, there was the possibility that she might have had some feeling towards Wallingford, in which case she would probably have been acting in collusion with him and her absence from home on each occasion when the poisoning took place would have been part of the arrangement. But, excluding Wallingford, and supposing her to be concerned with some other man, did her absence from home absolutely exclude the possibility of her being the poisoner? There were suggestions of skilful and ingenious arrangements to create false appearances. Was it possible that those arrangements included some method by which the poison could be administered during her absence without the connivance or knowledge of any other person?

"I pondered this question carefully by the light of all the details disclosed at the inquest; and the conclusion that I reached was that, given a certain amount of knowledge, skill and executive ability, the thing was possible. But as soon as I had admitted the possibility, I was impressed by the way in which the suggestion fitted in with the known facts and served to explain them. For all the arranged appearances pointed to the use of Fowler's Solution, administered by the mouth. But this could not possibly have been the method if the poisoner were a hundred miles away. And as I have said, I was strongly inclined to infer, from the patient's symptoms and the condition of the body, that the poison had not been administered by the mouth.

"But all this, as you will realize, was purely hypothetical. None of the assumptions was supported by a particle of positive evidence. They merely represented possibilities which I proposed to bear in mind in the interpretation of any new evidence that might come into view.

"This brings us to the end of the first stage; the conclusions arrived at by a careful study of the depositions. But following hard on the inquest was your visit to me when you gave me the particulars of your past life and your relations with Barbara and Monkhouse. Now your little autobiographical sketch was extremely enlightening, and, as it has turned out, of vital importance. In the first place, it made clear to me that your relations with Barbara were much more intimate than I had supposed. You were not merely friends of long standing; you were virtually in the relation of brother and sister. But with this very important difference: that you were not brother and sister. An adopted brother is a possible husband; an adopted sister is a possible wife. And when I considered your departure to Canada with the intention of remaining there for life, and your unexpected return, I found that the bare possibility that Barbara might wish to be released from her marriage had acquired a certain measure of probability.

"But further; your narrative brought into view another person who had died. And the death of that person presented a certain analogy with the death of Monkhouse. For if Barbara had wished to be your wife, both these persons stood immovably in the way of her wishes. Of course there was no evidence that she had any such wish, and the death of Stella was alleged to have been due to natural causes. Nevertheless, the faint, hypothetical suggestions offered by these new facts were strikingly similar to those offered by the previous facts.

"The next stage opened when I read your diary, especially the volume written during the last year of Stella's life. But now one came out of the region of mere speculative hypothesis into that of very definite suspicion. I had not read very far when, from your chance references to the symptoms of Stella's illness, I came to the decided conclusion that, possibly mingled with the symptoms of real disease, were those of more or less chronic arsenical poisoning. And what was even more impressive, those symptoms seemed to be closely comparable with Monkhouse's symptoms, particularly in the suggestion of a mixed poisoning partly due to minute doses of arsine. I need not go into details, but you will remember that you make occasional references to slight attacks of jaundice (which is very characteristic of arsine poisoning) and to 'eye-strain' which the spectacles failed to relieve. But, redness, smarting and watering of the eyes is an almost constant symptom of chronic arsenic poisoning. And there were various other symptoms of a decidedly suspicious character to which you refer and which I need not go into now.

"Then a careful study of the diary brought into view another very impressive fact. There were considerable fluctuations in Stella's condition. Sometimes she appeared to be so far improving as to lead you to some hopes of her actual recovery. Then there would be a rather sudden change for the worse and she would lose more than she had gained. Now, at this time Barbara had already become connected with the political movement which periodically called her away from home for periods varying from one to four weeks; and when I drew up a table of the dates of her departures and returns, I found that the periods included between them – that is the periods during which she was absent from home – coincided most singularly with Stella's relapses. The coincidence was so complete that, when I had set the data out in a pair of diagrams in the form of graphs, the resemblance of the two diagrams was most striking. I will show you the diagrams presently.

"But there was something else that I was on the look-out for in the diary, but it was only quite near the end that I found it. Quite early, I learned that Stella was accustomed to read and work at night by the light of a candle. But I could not discover what sort of candle she used; whether it was an ordinary household candle or one of some special kind. At last I came on the entry in which you describe the making of the wax mould; and then I had the information that I had been looking for. In that entry you mention that you began by lifting the reflector off the candle, by which I learned that the receptacle used was not an ordinary candlestick. Then you remark that the candle was of 'good hard wax'; by which I learned that it was not an ordinary household candle-these being usually composed of a rather soft paraffin wax. Apparently, it was a stearine candle such as is made for use in candlelamps."

"But," I expostulated, "how could it possibly matter what sort of candle she used? The point seems to be quite irrelevant."

"The point," he replied, "was not only relevant; it was of crucial importance. But I had better explain. When I was considering the circumstances surrounding the poisoning of Monkhouse, I decided that the probabilities pointed to Barbara as the poisoner. But she was a hundred miles away when the poisoning occurred; hence the question that I asked myself was this: Was there any method that was possible and practicable in the existing circumstances by which Barbara could have arranged that the poisoning could be effected during her absence? And the answer was that there was such a method, but only one. The food and the medicine were prepared and administered by those who were on the spot. But the candles were supplied by Barbara and by her put into the bedside candle-box before she went away. And they would operate during her absence."

"But," I exclaimed, "do I understand you to suggest that it is possible to administer poison by means of a candle?"

"Certainly," he replied. "It is quite possible and quite practicable. If a candle is charged with finely powdered arsenious acid – 'white arsenic' – when that candle is burnt, the arsenious acid will be partly vaporized and partly converted into arsine, or arseniureted hydrogen. Most of the arsine will be burnt in the flame and reconverted into arsenious acid, which will float in the air, as it condenses, in the form of an almost invisible white cloud. The actual result will be that the air in the neighbourhood of the candle will contain small traces of arsine – which is an intensely poisonous gas – and considerable quantities of arsenious acid, floating about in the form of infinitely minute crystals. This impalpable dust will be breathed into the lungs of any person near the candle and will settle on the skin, from which it will be readily absorbed into the blood and produce all the poisonous effects of arsenic.

"Now, in the case of Harold Monkhouse, not only was there a special kind of candle, supplied by the suspected person, but, as I have told you, the symptoms during life and the appearances of the dead body, all seemed to me to point to some method of poisoning through the lungs and skin rather than by way of the stomach, and also suggested a mixed poisoning in which arsine played some part. So that the candle was not only a possible medium of the poisoning; it was by far the most probable.

"Hence, when I came to consider Stella's illness and noted the strong suggestion of arsenic poisoning; and when I noted the parallelism of her illness with that of Monkhouse; I naturally kept a watchful eye for a possible parallelism in the method of administering the poison. And not only did I find that parallelism; but in that very entry, I found strong confirmation of my suspicion that the candle was poisoned. You will remember that you mention the circumstance that on the night following the making of the wax mould you were quite seriously unwell. Apparently you were suffering from a slight attack of acute arsenical poisoning, due to your having inhaled some of the fumes from the burning candle."

"Yes, I remember that," said I. "But what is puzzling me is how the candles could have been obtained. Surely it is not possible to buy arsenical candles?"

"No," he replied, "it is not. But it is possible to buy a candle-mould, with which it is quite easy to make them. Remember that, not so very long ago, most country people used to make their own candles, and the hinged moulds that they used are still by no means rare. You will find specimens in most local museums and in curio shops in country towns and you can often pick them up in farmhouse sales. And if you have a candle-mould, the making of arsenical candles is quite a simple affair. Barbara, as we know, used to buy a particular German brand of stearine candles. All that she had to do was to melt the candles, put the separated wicks into the mould, stir some finely-powdered white arsenic into the melted wax and pour it into the mould. When the wax was cool, the mould would be opened and the candles taken out – these hinged moulds usually made about six candles at a time. Then it would be necessary to scrape off the seam left by the mould and smooth the candles to make them look like those sold in the shops."

"It was a most diabolically ingenious scheme," said I.

"It was," he agreed. "The whole villainous plan was very completely conceived and most efficiently carried out. But to return to our argument. The discovery that Stella had used a special form of candle left me in very little doubt that Barbara was the poisoner and that poisoned candles had been the medium used in both crimes. For we were now out of the region of mere hypothesis. We were dealing with genuine circumstantial evidence. But that evidence was still much too largely inferential to serve as the material for a prosecution. We still needed some facts of a definite and tangible kind; and as soon as you came back from your travels on the Southeastern Circuit, fresh facts began to accumulate. Passing over the proceedings of Wallingford and his follower and the infernal machine – all of which were encouraging, as offering corroboration, but of no immediate assistance – the first really important accretion of evidence occurred in connection with our visit to the empty house in Hilborough Square."

"Ha!" I exclaimed. "Then you did find something significant, in spite of your pessimistic tone at the time? I may say, Thorndyke, that I had a feeling that you went to that house with the definite expectation of finding some specific thing. Was I wrong?"

"No. You were quite right. I went there with the expectation of finding one thing and a faint hope of finding another; and both the expectation and the hope were justified by the event. My main purpose in that expedition was to obtain samples of the wallpaper from Monkhouse's room, but I thought it just possible that the soot from the bedroom chimneys might yield some information. And it did.

"To begin with the wallpaper: the condition of the room made it easy to secure specimens. I tore off about a dozen pieces and wrote a number on each, to correspond with numbers that I marked on a rough sketch-plan of the room which I drew first. My expectation was that if – as I believed – arsenical candles had been burnt in that room, arsenic would have been deposited on all the walls, but in varying amounts, proportionate to the distance of the wall from the candle. The loose piece of paper on the wall by the bed was, of course, the real touchstone of the case, for if there were no arsenic in it, the theory of the arsenical candle would hardly be tenable. I therefore took the extra precaution of writing a full description of its position on the back of the piece and deposited it for greater safety in my letter-case.

"As soon as I reached home that day I spread out the torn fragment on the wide stage of a culture microscope and examined its outer surface with a strong top light. And the very first glance settled the question. The whole surface was spangled over with minute crystals, many of them hardly a ten-thousandth of an inch in diameter, sparkling in the strong light like diamonds and perfectly unmistakable; the characteristic octahedral crystals of arsenious acid.

"But distinctive as they were, I took nothing for granted. Snipping off a good-sized piece of the paper, I submitted it to the Marsh-Berzelius test and got a very pronounced 'arsenical mirror,' which put the matter beyond any possible doubt or question. I may add that I tested all the other pieces and got an arsenic reaction from them all, varying, roughly, according to their distance from the table on which the candle stood.

"Thus the existence of the arsenical candle was no longer a matter of hypothesis or even of mere probability; it was virtually a demonstrated fact. The next question was, who put the arsenic into the candle? All the evidence, such as it was, pointed to Barbara. But there was not enough of it. No single fact connected her quite definitely with the candles, and it had to be admitted that they had passed through other hands than hers and that the candle-box was accessible to several people, especially during her absence. Clear evidence, then, was required to associate her – or someone else – with those poisoned candles, and I had just a faint hope that such evidence might be forthcoming. This was how I reasoned:

"Here was a case of poisoning in which the poison was self-administered and the actual poisoner was absent. Consequently it was impossible to give a calculated dose on a given occasion, nor was it possible to estimate in advance the amount that would be necessary to produce the desired result. Since the poison was to be left within reach of the victim, to be taken from time to time, it would be necessary to leave a quantity considerably in excess of the amount actually required to produce death on any one occasion. It is probable that all the candles in the box were poisoned. In any case, most of them must have been; and as the box was filled to last for the whole intended time of Barbara's absence, there would be a remainder of poisoned candles in the box when Monkhouse died. But the incident of the 'faked' medicine showed that the poisoner was fully alive to the possibility of an examination of the room. It was not likely that so cautious a criminal would leave such damning evidence as the arsenical candles in full view. For if, by chance, one of them had been lighted and the bearer had developed symptoms of poisoning, the murder would almost certainly have been out. In any case, we could assume that the poisoner would remove them and destroy them after putting ordinary candles in their place.

"But a candle is not a very easy thing to destroy. You can't throw it down a sink, or smash it up and cast it into the rubbish-bin. It must be burnt; and owing to its inflammability, it must be burnt carefully and rather slowly; and if it contains a big charge of arsenic, the operator must take considerable precautions. And finally, these particular candles had to be burnt secretly.

"Having regard to these considerations, I decided that the only safe and practicable way to get rid of them was to burn them in a fireplace with the window wide open. This would have to be done at night when all the household was asleep, so as to be safe from interruption and discovery; and a screen would have to be put before the fireplace to prevent the glare from being visible through the open window. If there were a fire in the grate, so much the better. The candles could be cut up into small pieces and thrown into the fire one at a time.

"Of course the whole matter was speculative. There might have been no surplus candles, or if there were, they might have been taken out of the house and disposed of in some other way. But one could only act on the obvious probabilities and examine the chimneys, remembering that whereas a negative result would prove nothing for or against any particular person, a positive result would furnish very weighty evidence. Accordingly I collected samples of soot from the various bedroom chimneys and from that of Barbara's boudoir, labelling each of them with the aid of the cards which you had left in the respective rooms.

"The results were, I think, quite conclusive. When I submitted the samples to analysis I found them all practically free from arsenic – disregarding the minute traces that one expects to find in ordinary soot – with one exception. The soot from Barbara's bedroom chimney yielded, not mere traces, but an easily measurable quantity – much too large to have been attributable to the coal burnt in the grate.

"Thus, you see, so far as the murder of Monkhouse was concerned, there was a fairly conclusive case against Barbara. It left not a shadow of doubt in my mind that she was the guilty person. But you will also see that it was not a satisfactory case to take into court. The whole of the evidence was scientific and might have appeared rather unconvincing to the ordinary juryman, though it would have been convincing enough to the judge. I debated with myself whether I should communicate my discoveries to the police and leave them to decide for or against a prosecution, or whether I should keep silence and seek for further evidence. And finally I decided, for the present, to keep my own counsel. You will understand why."

"Yes," said I. "You suspected that Stella, too, had been poisoned."

"Exactly. I had very little doubt of it. And you notice that in this case there was available evidence of a kind that would be quite convincing to a jury – evidence obtainable from an examination of the victim's body. But here again I was disposed to adopt a waiting policy for three reasons. First, I should have liked to avoid the exhumation if possible. Second, if the exhumation were unavoidable, I was unwilling to apply for it until I was certain that arsenic would be found in the body; and third, although the proof that Stella had been poisoned would have strengthened the case enormously against Barbara, it would yet have added nothing to the evidence that a poisoned candle had been used.

"But the proof of the poisoned candle was the kernel of the case against Barbara. If I could prove that Stella had been poisoned by means of a candle, that would render the evidence absolutely irresistible. This I was not at present able to do. But I had some slight hopes that the deficiency might be made up; that some new facts might come into view if I waited. And, as there was nothing that called for immediate action, I decided to wait, and in due course, the deficiency was made up and the new facts did come into view."

As he paused, I picked up Stella's medallion and looked at it with a new and sombre interest. Holding it up before him, I said: "I am assuming, Thorndyke, that the new facts were in some way connected with this. Am I right?"

"Yes," he replied, "you are entirely right. The connection between that charming little work and the evidence that sent that monster of wickedness to her death is one of the strangest and most impressive circumstances that has become known to me in the whole of my experience. It is no exaggeration to say that when you and Stella were working on that medallion, you were forging the last link in the chain of evidence that could have dragged the murderess to the gallows."

He paused, and, having replenished my glass, took the medallion in his hand and looked at it thoughtfully. Then he knocked out and refilled his pipe and I waited expectantly for the completion of this singular story.

Chapter Eighteen
The Final Proof

"We now," Thorndyke resumed, "enter the final stage of the inquiry. Hitherto we have dealt with purely scientific evidence which would have had to be communicated to the jury and which they would have had to take on trust with no convincing help from their own eyes. We had evidence, conclusive to ourselves, that Monkhouse had been murdered by means of a poisoned candle. But we could not produce the candle or any part of it. We had nothing visible or tangible to show to the jury to give them the feeling of confidence and firm conviction which they rightly demand when they have to decide an issue involving the life or death of the accused. It was this something that could be seen and handled that I sought, and sought in vain until that momentous evening when I called at your chambers to return your diary.

"I remember that as I entered the room and cast my eyes over the things that were spread out on the table, I received quite a shock. For the first glance showed me that, amongst those things were two objects that exactly fulfilled the conditions of the final test. There was the wax mould – a part, and the greater part, of one of the suspected candles; and there was the tress of hair – a portion of the body of the person suspected to have been poisoned. With these two objects it was possible to determine with absolute certainty whether that person had or had not been poisoned with arsenic, and if she had, whether the candle had or had not been the medium by which the poison was administered."

"But," I said, "you knew from the diary of the existence of the wax mould."

"I knew that it *had* existed. But I naturally supposed that the cast had been taken and the mould destroyed years ago, though I had intended to ask you about it. However, here it was, miraculously preserved, against all probabilities, still awaiting completion. Of course, I recognized it instantly, and began to cast about in my mind for some means of making the necessary examination without disclosing my suspicions. For you will realize that I was unwilling to say anything to you about Stella's death until the question was settled one way or the other. If the examination had shown no arsenic either in the candle or in the hair, it would not have been necessary to say anything to you at all.

"But while I was debating the matter, the problem solved itself. As soon as I came to look at Stella's unfinished works, I saw that they cried aloud to be completed and that Polton was the proper person to carry out the work. I made the suggestion, which I should have made in any case, and when you adopted it, I decided to say nothing but to apply the tests when the opportunity offered."

"I am glad," said I, "to hear you say that you would have made the suggestion in any case. It looked at first like a rather cold-blooded pretext to get possession of the things. But you were speaking of the hair. Can you depend on finding recognizable traces of arsenic in the hair of a person who has been poisoned?"

"Certainly, you can," he replied. "The position is this: when arsenic is taken it becomes diffused throughout the whole body, including the blood, the bones and the skin. But as soon as a dose of arsenic is taken, the poison begins to be eliminated from the body, and, if no further dose is taken, the whole of the poison is thrown off in a comparatively short time until none remains in the tissues – with one exception. That exception is the epidermis, or outer skin, with its appendages – the finger and toe nails and the hair. These structures differ from all others in that, instead of growing interstitially and being alive throughout, they grow at a certain growing-point and then become practically dead structures. Thus a hair grows at the growing-point where the bulb joins the true skin. Each day a new piece of hair is produced at the living root, but when once it has come into being it grows no more, but is simply pushed up from below by the next portion. Thenceforward it undergoes no change, excepting that it gradually moves upwards as new portions are added at the root. It is virtually a dead, unchanging structure.

"Now suppose a person to take a considerable dose of arsenic. That arsenic becomes diffused throughout all the living tissues and is for a time deposited in them. The growing-point of the hair is a living tissue and of course the arsenic becomes deposited in it. Then the process of elimination begins and the arsenic is gradually removed from the living tissues. But in twenty-four hours, what was the growing-point of the hair has been pushed up about the fiftieth of an inch and is no longer a growing structure. It is losing its vitality. And as it ceases to be a living tissue it ceases to be affected by the process of elimination. Hence the arsenic which was deposited in it when it was a living tissue is never removed. It remains as a permanent constituent of that part of the hair, slowly moving up as the hair grows from below, until at last it is snipped off by the barber; or, if the owner is a long-haired woman, it continues to creep along until the hair is full-grown and drops out."

"Then the arsenic remains always in the same spot?"

"Yes. It is a local deposit at a particular point in the hair. And this, Mayfield, is a most important fact, as you will see presently. For observe what follows. Hair grows at a uniform rate – roughly, a fiftieth of an inch in twenty-four hours. It is consequently possible, by measurement, to fix nearly exactly, the age of any given point on a hair. Thus if we have a complete hair and we find at any point in it a deposit of arsenic, by measuring from that point to the root we can fix, within quite narrow limits, the date on which that dose of arsenic was taken."

"But is it possible to do this?" I asked.

"Not in the case of a single hair," he replied. "But in the case of a tress, in which all the hairs are of the same age, it is perfectly possible. You will see the important bearing of this presently.

"To return now to my investigation. I had the bulk of a candle and a tress of Stella's hair The questions to be settled were, 1. Was there arsenic in the candle? and 2. Had Stella been poisoned with arsenic? I began by trimming the wax mould in readiness for casting and then I made an analysis of the trimmings. The result was the discovery of considerable quantities of arsenic in the wax.

"That answered the first question. Next, as the tress of hair was larger than was required for your purpose, I ventured to sacrifice a portion of it for a preliminary test. That test also gave a positive result. The quantity of arsenic was, of course, very minute, but still it was measurable by the delicate methods that are possible in dealing with arsenic; and the amount that I found pointed either to one large dose or to repeated smaller ones.

"The two questions were now answered definitely. It was certain – and the certainty could be demonstrated to a jury – that Stella had been poisoned by arsenic, and that the arsenic had been administered by means of poisoned candles. The complete proof in this case lent added weight to the less complete proof in the case of Monkhouse; and the two cases served to corroborate one another in pointing to Barbara as the poisoner. For she was the common factor in the two cases. The other persons – Wallingford, Madeline and the others – who appeared in the Monkhouse case, made no appearance in the case of Stella; and the persons who were associated with Stella were not associated with Monkhouse. But Barbara was associated with both. And her absence from home was no answer to the charge if death was caused by the candles which she had admittedly supplied.

"But complete as the proof was, I wished, if possible, to make it yet more complete: to associate Barbara still more definitely with the crime. In the case of Monkhouse, it was clear that the poisoning always occurred when she was absent from home. But this was not so clear in the case of Stella. Your diary showed that Stella's relapses coincided pretty regularly with Barbara's absences; but it was not certain (though obviously probable) that the relapses coincided with the periods of poisoning. If it could be proved that they did coincide, that proof would furnish corroboration of the greatest possible weight. It would show that the two cases were parallel in all respects.

"But could it be proved? If the tress of Stella's hair had been at my disposal, I had no doubt that I could have decided the question. But the tress was yours, and it had to be preserved. Whatever was to be done must be done without destroying or injuring the hair, and I set myself the task of finding some practicable method. Eventually, I decided, without much hope of success, to try the X-rays. As arsenic is a fairly dense metal and the quantity of it in the deposits quite considerable, it seemed to me possible that it might increase the density of the hairs at those points sufficiently to affect the X-ray shadow. At any rate, I decided to give the method a trial.

"Accordingly, Polton and I set to work at it. First, in order to get the densest shadow possible, we made the tress up into a close cylinder, carefully arranging it so that all the cut ends were in exactly the same plane. Then we made a number of graduated exposures on 'process' plates, developing and intensifying with the object of getting the greatest possible degree of contrast. The result was unexpectedly successful. In the best negative, the shape of the tress was faintly visible and was soon to be crossed by a number of perfectly distinct pale bands. Those bands were the shadows of the deposits of arsenic. There could be no doubt on the subject. For, apart from the fact that there was nothing else that they could be, their appearance agreed exactly with what one would have expected. Each band presented a sharp, distinct edge towards the tips of the hairs and faded away imperceptibly towards the roots. The sharp edge corresponded to the sudden appearance of arsenic in the blood when the poisoning began. The gradual fading-away corresponded to the period of elimination when the poisoning had ceased and the quantity of arsenic in the blood was becoming less and less from day to day.

"Now, since hair grows at a known, uniform rate, it was possible to convert the distances between these arsenical bands into periods of time; not with perfect exactness, because the rate of growth varies slightly in different persons, but with sufficient exactness for our present purpose. As soon as I looked at those bands, I saw that they told the whole story. But let us follow the method of proof.

"Assuming the rate of growth to be one fiftieth of an inch in twenty-four hours – which was probably correct for a person of Stella's age – I measured off on the photograph seven inches and a quarter from the cut ends as representing the last year of her life. Of course, I did not know how close to the head the hair had been cut, but, judging by the bands, I assumed that it had been cut quite close to the skin – within a quarter of an inch."

"I happen to know that you were quite right," said I, "but I can't imagine how you arrived at your conclusion."

"It was quite a simple inference," he replied, "as you will see, presently. But to return to the photograph. Of the measured space of seven inches and a quarter I took a tracing on sheet celluloid, marking the sharp edges of the bands, the points at which the fading began and the points at which the band ceased to be visible. This tracing I transferred to paper ruled in tenths of an inch – a tenth of an inch representing five days – and I joined the points where the fading began and ended by a sloping line. I now had a diagram, or chart, which showed, with something approaching to accuracy, the duration of each administration of arsenic and the time which elapsed between the successive poisonings. This is the chart. The sloping lines show the fading of the bands."

He handed me a paper which he had just taken from a drawer and I looked at it curiously but with no great interest. As I returned it after a brief inspection I remarked: "It is quite clear and intelligible, but I don't quite see why you took the considerable trouble of making it. Does it show anything that could not be stated in a few words?"

"Not by itself," he replied. "But you remember that I mentioned having made two other charts, one showing the fluctuations in Stella's illness and the other showing Barbara's absences from home during the same period. Here are those other two charts; and now, if you put the three together, your eye can take in at a glance a fact of fundamental importance; which is that the relapses, the absences and the poisonings all coincided in time. The periodicity is strikingly irregular; but it is identical in all three charts. I made these to hand to the jury, and I think they would have been quite convincing, since any juryman could check them by the dates given in evidence, and by inspection of the radiograph of the hair."

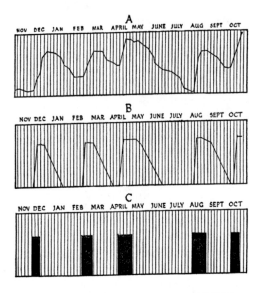

EXPLANATION OF THE CHARTS

CHART A shows the fluctuations in the illness of Stella Keene during the year preceding her death in October. Divided into intervals of five days.

CHART B shows the distribution of the arsenical bands in Stella Keene's hair. The steep sides of the curves, towards the tips of the hairs, show the sudden appearance of the deposit, and the sloping sides, towards the roots of the hairs, represent its more gradual fading. Each of the narrow divisions represents five days' growth.

CHART C shows the periods during which Barbara was absent from home, each absence being represented by a black column. Divided into intervals of five days.

I gazed at the three charts and was profoundly impressed by the convincing way in which they demonstrated the connection between Barbara's movements and the results of her diabolical activities. But what impressed me still more was the amazing ingenuity with which Thorndyke had contrived to build up a case of the most deadly precision and completeness out of what seemed, even to my trained intelligence, no more than a few chance facts, apparently quite trivial and irrelevant.

"It seems," I said, "that, so far as you were concerned, the exhumation was really unnecessary."

"Quite," he replied. "It proved nothing that was not already certain. Still, the Commissioner was quite right. For the purposes of a trial, evidence obtained from the actual body of the victim is of immeasurably more weight than indirect scientific evidence, no matter how complete. An ordinary juryman might have difficulty in realizing that the hair is part of the body and that proof of arsenical deposit in the hair is proof of arsenic in the body. But the mistake that he made, as events turned out, was in refusing to make the arrest until my statements had been confirmed by the autopsy and the analysis. That delay allowed the criminal to escape. Not that I complain. To me, personally, her suicide came as a blessed release from an almost intolerable position. But if I had been in his place, I would have taken no chances. She would have gone to trial and to the gallows."

"Yes," I admitted; "that was what justice demanded. But I cannot be thankful enough for the delay that let her escape. Fiend as she was, it would have been a frightful thing to have had to give the evidence that would have hanged her."

"It would," he agreed; "and the thought of it was a nightmare to me. However, we have escaped that; and after all, justice has been done."

We were silent for a few minutes, during which Thorndyke smoked his pipe with a certain air of attention as if he expected me to put some further questions. And, in fact, there were one or two questions that I wanted to have answered. I began with the simplest.

"I am still a little puzzled by some of the circumstances in this case. The infernal machine I happen to know to have been sent by Barbara, though I don't understand why she sent it. But Wallingford's proceedings are a complete mystery to me. What do you suppose induced him to keep a watch on you in that extraordinary fashion? And who was the man who shadowed him? There certainly was such a man, for I saw him, myself. And the same man had been shadowing Miss Norris. What do you make of it all?"

"One can only reason from past experiences," he replied. "It seems to be a rule that a person who has committed a crime cannot remain quiet and let things take their course. There appears to be an irresistible impulse to lay down false clues and create misleading appearances. It is always a mistake, unless the false clues are laid down in advance, and even then it is apt to fail and unexpectedly furnish a real clue.

"Now Barbara, with all her astonishing cleverness, made that mistake. She laid down a false clue in advance by her absences from home, and the trick certainly worked successfully at the inquest. But it was precisely those absences that put me on the track of the candle, which otherwise might have passed unsuspected. The faked medicine was another false clue which attracted my attention and added to my suspicion concerning the candle. Then, after the event came these other endeavours to mislead. They did neither harm nor good, as it happened, since I had already marked her down as the principal suspect. But if I had been in doubt, I should have followed up those clues and found her at the end of them.

"As to Wallingford, I imagine that she led him to believe that I was employed by you to fix the crime on him and that he was advised to watch me and be ready to anticipate any move on my part; her actual object being to cause him to behave in such a manner as to attract suspicious attention. The function of the private detective – for that is what he must have been – would be to keep Wallingford's nerves – and Miss Norris', too – in such a state that they would appear anxious and terrified and tend to attract attention. The infernal machine was primarily intended, I think, to cast suspicion on one or both of them.

That was what I inferred from the total absence of finger-prints and the flagrantly identifiable character of the pistol and the wool.

"But the greatest, the most fatal mistake that Barbara made was the one that is absolutely characteristic of the criminal. She repeated the procedure of a previous crime that had been successful. It was that repetition that was her undoing. Either crime, separately, might have been difficult to fix on her. As it was, each crime was proof of the other."

Once more we fell silent; and still Thorndyke had the air of expecting some further question from me. I looked at him nervously; for there was something that I wanted to ask and yet I hardly dared to put it into words. For, as I had looked at those charts, a horrid suspicion had taken hold of me. I feared to have it confirmed, and yet I could not let it rest. At last, I summoned courage enough to put the question.

"Thorndyke," I said, "I want you to tell me something. I expect you know what it is."

He looked up and nodded gravely.

"You mean about Stella?" said he.

"Yes. How long would she have lived if she had not been poisoned?"

He looked away for a few moments, and, impassive as his face was, I could see that he was deeply moved. At length he replied: "I was afraid you were going to ask me that. But since you have, I can only answer you honestly. So far as I can judge, but for that accursed ghoul, the poor girl might have been alive and well at this moment."

I stared at him in amazement. "Do you mean," I demanded, "that she was not really suffering from consumption at all?"

"That is what it amounts to," he replied. "There were signs of old tubercular trouble, but there was nothing recent. Evidently she had good powers of resistance, and the disease had not only become stationary, but was practically extinct. The old lesions had undergone complete repair, and there is no reason to suppose that any recurrence would have taken place under ordinary conditions."

"But," I exclaimed, hardly able to believe that the disaster had been so overwhelmingly complete, "what about the cough? I know that she always had a more or less troublesome cough."

"So had Monkhouse," he replied; "and so would anyone have had whose lungs were periodically irritated by inhaling particles of arsenious acid. But the tubercular mischief was quite limited and recovery must have commenced early. And Barbara, watching eagerly the symptoms of the disease which was to rid her of her rival, must have noted with despair the signs of commencing recovery and at last resolved to do for herself what nature was failing to do. Doubtless, the special method of poisoning was devised to imitate the symptoms of the disease; which it did well enough to deceive those whose minds were prepared by the antecedent illness to receive the suggestion. It was a horribly, fiendishly ingenious crime; calmly, callously devised and carried out to its appalling end with the most hideous efficiency."

After he had finished speaking, I remained gazing at him dumbly, stupefied, stunned by the realization of the enormity of this frightful thing that had befallen. He, too, seemed quite overcome, for he sat silently, grasping his extinct pipe and looking sternly and fixedly into the fire. At length he spoke, but without removing his gaze from the bright embers.

"I am trying, Mayfield," he said, gently, "to think of something to say to you. But there is nothing to say. The disaster is too complete, too irretrievable. This terrible woman has, so far, wrecked your life, and I recognize that you will carry the burden of your loss so long as you live. It would be a mere impertinence to utter futile and banal condolences. You know what I, your friend, am feeling and I need say no more of that; and I have too much confidence in your wisdom and courage to think of exhortations.

"But, though you have been robbed of the future that might have been, there is still a future that may be. It remains to you now only to shoulder your fardel and begin your pilgrimage anew; and if the road shall seem at first a dreary one, you need not travel it alone. You have friends; and one of them will think it a privilege to bear you company and try to hearten you by the way."

He held out his hand and I grasped it silently and with a full heart. And the closer friendship that was inaugurated in that hand-clasp has endured through the passing years, ever more precious and more helpful.

R Austin Freeman

The D'Arblay Mystery
A Dr Thorndyke Mystery

When a man is found floating beneath the skin of a green-skimmed pond one morning, Dr Thorndyke becomes embroiled in an astonishing case. This wickedly entertaining detective fiction reveals that the victim was murdered through a lethal injection and someone out there is trying a cover-up.

Dr Thorndyke Intervenes
A Dr Thorndyke Mystery

What would you do if you opened a package to find a man's head? What would you do if the headless corpse had been swapped for a case of bullion? What would you do if you knew a brutal murderer was out there, somewhere, and waiting for you? Some people would run. Dr Thorndyke intervenes.

R Austin Freeman

Felo De Se
A Dr Thorndyke Mystery

John Gillam was a gambler. John Gillam faced financial ruin and was the victim of a sinister blackmail attempt. John Gillam is now dead. In this exceptional mystery, Dr Thorndyke is brought in to untangle the secrecy surrounding the death of John Gillam, a man not known for insanity and thoughts of suicide.

Flighty Phyllis

Chronicling the adventures and misadventures of Phyllis Dudley, Richard Austin Freeman brings to life a charming character always getting into scrapes. From impersonating a man to discovering mysterious trapdoors, *Flighty Phyllis* is an entertaining glimpse at the times and trials of a wayward woman.

R Austin Freeman

Helen Vardon's Confession
A Dr Thorndyke Mystery

Through the open door of a library, Helen Vardon hears an argument that changes her life forever. Helen's father and a man called Otway argue over missing funds in a trust one night. Otway proposes a marriage between him and Helen in exchange for his co-operation and silence. What transpires is a captivating tale of blackmail, fraud and death. Dr Thorndyke is left to piece together the clues in this enticing mystery.

Mr Pottermack's Oversight

Mr Pottermack is a law-abiding, settled homebody who has nothing to hide until the appearance of the shadowy Lewison, a gambler and blackmailer with an incredible story. It appears that Pottermack is in fact a runaway prisoner, convicted of fraud, and Lewison is about to spill the beans unless he receives a large bribe in return for his silence. But Pottermack protests his innocence, and resolves to shut Lewison up once and for all. Will he do it? And if he does, will he get away with it?

OTHER TITLES BY R AUSTIN FREEMAN AVAILABLE DIRECT FROM HOUSE OF STRATUS

Quantity	£	$(US)	$(CAN)	€
THE ADVENTURES OF ROMNEY PRINGLE	6.99	12.95	19.95	13.50
THE CAT'S EYE	6.99	12.95	19.95	13.50
A CERTAIN DR THORNDYKE	6.99	12.95	19.95	13.50
THE D'ARBLAY MYSTERY	6.99	12.95	19.95	13.50
DR THORNDYKE INTERVENES	6.99	12.95	19.95	13.50
DR THORNDYKE'S CASEBOOK	6.99	12.95	19.95	13.50
DR THORNDYKE'S CRIME FILE	6.99	12.95	19.95	13.50
THE EXPLOITS OF DANBY CROKER	6.99	12.95	19.95	13.50
THE EYE OF OSIRIS	6.99	12.95	19.95	13.50
FELO DE SE	6.99	12.95	19.95	13.50
FLIGHTY PHYLLIS	6.99	12.95	19.95	13.50
FOR THE DEFENCE: DR THORNDYKE	6.99	12.95	19.95	13.50
FROM A SURGEON'S DIARY	6.99	12.95	19.95	13.50
THE FURTHER ADVENTURES OF ROMNEY PRINGLE	6.99	12.95	19.95	13.50
THE GOLDEN POOL: A STORY OF A FORGOTTEN MINE	6.99	12.95	19.95	13.50
THE GREAT PORTRAIT MYSTERY	6.99	12.95	19.95	13.50
HELEN VARDON'S CONFESSION	6.99	12.95	19.95	13.50

ALL HOUSE OF STRATUS BOOKS ARE AVAILABLE FROM GOOD BOOKSHOPS OR DIRECT FROM THE PUBLISHER:

Internet: www.houseofstratus.com including synopses and features.

Email: sales@houseofstratus.com
info@houseofstratus.com
(please quote author, title and credit card details.)

OTHER TITLES BY R AUSTIN FREEMAN AVAILABLE DIRECT
FROM HOUSE OF STRATUS

Quantity		£	$(US)	$(CAN)	€
	THE JACOB STREET MYSTERY	6.99	12.95	19.95	13.50
	JOHN THORNDYKE'S CASES	6.99	12.95	19.95	13.50
	THE MAGIC CASKET	6.99	12.95	19.95	13.50
	MR POLTON EXPLAINS	6.99	12.95	19.95	13.50
	MR POTTERMACK'S OVERSIGHT	6.99	12.95	19.95	13.50
	THE MYSTERY OF 31 NEW INN	6.99	12.95	19.95	13.50
	THE MYSTERY OF ANGELINA FROOD	6.99	12.95	19.95	13.50
	THE PENROSE MYSTERY	6.99	12.95	19.95	13.50
	PONTIFAX, SON AND THORNDYKE	6.99	12.95	19.95	13.50
	THE PUZZLE LOCK	6.99	12.95	19.95	13.50
	THE RED THUMB MARK	6.99	12.95	19.95	13.50
	A SAVANT'S VENDETTA	6.99	12.95	19.95	13.50
	THE SHADOW OF THE WOLF	6.99	12.95	19.95	13.50
	A SILENT WITNESS	6.99	12.95	19.95	13.50
	THE SINGING BONE	6.99	12.95	19.95	13.50
	THE STONEWARE MONKEY	6.99	12.95	19.95	13.50
	THE SURPRISING EXPERIENCES OF MR SHUTTLEBURY COBB	6.99	12.95	19.95	13.50
	THE UNWILLING ADVENTURER	6.99	12.95	19.95	13.50
	WHEN ROGUES FALL OUT	6.99	12.95	19.95	13.50

ALL HOUSE OF STRATUS BOOKS ARE AVAILABLE FROM GOOD BOOKSHOPS
OR DIRECT FROM THE PUBLISHER:

Tel: Order Line
  0800 169 1780 (UK)
   800 724 1100 (USA)
  International
  +44 (0) 1845 527700 (UK)
  +01 845 463 1100 (USA)

Fax: +44 (0) 1845 527711 (UK)
  +01 845 463 0018 (USA)
  (please quote author, title and credit card details.)

Send to: House of Stratus Sales Department House of Stratus Inc.
    Thirsk Industrial Park   2 Neptune Road
    York Road, Thirsk   Poughkeepsie
    North Yorkshire, YO7 3BX   NY 12601
    UK   USA

PAYMENT

Please tick currency you wish to use:

☐ £ (Sterling)　☐ $ (US)　☐ $ (CAN)　☐ € (Euros)

Allow for shipping costs charged per order plus an amount per book as set out in the tables below:

CURRENCY/DESTINATION

	£(Sterling)	$(US)	$(CAN)	€(Euros)
Cost per order				
UK	1.50	2.25	3.50	2.50
Europe	3.00	4.50	6.75	5.00
North America	3.00	3.50	5.25	5.00
Rest of World	3.00	4.50	6.75	5.00
Additional cost per book				
UK	0.50	0.75	1.15	0.85
Europe	1.00	1.50	2.25	1.70
North America	1.00	1.00	1.50	1.70
Rest of World	1.50	2.25	3.50	3.00

PLEASE SEND CHEQUE OR INTERNATIONAL MONEY ORDER
payable to: HOUSE OF STRATUS LTD or HOUSE OF STRATUS INC. or card payment as indicated

STERLING EXAMPLE

Cost of book(s):..................... Example: 3 x books at £6.99 each: £20.97

Cost of order: .... Example: £1.50 (Delivery to UK address)

Additional cost per book:.............. Example: 3 x £0.50: £1.50

Order total including shipping:.......... Example: £23.97

VISA, MASTERCARD, SWITCH, AMEX:

☐☐☐☐☐☐☐☐☐☐☐☐☐☐☐☐☐☐☐☐

Issue number (Switch only):

☐☐☐

Start Date:　　　　　　**Expiry Date:**

☐☐/☐☐　　　　　　☐☐/☐☐

Signature: _____

NAME: _____

ADDRESS: _____

COUNTRY: _____

ZIP/POSTCODE: _____

Please allow 28 days for delivery. Despatch normally within 48 hours.

Prices subject to change without notice.
Please tick box if you do not wish to receive any additional information. ☐

House of Stratus publishes many other titles in this genre; please check our website (**www.houseofstratus.com**) for more details.